Astrid Cane

Anonymous

Erotica Biblion Society
of
London and New York 1891

Anonymous

Copyright © ThesecretBookshelf

All rights reserved.

ISBN-13:978-1530933051

ISBN-10:1530933056

Astrid Cane

CHAPTER 1 4

CHAPTER 2 12

CHAPTER 3 23

CHAPTER 4 33

CHAPTER 5 42

CHAPTER 6 51

CHAPTER 7 63

CHAPTER 8 76

CHAPTER 9 89

CHAPTER 10 100

CHAPTER 11 111

CHAPTER 12 121

CHAPTER 13 133

CHAPTER 14 143

CHAPTER 15 152

CHAPTER 16 162

CHAPTER 17 175

CHAPTER 18 184

CHAPTER 19 194

ENVOI 204

CHAPTER 1

Astrid Cane adjusted the folds of her blue velvet gown and gazed curiously around her as she descended from her carriage assisted by a footman who had hastened down the broad stone steps of the country manor. Never before had Astrid made a social call on her own, but this first sight of Hardcastle-as the manor was called-pleased her. Its stone walls, latticed by Nature with ivy, had long mellowed with age, as if to avow their proud permanence in the county of Buckinghamshire. Glittering in the afternoon sunlight, the trellised windows offered their discreet greeting.

Unaccustomed to hurrying, the aristocratic young lady slowly ascended the steps, where a housemaid awaited her.

'Lady Tingle waits in the drawing room to welcome you, Miss'.

'Very well, you may show me through', replied Astrid languidly, dangling a small, blue parasol from her wrist.

The house was cool, smelling pleasantly of lavender and wood polish. The fragrance of newly baked bread wafted through from some distant kitchen, making Astrid's finely cut nostrils twitch agreeably. Opening two inner doors-since Society will oddly have it that it is impolite for servants to knock before entering drawing rooms-the maid announced Astrid briefly and then left her to be welcomed by her hostess.

Lady Tingle, who had just entered her fortieth year was a woman of imposing figure. A little above medium height, she bore herself like a queen. She was attired in a black gown whose sombreness was relieved by a subtle patterning of silvery threads interwoven in the material. Her auburn hair was bunched high, her swan-like neck adorned with a black-velvet choker set in the middle with a single diamond. Her bust, being prominent, announced a rich firmness of flesh beneath, as did the arrogant thrusting of her derriere.

'You are most welcome, my dear', Lady Tingle said in a voice as soft as a dove's feathers. Without seeming to, her eyes drank in the svelte curves which the clinging of Astrid's dress accentuated. Slender, and of equal stature to her hostess, Astrid was in her twenty-third year. Her complexion was marble smooth and clear, with a pretty hint of pink in her face that was enhanced by the noble lines of her cheekbones. Her mouth was full, her lower lip being particularly voluptuous. An aquiline nose, neither long nor short, large hazel eyes, and an abundance of soft, dark hair completed the most pleasing nubile curves of her figure.

'I fear that I know little enough of the purpose of my visit, save what Mama wrote to me', Astrid said.

'We must have tea and talk', Julie Tingle answered comfortably, and motioned her guest to a chair. 'You need experience no embarrassment, my dear, at the fact that we have not previously been introduced. Your dear Mama is in Switzerland, of course, and, I gather, may remain there for some time. She has naturally been concerned as to your future. You are, after all, the oldest of her daughters and the one whom she cherishes the most. Ah, here is the tea!'.

The afternoon comforts of the well-to-do having been served, and the Indian tea being of the finest, Astrid was set a little more at ease, though not a wrinkle of her clear brow betrayed the uncertainty she felt at journeying to make this visit as her mother had requested.

'I know not how long I can stay', Astrid said, failing no more than her hostess to drink in all that she saw, whether of Lady Tingle herself or of the superbly appointed drawing room with its glittering chandelier, its grey and blue silks, and the numerous pretty ornaments that lay everywhere. In particular, the eyes of her hostess attracted her glances, for they seemed to glitter with hidden lights.

'It will depend on your progress, my dear. From the little I have seen of you up to this moment, I would say that a month would suffice- perhaps less. You are here to be introduced to a world of disciplinary experiences all of which will benefit you as muchly as your dear Mama intends they shall'.

At this, Astrid's mouth dropped, for she could not believe that she had heard what she thought she had, all of Lady Tingle's words being uttered in the most casual fashion.

'I fear I do not quite understand', she responded.

'You have a fine, proud look, Astrid-I am pleased with that. You will not succumb easily, but then it is for the best if you do not, as will come clear to you. Those who do, often prove useless'. Rising, Julia placed her hand beneath Astrid's chin and lifted it. 'Marie, the maid, will show you to your room', she added.

Appearing at first lost for words, Astrid returned her gaze with total wonderment. 'I... I fail to understand, Lady Tingle. I cannot possibly stay more than a day or two. Papa expects...'.

'What your Papa expects and what he receives are possibly two different things, Astrid. Do, please, call me Julia. Your clothes will have been wardrobed by now and you will naturally wish to change after your journey. We have much to talk of. There are few enough young men and young women who are sent to me for whom I have any true affection. In your case, I believe I find immediately a charming exception. Ah, Marie-yes, come in. Escort Miss Cane to her room'.

'Yes, Ma'am'.

The maid had entered so silently that Astrid started and then gazed all about her as though in a dream.

'I cannot believe that Mama had any intentions other than that I should make a social call upon you', she said stiffly.

'An extremely social call, yes', Julia laughed, 'but perhaps rather more prolonged than you anticipated and certainly of a nature that you least expected. Marie, I think you had best call Tom. The young lady appears unwilling to rise. You will both assist her upstairs'.

'Madam-no!', gasped Astrid, rising quickly and utterly bewildered. 'I believe you fail to understand who I am. If you will be so kind as to have my carriage recalled, I shall leave'.

'Your carriage has long left, my dear. There is no way that you are going to leave until I judge you fit to do so. Now, Marie and Tom, take her up!'.

'How dare you! No!', screamed Astrid, who in that moment found herself in the close presence of a burly male servant and Marie. Unheard of as it was to be touched by mere servants, she felt the outrage of having her wrists seized and drawn behind her by Tom, whose grip she could find no way of escaping from without utter indignity. At the same tune, Marie took her elbow.

'To be bathed, Ma'am?', Marie asked her mistress.

'Yes, you and Amy will see to it. Have me called when it is done', Julia replied to screams from Astrid who was being propelled towards the double doors of the drawing room. Hustled into the great hallway, Astrid fought bitterly against the hands that, as she felt then, were impelling her to her doom.

'Release me! Ah, you beasts, how dare you lay hands on me!', she screeched to no avail. Bundled slowly upstairs, her feet kicked frantically until Tom wheeled her about and, with no more effort than it would take to lift a kitten, slung her over his shoulder. 'No! No! No!', moaned Astrid, beating with her fists upon his broad back the while that he reached the first landing, with Marie following. He then bore her towards a bedroom.

Meanwhile Lady Tingle languidly lit a Turkish cigarette and took from a small chest of drawers a letter which bore a Swiss stamp and which she had already perused several tunes. Astrid's cries reached her but faintly as she unfolded the delicately scented pages and regained her seat to engage herself anew in the message.

'My dearest Julia', she read, 'I write to you with a purpose that you have for several years wished and which we have not infrequently discussed. My sojourn here will be considerably extended, for the air and all about suits me as well as does that engaging rascal, Rudolph, for whose sake I have put England behind me. He and I are of mutual mind, as you well know, and thoroughly enjoy what you are occasionally pleased to call our "sporting activities" together. He is as thorough, my dear, with the strap, the cane, and the crop as ever you were, though his own sturdy buttocks are put to such in turn when I am so minded.

'His daughters, Amanda and Rose, are perfect darlings, the former being now nineteen and her sister just attaining her sixteenth year. The little devils have been well bottom-trained, I can tell you. 'Tis a pure delight to unveil their lovely round derrieres and apply the strap or birch or what you will to their refulgent cheeks. Rose is naturally a trifle more hesitant than her sister and occasionally must be held. In such matters your frequent counsels to me are well taken. "An air of mystery should attend all , I hear you saying. For this purpose an upper room of the house is set aside, all daylight being excluded by thick drapes. How delightfully the soft glow of but three oil lamps casts its subdued glimmerings over their naughty bottoms!

'Rose is not yet broken in. I would have it so in a few weeks time upon her sixteenth birthday. As yet the dear girl knows only the occasional brushing of my lips over her heated nether cheeks when the birch has swished across them a full dozen times. In coddling her afterwards, I have naturally soothed her blubberings by moving my mouth lightly upon her own. Her eyes in that mysterious gloom beseech a little more, but 'tis best to keep her for the nonce on tenterhooks. I have but flirted my fingers about her moist cunny once. How ardently her hips writhed, though naturally this sensuous movement was unspokenly understood to be solely the result of her birching!

'Amanda is quite other. We are as sisters of occasion. Her pleasure in being bound tightly, attired in a short chemise, stockings, and shoes, and with her drawers lowered just sufficiently to display the pretty muff of her pubis, is quite delightful. Thus secured, I bring her to lie upon the bed in the selfsame room of mystery, and, having kissed her once or twice upon her ruby lips, I leave her to her anticipations, frequently for a full hour or more. Her waist is slender, as are her calves and ankles, but she is otherwise plumpish, which pleases me, for she beds well thus under a male. Her nipples are thick and conical, her mouth sultry, her titties exceedingly full and firm. You would find it a rare pleasure to possess her.

'But before I am lost in such diverting details, I hasten to the matter of my darling Astrid, whose education in all these respects has been too long neglected. I need scarcely repeat what I have so often said, that my husband, Ralph, is a weakling and totally unimaginative in all matters as concern you and me intimately. Can you conceive, Julia, that, unlike his sterner brethren, he has never once put the girls to the birch? In all such respects they are complete muffs who know not the lingering pleasures that bind the more knowing of us together. As to Astrid herself, she has the core of strength that you will not fail to recognise and must take her place among such womanly ranks as you and I realise to be the only ones worthy of attainment.

'Take her, train her, my love, as you yourself once trained me in my state of unknowing. To no other could I entrust such a mission. She will emerge from the fire well tempered and perfectly understanding of the future delights to which you will have awoken her. Judging the moment as you will, you may then return her home. I expect not to hear from her until then, by which time she will surely be among the chosen, as imperious to give as she is willing to receive. That you will privately apprise me of her progress I doubt not. For the moment I must attend to that of Amanda and Rose. Deprived of the prick for a full week, Amanda's mouth has a deliciously sulky look. Her bottom must be attended to with the martinet before she receives again the manly weapon. As to Rose, I shall leave it to her papa to spank her, for he truly adores bouncing his palm off those resilient cheeks. Once he has concluded that entertaining chore, he will be in a fine, stiff condition to perform his next!

'Au 'voir, my darling Julia. I wait breathlessly upon your first report'.

Your ever adoring,

Cynthia

Bringing the perfumed pages to her lips in a token salute, Julia smiled reminiscently. It was she indeed who more than twenty years before had first put Lady Cynthia Cane's bottom to the crop before it received its first libation of sperm. Ever before Julia's eyes was the sight of Cynthia's red-streaked bottom, her howls and cries resounding through the stable to which she had been taken. Wrists bound-'to prevent any nonsense', as Julia put it-Cynthia had been hauled over a bale of straw, drawers at the ankles, and her skirts piled well up above her hips.

'No, Julia, no-oh my God, you cannot!', Cynthia had screeched to no avail whatever while a silent housemaid held her down and the first slicing cut of the crop swished across her bared cheeks. 'AAAARGH!', had come Cynthia's agonised shriek, though each swish was controlled with such moderation as marked but did not otherwise harm the luscious moon which her naked bottom presented. Bucking, sobbing, and protesting, Cynthia had received the full dozen before the rubicund knob of a prick was urged between her heated, throbbing cheeks, the possessor of that initiating penis being none other than Julia's older brother, Henry, who had become totally subservient to her whims.

Tight as the entry was, he had effected it until Cynthia's scorched bottom was held rammed to his stomach. The maid was then dismissed and Julia held and coaxed her friend, whose tear-streaked face swung from side to side as she endeavoured to contain the throbbing weapon.

'Forty strokes, Henry', Julia had then commanded crisply, holding her left hand clamped down firmly over the nape of Cynthia's neck. Groaning at the sheer bliss of being so tightly ensconced in a bottom he had often eyed but had never seen unveiled before, Henry had commenced his duty, ramming his fiery shaft slowly back and forth within Cynthia's clinging orifice while Julia-beholding all with an expression of great calm- failed not to count each forward plunge as silently as he.

Well-rewarded for her silence upon the matter, the housemaid had thereafter attended frequently upon Cynthia's training. She took such a taste for it that within a month she had bedded with the two friends and become the object of their lascivious toyings. By then Cynthia had brought herself more willingly to all that Julia had taught her to suffer and enjoy, and had been so frequently spermed by all the subservient males of the household, that she could, as Julia of times said, have bathed her in the throbbing liquor, had been preserved.

Now from her musings of the past, Julia rose and smoothed her faultless coiffure. Astrid's cries still came from above, as she had expected. It was time for her first lesson.

CHAPTER 2

Astrid's experiences in the time that had passed since she had been carried upstairs had brought her almost to a point of dumbness. At home, her personal maid, Mary, frequently assisted her in her boudoir, lacing her corsets and such. Not infrequently Mary would dare to allow her warm palms to linger around the smooth silky globe of her young mistress's bottom, while adjusting the straps of Astrid's corsets to her stockings or smoothing out her drawers. Astrid suffered such touches, though they would sometimes cause her to flush and to stir her hips as the delicate fingertips assailed her naked cheeks, bringing curious longings to her mind.

Never before, however, had Astrid been stripped by force, as Marie and Amy now saw to it that she was. Thankful only that the manservant had been dismissed, Astrid spat and hissed while the remaining garment of her white-batiste drawers was removed.

'You beasts, you shall suffer for this!', she moaned. Held down on her back upon a huge bed, her superb titties rolled and quivered while Marie held her arms above her head and Amy, at the foot of the bed, maintained such pressure on her ankles that only her hips were allowed to undulate. Her eyes wild and haggard, Astrid uttered a piercing cry as Lady Tingle entered and gazed down approvingly upon her.

All revealed to her gaze, Julia saw how beauteous was the prize. Astrid's tits were already noble in form, as firm as blancmanges with adorable pinky-brown nipples that quivered with rage to be so offered to view. Her hips possessed that perfect violin curve which marks the most shapely of women well proportioned in the lower half. Her legs were long and as sweetly shaped as any that the finest Italian sculptor might have fashioned, the calves and ankles slender and the thighs fulsome and plump. Between them, and thoroughly well-displayed, the shell-like lips of her cunt lay enfolded by a mass of light brown curls that frothed and massed all about her mount. In a word,

Astrid looked a perfect goddess of desire over whose valleys and hillocks Julia's lascivious tongue longed to roam.

'I cannot bear this! My God, let me dress! The shame-oh, the shame!', Astrid cried.

'Have pity and let me cover myself!'.

'Straddle her, Amy', Julia commanded, the words causing Astrid to buck madly.

'You dare not!', she cried, but all was effected so rapidly that in a trice the maid had leapt nimbly upon the bed, casting her legs on either side of Astrid's body. Facing her feet, and squatting her bottom lightly upon the outraged young woman, Amy looped both arms beneath Astrid's thighs and drew them back so that the exposure of her most ultimate parts was then complete. As Astrid's bottom was half-lifted, Julia moved smoothly to the end of the bed at the position which Amy had so quickly vacated, and slid her palms beneath the luscious half-moons.

'NO-OH! You will be punished for this!', came Astrid's screech.

Her arms were still held by Marie, who knelt attentively beside her. She was unable to wrench her drawn-back thighs from Amy's tight grasp, and was held completely immobile, the full prey of Julia, who had commenced taming other wilful young ladies in much this wise.

Cupping the wriggling cheeks of Astrid's bottom firmly, Julia bent farther forward and slid her face up between the heavenly columns until her warm breath approached and wafted around the haven of Astrid's cunny. Longingly, her pink tongue extended itself, moving in slow and snake-like fashion about the puffy lips, causing Astrid to moan beseechingly since no tongue or finger had ever touched her there. Slow and subtle in her ministrations, Julia sought with the very tip of her tongue to part the lovelips, whose oily secretions already announced themselves. The salty, tangy flavour, intoxicating as it was, caused Julia then to insert a full four inches of her tongue into the velvety cleft, where she wriggled it about, causing Astrid's plump, tight bottom to gyrate upon her hands.

'Do not, do not, do NOT!', Astrid sobbed unceasingly, her arms and legs constantly trying to loose themselves from her captors.

'What a delicious cunt she has', murmured Julia, whose tongue sought the moist cleft where the little button of Astrid's clitoris had already swelled a trifle. Like a tiny penis, it poised there, silently imploring of its own accord the labial caresses that Julia artfully brought to it.

'HAH-OOOOH!', Astrid moaned. Slivers of white fire seemed to shoot through her belly at this lascivious attention. Unknowing even that she possessed such a titillating little organ, she found herself enduring indescribable sensations under the circular working of her hostess's tongue.

Is she coming yet, Madame', Amy asked excitedly, seeing her mistress's nose rubbing all around the young woman's plump mount as her mouth worked.

'In but a moment or two. She will sprinkle well, this one', came the husky, muffled response.

Already the seepings of Astrid's juices swam over and around Julia's mouth, which received them with perfect glee, for no nectar was ever sweeter to Lady Tingle. Finery attuned as her ears were, she recognised a changing note in Astrid's sobbings and breathings, and could feel, too, the anticipatory tightening of the young woman's marbled bottom cheeks as the delicious crisis approached. Within seconds, as Julia's tongue continued lapping, a gritty whine emitted itself from Astrid's throat. Her whole belly and cunt, as it seemed to her, were melting in a fire of bliss, and her thighs no longer strove against the ringing of Amy's arms.

'THOOO-OOOH-OOH!', came her whine. Her clitoris-long, fully erect-seemed to appeal for one last sweeping of Julia's tongue. Receiving it, and feeling it then plunge its full, snaking length within her oozing grotto, Astrid came. Her hips bucked violently, her back rippling, and then from her longing cunny spurted a fine milky rain which spattered

Julia's nose and flooded her mouth with its creamy essence.

'HAAAAAR!', Astrid shuddered. Despite herself, she could not help but grind her slit passionately to Julia's open mouth while yet again and again her climactic bliss repeated itself until, weakening and sobbing, she found herself released, her legs falling as limp as her arms, her face flushed then pale, her belly heaving.

'What a froth! One would think that a young stallion had mounted her!', murmured Julia. Take her now to the bathroom and sponge and perfume her well'.

'Stop, oh stop!', Astrid moaned, though her protests were now so feeble and her divine form so throbbing still with pleasure that she was but as a limp doll. She permitted herself to be weakly drawn off the bed by the two maids, her knees buckling as she was led along the corridor to a bathroom of such curious aspect as Astrid had never seen before.

The bath itself was marble and like no other she had encountered. It so shallow that it seemed but a trough of elongated oval shape set upon four short and gilded plinths. Warm and scented water lay already within it to a depth of scarce more than eighteen inches. Immediately above the bath hung gilded chains which extended down from hooks. On seeing these, Astrid uttered a cry of alarm and would have urged herself back again towards the door had not the two maids forced her into the bath holding her in a standing posture. Marie clasped her tightly about her slender waist, while her companion took the chains and fastened them with circlets of iron about Astrid's wrists. Held upright thus, Astrid commenced beseeching the pair as she would never otherwise have deigned to do with servants.

'Let me go, I beg you! My father will reward you well! Oh, why am I chained?'.

'Tut, tut, how the young lady questions things', laughed Marie, taking a fine, large sponge and lathering it well with perfumed soap. 'Whether your Papa will reward you or you him is something for the future to decide. As to your bonds, they are but to keep you still while you are bathed. Open your legs now, Miss!'.

Uttering a rattling cry, Astrid could but hang her head back in quivering shame and wonder as the warm sponge laved her legs, moving ever upwards until its sensuous surface was worked by Marie's subtle hand beneath her dell. Feeling the warm water, Astrid haplessly rotated her bottom. The sensations she had already endured under Julia's caresses had been exquisite, yet that they were the devil's work she was convinced and strove still to suppress them.

'What would I not give to kiss her!', Amy exclaimed, while she herself saw to the additional sponging of Astrid's body above her hips.

'Madam will be very angry if you do', Marie scolded, though she herself could not resist slipping her middle finger up past the sponge and letting it brush beneath the lips of Astrid's cunt, making her quiver adorably. Occasionally Lady Tingle permitted them to sport with some of the girls who were brought to Hardcastle for training, but only those whom their mistress considered to be naughty but submissive, having no streaks of arrogance in them and being fit only for 'harem games', as her Ladyship would declare. Instinctively, Marie had already divined that Miss Astrid Cane was not one such. Had she been, Lady Tingle might well have birched her first, for it was thought to be 'as fine a way of bringing a young lady on as any. That she had accorded Astrid much more intimate attentions was a sign of more loving devotion.

Astrid by now had ceased to protest, knowing well enough that there was no purpose to it. Thoroughly washed, she was dried and powdered in the bath before the chains were released and her aching arms allowed to fall. That she would soon enough escape she had no doubt and therefore permitted herself to be taken in silence back to the boudoir, where her hostess had been amusing herself by reading a novelette of a kind that may only be purchased in Paris or from certain discreet establishments in London. The change of expression in Astrid's face amused her but did not surprise her. The mettle of her mama showed more clearly now, save for a slight trembling of Astrid's fingers as she was sat upon the bed.

Julia's nostrils twitched at the fresh and perfumed aromas that exuded from the young woman's naked body. 'Your first experience, my dear, has, I trust, not been too alarming?', Julia asked without a trace of irony in her voice. Women were ever more intriguing to handle than males, for the subtlety of their minds was greater and their instincts more finely attuned. A battle of mind and soul with a male could be won briefly by a determined female. With her own kind the matter was often different.

'Will they not leave?', Astrid asked in as calm a voice as she could muster, for she sat now at least untouched.

'If you will have it so', Julia sighed. She had no illusions that Astrid might attempt to overpower her. It had been attempted but once before by a young aristocrat who had fought like a tigress for a minute until the snarling of a whip around her naked bottom had finally quelled her. 'You will not mind if I take precautions, Astrid?', she asked, letting her book fall upon her chair as she rose. Astrid's momentary curiosity in that moment was her undoing, for her eyes chanced to fall upon an illustration which the open book revealed. In so doing, a fierce blush rose into her cheeks since that which she saw seemed to her the most infinitely shameful thing she had ever encountered.

Alas, that moment of inattention proved her further undoing, for in a trice Marie and Amy were upon her, binding her arms to her sides with a fine rope which had lain in readiness under the bed. While Astrid, now laid full-length, screamed her protests, which were as much of anger as humiliation, her long and beautiful legs were similarly secured until she lay completely trussed and panting.

'That will do', Julia declared, having watched the struggle with passionate interest.

'Oh, my God, you will surely suffer for this! The moment that Papa learns of how shamefully you have treated me he will...'.

'He will do nothing', her hostess declared, seating herself beside the writhing girl and quelling her further words by placing her hand over her mouth while Astrid's noble eyes blazed into hers. 'Cry and scream as you will, my love, for no one will hear you, save those whose pleasure it is to do so. I refer to the servants, of course. They are completely in my thrall, as are you now, Astrid, until it pleases me to release you. Listen and listen well, girl. You are not here to be tortured, as you appear to think.

Did my tongue torture you? Only to a point of exquisite delight, yes. Were the chains in the bathroom rough? They but held you still and prevented unseemly struggling. You do not wish to appear undignified, I am sure, whatever trials you may be put to. There is a purpose to them which you will soon enough understand. Be civilised, Astrid, for I mean to bring you nothing but pleasure and enduring happiness'.

'Don't! No! AH!', Astrid spluttered, for in that selfsame moment Julia removed her hand and held her ripe mouth down firmly over the young woman's while gripping her chin so that her lips were unable to escape the wanton salute. Little by little, under the squashing of Julia's mouth, Astrid's upper lip rolled back, her white teeth parting haplessly to receive the gliding of Julia's tongue within. Therewith, pinching the girl's nostrils, Julia ensured that Astrid's mouth remained open while her tongue swirled about hers.

Long, long did this kiss of illicit passion last, while Astrid quivered in her every vein. Not even her dear mama had kissed her upon the mouth before and the experience flooded her mind with unwonted pleasure against which she still wilfully fought. Knowing her victim better even than she did herself, however, Julia relinquished her grip upon Astrid's chin and allowed her palm to float lightly and in the most teasing manner over the rosebud nipples, which peeped amid the binding ropes.

Her nose still pinched twixt Julia's finger and thumb, Astrid gurgled and twisted. Their salivas mingled as did their tongues. Electric thrills coursed through her tits, which the bonds caused to swell even more. Her nipples rose like thorns and her scented cunt moistened anew. Bubbling out her breath, she gave a long, low sob that throbbed with untold passions, as Julia slowly withdrew her mouth and hands.

'A kiss between women-is it not the most voluptuous thing?', Julia asked softly while yet Astrid endeavoured to gather both her breath and her mind. Before she could do either, Julia had rolled her over so that she lay helpless upon her belly.

'You must, must, must let me go-please, oh please!', Astrid whimpered.

'No., my dear, that is the last thing I shall do. Rather, I shall bring you to me, but these are words you will not understand yet, for your mind and your soul are not yet broken away from the dull, meddlesome world you would otherwise have inhabited'.

So saying, Julia slowly divested herself of her gown, beneath which she wore naught but a black waist corset which left her mammalian beauties completely bared, and patterned stockings of the sheerest black silk. Going then to an armoire, she drew forth a martinet whose thongs hissed menacingly as they sleeked down one noble thigh.

'Has no part of your adorable body been caressed before, Astrid?', she asked.

'My God, no-how dare you ask me such a thing! YEEE-AAAARGH!', screeched the tightly bound young woman, as, without further ado, the thongs hissed across her naked bottom cheeks, leaving in their path a fierce singeing of fire.

'Never, Astrid? By no one?', came Julia's voice insistently. "Think carefully before you reply. Let me give you something to stir your thoughts, my pet'.

'OW-OUCH! NEEE-YNNNNG! Stop it! Don't Ah, it burns! You beast, you beast-OUCH!'.

Again and again the martinet sang its song now, sweeping this way and that as the tortured orb of Astrid's bottom writhed and jerked. Streaks of white fire seemed to be invading her ardent buttocks, the long tongues of heat reaching into her every crevice.

'NEVER, Astrid? Mark carefully your reply or a dozen more will fall!'

'BOO-BOO-BOO-BOOO!', Astrid sobbed, for with each word the thongs hissed their paths across her blazing cheeks, which tightened visibly at every stroke. 'Ah! AH! Ah, God, stop, Yes! My... my... MY maid... she... she has touched my bottom in assisting m... me to dress. YOOOOH!'.

'Indelicately, nicely, has she touched you, Astrid?'.

'YA-AH-AAAAH! Oh, stop, please, stop, YES! She f... f... feels me there-oh, I am ashamed to tell it! OH!'.

Sobbing uncontrollably, Astrid was spun over once more onto her back, her scorched bottom throbbing and jerking to the unwonted contact with the silky bedcover upon which Julia nevertheless firmly pressed her so that Astrid's agonised and weeping eyes stared up into her own.

'You are not untruthful, then', Julia purred. 'No, do not struggle, my girl, for a hot bottom is best alleviated by being pressed into something-preferably the torso of a male with a hard prick. The sensation is torturous but yet quite delicious when the waiting knob slips in. Every wriggle of the bottom but assists the invasion that follows. It is called corking, or sheathing, or ramming, or what you will-exactly as in the drawing in my book upon which your eyes fell. Look again, Astrid!', Julia commanded, picking up the volume and holding it before the young woman's bleared eyes.

'It is h... hateful, wicked, oh, I cannot! Take it away!', Astrid pleaded while with a taunting smile Julia traced the outlines of the drawing with her finger. Perfectly delineated, it showed a young woman bent over the back of a chair in the seat of which knelt an older one holding her arms. On the floor lay a cane whose handiwork was evinced by the parallel stripes marking the girl's round bottom. To the rear of her, his knees slightly bent and his trousers at his ankles, crouched a man whose rearing penis was pointed directly between her nether checks.

'Wicked, indeed! Such pleasures', Julia laughed throatily, and then, with a sinuous wriggle, slid full down upon Astrid so that every inch of their warm bodies curved into one another's.

'No! Please, no!', Astrid sobbed. Unable now to squirm her blazing bottom as she wished, she was forced to lie still under the heavy, voluptuous weight of Julia, whose stiff nipples rubbed upon her own and whose hairy bush was couched upon hers. 'Lie still, lie still, and say nothing. NOTHING, do you hear? Or I shall whip you more fiercely, my naughty one', Julia both chided and soothed in the same breath.

'I c... cannot! It is wicked, wicked, wicked!', Astrid choked. Her cheeks, wet with tears, were stroked by Julia's hand. Julia's mouth brushed hers softly.

'Many are the delights of the world that are wicked, my love. Be certain only that mine will eventually prove the most delightful. In but a moment, when the warmth of my breasts and belly and thighs and the hungry heat of my cunt have fully invaded you, I shall leave you here to lie still. Wine and food will be brought to you and then you will sleep. When you awake it will be to find yourself as helplessly bound as you are now'.

'No, no! Oh, Lady Tingle-Julia-let me go, let me go home, please! I swear to say nothing of this if only you will!'

'SHUSH!', Julia commanded her softly. 'There is much for you to learn. Think upon it, Astrid. You will not know what will happen to you when you awake, though it shall not be dire. You will remain a victim of my pleasures until you discover your own'.

'NO-OH!', Astrid's wail came then, but, even as her cry echoed through the sumptuous boudoir, so Julia gathered up her gown and departed smoothly and silently, closing and locking the door behind her.

Eyes glazed and bottom cheeks still twitching from their unaccustomed basting, Astrid wriggled, and then with a sobbing sigh lay still once more. With the closing of the door a terrible silence reigned about her. Once or twice she fancied that she heard muffled footsteps and a murmuring of voices. Each time they appeared to approach, she stiffened within herself and then relaxed again. The stinging feeling in her nether cheeks changed gradually to a warm glow that infused even her sticky quim. From moment to moment, she felt as though she were falling into dreams of her maid's hands soothing subtly under the bare flesh of her bottom. After a seeming eternity, the door opened and her haunted state went to the door. Marie and Amy entered, Marie carrying a large silver tray of food and wine which she rested upon her knees as she sat close to Astrid.

Lifted into a sitting position by Amy, who stroked her hair fondly, Astrid dumbly allowed herself to be fed with smoked salmon and other delicacies. Between bites, wine was gurgled down her throat.

'She eats well-that is the best of signs', Marie said contentedly when Astrid was laid back again, her head on a pillow, her eyes closed. The draught she had been given would ensure that she slept for an hour at least. Her pretty lips quivered and then were still. Falling, as it seemed to her, down a long, black-velvet tunnel she slept.

CHAPTER 3

Having entered her dressing room to don a pair of blue-silk directoire drawers and to cast about her voluptuous form a tea gown of matching material, Julia descended with a pleased smile upon her lips. The venture had gone as well as she had expected it to, and perhaps a trifle better. Every scornful of those whom she considered the oafs of Society-whether poor or rich-Julia admired above all young women of high-tempered spirit such as she now knew Astrid to be. The girl would be a perfect treasure.

Upon reaching the foot of the stairs she was met by Amy, who now wore an expression of greater humbleness on her face, for while their mistress allowed them certain pleasures she could also be exceedingly strict.

'Lady Dunnit is here to see you, Ma'am'.

'Alone, Amy?'

'No, Ma'am, she has her nephew with her-the one who...'.

'That will do, Amy. You may bring in some wine', Julia interrupted, for she was aware that the maid was about to attempt some familiar reminiscing. Lady Dun-nit was an infrequent visitor, but the occasions that she spent with Julia were often memorable, as they were for her nephew, Anthony. He had attained now to the age of seventeen and was a slender youth with a somewhat girlish face and blond hair, which Julia had insisted must be allowed to grow. Not having seen him for over a month, she was pleased, upon entering the drawing room, to find that it now almost reached his shoulders and went rather fetchingly with the blue velvet suit he wore.

Lady Esmeralda Dunnit was a lady in her early forties, who led the local hunt with her husband. Despite her commanding looks and her fiery figure, she acceded to Julia in all matters. The two had been at boarding school together and knew each other's ways. Embracing fondly, they kissed, pecking and cooing at one another's lips while Anthony sat silent and not a little fearful in the presence of their hostess.

'He looks a trifle pale. Have you been over-milking him?', Julia asked distantly while taking good care not to look at Anthony directly.

'Why, no', simpered Esmeralda. 'There has been very little opportunity for it. His mama is too often about and keeps a most careful eye on him'.

'Oh, tush! You should have brought her to rein long ago with as much ease as you do your horses, Esmeralda. It would appear that I shall have to intervene in that. You have been lost for pleasure then, I suppose?'.

A perfect shyness then appeared to come over her lady visitor, who had the grace to blush a little. Julia knew her well enough, however, not to pursue the matter too vocally and merely whispered something in her ear which caused Esmeralda to tremble inwardly with pleasure. At this moment, Marie entered with the wine, which, being a good Chateau neuf du Pape, afforded Lady Dunnit the sense of headiness she preferred to enjoy at such moments in Julia's presence. On purpose, nothing whatever was said to her nephew, who was but given a glass of milk while the two ladies sat and chatted as two might do in any English drawing room. After his second glass, however, Julia saw fit to take action. Summoning Marie again with a small hand bell, she nodded to Esmeralda, who, with excitement pulsing in her veins, rose and followed the maid out.

Esmeralda knew well enough where she was to go and having ascended to the second floor-unknowingly skirting the very door behind which Astrid lay-entered a room that was most curiously furnished. The walls on three sides were covered in rucked velvet drapes of dark blue, which completely concealed the windows, thus making it necessary to have lamps continually burning within. Upon the other wall, which was painted smoothly in cream, hung an assortment of whips, crops, leather paddles, and other devices that included chains, cuffs, and elaborate leather gags, some of which caused a ball to be held in the mouth of such miscreants as must be kept silent. Along one wall was a huge divan whose velvet surface offered comfort and ease. This, however, was not to be forthcoming until one had suffered certain torments, as Esmeralda well knew. The principal object of her attention was a whipping horse that stood in the centre of the room. Its bulk, supported upon four stout legs, resembled a huge bolster, covered in leather and cylindrical in shape. Its length was almost five feet and its diameter two feet. By a cunning mechanical device, the legs were adjustable in height and could be wound up or down at will. To one side of this apparatus was a more simple but stoutly built wooden trestle that but for its padded top might have been taken for a sawing horse, its triangular legs fastened securely to the floor.

'Madam will remove her dress', Marie said. She had dealt with Lady Dunnit before and knew something of her tastes and whims. Like many fine ladies whose exotic and lewd ideas could not be fulfilled in their own domestic surroundings, Esmeralda sought the assistance and encouragement of one as knowing as Julia, who, being as wealthy as herself, required no fees for her attendances, as she was pleased to call them. Having stripped the voluptuous dame of her dress, Marie next removed Tier petticoat and her knickers, which she drew carefully off over the tight-laced boots that Lady Dunnit wore. That left her attired in black, patterned stockings and a small corset, which left nothing of her monumental bottom and breasts concealed.

Stepping back, Marie surveyed the wondrous half-moons, which gleamed pale and full, nobly supported as they were on her stout thighs.

'You may turn, Madam', she said, whereat Esmeralda did so, displaying her fine black bush of thick curls beneath a swelling belly.

'You may lick me, Marie',

The words came softly and pleadingly in a tone that the noble dame would never otherwise have used to a servant. Here, however, she had knowingly entered a different realm, one in which she could play a submissive or supplicating role in order to appease her amorous desires. Her legs quivered visibly as the maid knelt and first sniffed appreciatively under Esmeralda's quim.

'How nice you smell, Madam. Have you received a cock here lately?'.

'No, my dear, for my husband is lax in his attentions. Put out your tongue now, I beg you, and slip it up between the lips. Ah! How delicious! A little farther in. Now twirl it around! Oh, what a good girl you are. Yes, press your lips up close. Ah, you make me tremble!'.

'My mistress will see to you properly in but a moment, Madam. Tom may be put to you also, if you wish, though that is not of course for me to say. Ah, Madam, you are coming! What a lovely spurting! The very thought of their cocks makes your juices flow, does it not', spluttered Marie, whose tongue continued to work steadily within and about the rolled lips of Lady Dunnit's cunt the while that her mouth and the tip of her nose became oiled with the damsel's effusions.

'Oh, my dear girl, do it more!'.

Esmeralda's legs stiffened and widened, her head falling back and her fingers coursing about her thick, brown nipples, which stood out upon her gelatinous gourds as she awaited the second coming of pleasure which seemed to set her belly and cunt on fire.

Meanwhile, downstairs, Anthony had, under Julia's command, removed all save his shirt and the batiste knickers, which she had been pleased to find he was wearing under his trousers. His limbs were strong but slender, the skin shaven everywhere and as smooth as a girl's.

'They are your elder sister's, I trust', Julia said, while making him stand to attention.

'Yes, Madam'.

'Expose your prick to me, you wretch, when I address you thus! Does she not make you get it out?'.

'Yes, Madam', Anthony trembled. He fumbled in the knickers which, being slit at the front as well as the rear, permitted him to work his penis out, where it lolled in a half-erect state, his balls remaining hid. The very presence of all females awed him. Those over twenty years of age seemed as veritable goddesses to him. He was as helpless in their hands as he now was with Julia. As she moved about him, much as one might examine a young stallion, he could glimpse through the gap in her gown the legs of her drawers and the luscious rims of her white thighs above her stocking tops. His jaw sagged and a squeal of surprise came from him as with one hand Julia wrenched his head back by taking hold of his hair and with the other cupped his balls tightly through the drawers.

'You are of service to her, Anthony?', she asked coldly, maintaining both her grips.

Anthony gulped and tried to nod. He dare not tell anyone the awful things that his sister, Maude, did to him. She was six years his senior and had been well-tutored by Julia, though he knew it not. Sometimes she would steal into his room at night while he slept and, drawing up his nightshirt to his armpits, bind him tightly from shoulders to knees while he lay in trembling dismay. Never speaking, Maude would then straddle his prone figure and raise her own nightdress to just above her hips. In the gloom he would see the whites of her thighs and the dark, mysterious triangle of hair about her plump mount. The bed would creak slightly as his sister settled her knees firmly, her cunt poised above his cock. Anthony always feared that the sound might arouse his parents, but no one ever came. Maude's hips were wide, and her tits-which he had never yet seen-were heavy. A musky perfume would come from between her thighs, making his prick stiffen rapidly.

Maude would never touch him until she deemed him stiff enough for his task, but would remain immobile, gazing down upon him. Anthony always tried to suppress the moan of pleasure that rose instinctively to his lips as then her warm clasp took his erect pego, brushing it under the waiting lips of her slit while her eyes appeared to burn down into his. Then with a contented sigh Maude would commence settling her cunt slowly on his cock, never bearing her weight down so much that he slipped in easily, but always keeping every tremor of her hips under control until at last the silky walls of her vagina absorbed him fully. Sheathed in her to the root, Anthony would feel the full impress of her round bottom on his thighs while she imperiously so held and contained him.

Sometimes Maude would bend over him and he would long for their lips to meet, but such never occurred. Straightening, she would commence jogging up and down on his prick, her motion slow and sensuous. Each time her breath hissed out through her nose, Anthony would know she was enjoying the delirium of orgasm, for his embedded tool would become wetter with her juices which would flow down onto his balls. He himself was not permitted to ejaculate his sperm until Maude uttered the single word 'NOW!'. Then at last the pent-up passions in him would find release and he would lie shaking and quivering in the tight enclosure of the ropes while his sperm jetted and throbbed within her.

Only when she had extolled the last drop would his sister dismount, wrinkling her nose in distaste at the spectacle of his sodden and weaking tool as it slipped from between her lovelips. Silently untying him, she would give his buttocks a sharp smack and tell him to go to sleep before departing as quietly as she had come.

Once, as Maude got off the bed, Anthony had heard to his frozen horror the voice of his mother coming from a farther bedroom.

'What are you doing, Maude? Is that you?'.

'Anthony needed a glass of water, Mama. I have seen to him'.

'Very well, Maude'.

His prick dripping into the sheet, he had then slept, though fearful that Maude might return in an hour or two, as she sometimes did, to waken him and put her to him again. This he knew was what was meant by being of service to her. The warmth and suction of his sister's cunt was heavenly and he longed to clasp her and kiss her while she was doing it, but such was never permitted. He was an instrument to be used for the pleasure of ladies. The very thought made Anthony feel swoony. Now when Julia stroked his cock while still holding his head back severely, tears of pleasure flooded into his eyes. Then her hold on his pego tightened and she led him out by it and upstairs. Hearing a scuffle from within the Attendance Room, Julia smiled and hesitated for a moment before entering. As she did so, Marie rose from her knees and Esmeralda quickly turned away.

'You have been naughty, Esmeralda', Julia intoned. Closing the door, she relinquished her grip on Anthony's cock and motioned him brusquely to stand in the corner. Marie wiped her mouth and smiled. Her shoulders quivering, Esmeralda dropped her head.

'Oh, how can you say such a thing!', she expostulated, though without any conviction whatever, thoroughly aware that her nephew's eyes, were feasting upon the exposed globe of her bottom as well as her tits, which he could see in profile.

'Marie-put her over!', came then Julia's crisp command, whereat Esmeralda uttered such a wail one might have thought she was being consigned to purgatory. The maid took her elbow firmly and led her, with her bottom cheeks wobbling heavily, to the trestle. '

'I beg you no! Oh, pray, do not whip my bottom! T shall never be wicked again, I do promise!', howled Esmeralda, though making no attempt whatever to escape her fate, as Marie bent her firmly over. Her belly was settled on the padded top, her wrists secured by clamps to the legs, thus forcing her arms to spread. Thus positioned, her bottom rose like a harvest moon glowing gloriously and exposing the full cleft for all to see. Beneath the lower bulge could be espied the smaller cleft of her cunt, whose ruby lips glistened in their nest of curls. Anthony, forced to stand with his arms at his sides in the corner, felt his cock quiver passionately. He had fucked his aunt but thrice before, each time on visits to Julia, and was ever eager to plunge his prick into whichever of her orifices was ordained for his attention.

'Your legs, Esmeralda-keep them full apart or by heavens I shall scorch your bottom until you scream for mercy!', said Julia, who had pondered which of her many instruments to use. For her own pleasure, as also for Esmeralda's, she sometimes brought the birch to her or even the cane, but in front of Anthony such would be unseemly. She therefore chose a paddle which was of thick leather, a large oval shape attached to a small, black handle. It made an exceedingly satisfying noise as well as affording a female sensations she could never otherwise obtain.

'Spare me, Julia, please!', Esmeralda whimpered, as out of the corner of her eye she saw her friend taking up position at her rear.

'I may spare you even your nephew's cock if you do not be quiet', Julia responded cynically, and therewith raised the leather paddle and brought it with a most resounding SMACK! and SPLATT! full across Esmeralda's full and fleshy bottom, causing her to yelp. Her nether cheeks contracted under the splatting smack which burned full into her. Her mouth open and her nose all but touching the floor, Esmeralda received with a screeching gasp a second and a third. Her hips waggled wildly, the heels of her boots digging frantically into the carpet. A pink glow spread across her cleft globe, the attractive hue merging into the pallor of her cheeks.

SPLATT! SMACK! SPLATT! SMACK! came the paddle again, each time bringing a more high-pitched cry from Esmeralda. Her hair drooped down one side of her face as her pins loosened. 'NOO-OOOH-OOOH!', came her plaintive wail, but all was ignored in the passion of the moment to which the deeply satisfying sound of the leather meeting her ardent flesh gave its salute.

The darling bitch was enjoying not only the sensations she was being afforded, but the spectacle she was giving, as Julia well knew. The very thought strengthened her arm and wrist. When Esmeralda received the next three it was first upon either cheek, from the side, and then beneath, causing her to jerk her hips up even more lewdly as the leather sought and seared into the lower and plumpest part of her bulge.

'Do not, Julia, do NOT! OW!', cried Esmeralda in such alarm as those are wont to offer who have appealed for punishment and yet feel themselves unable to sustain it. Her arms strained, causing the manacles which held her wrists to clink.

'Prepare the young male', Julia said curtly to Marie, who all the time had watched with deeply glowing eyes. Moving toward Anthony, who was trembling mightily, she removed first his drawers and then his shirt, leaving him naked for the fray. As was her custom then, she ringed his upstanding pego in her fingers and with her free hand cupped his balls, holding him steady while yet Julia, continuing to apply the paddle with expert sweeps of her arm, brought Esmeralda's ample derriere to a fine glow. The cheeks indeed looked positively glowing with heat and even larger than they had first appeared, their wriggling and writhing movements- accompanied by Esmeralda's ever-wilder cries- making Anthony's prick throb urgently in Marie's palm. She, however, merely tightened her grip upon it, causing his eyes to screw up.

'Ah, stop! Oh, stop! I cannot bear it, Julia! No-no more! Have pity!', came Esmeralda's screech, for her bottom felt now veritably like a brazier, her heaving cheeks clamping tightly upon one another in a hapless attempt to drive out the heat that was truly scorching her loins.

Julia then cast the paddle to one side, where it fell with a slight thud on the carpet. This was the signal for Marie, who led Anthony forward while his aunt's sobs filled the room. Her hair now cascaded full about her face upon which two pearly tears showed. As Anthony approached with his stiff pego pointing towards his aunt's hot rump, Julia stepped in front of her. So far over was Esmeralda bent that Julia had but to open her stately legs and then close them again in order to secure Esmeralda's back under her crotch. Leaning forward, she then parted the richly fleshed cheeks of Esmeralda's bottom and thereby fully exposed the crinkled brown ring of her anus.

'No! My god, not there!', came Esmeralda's croaking cry, which choked off into a hollow moan as Marie neatly placed the crest of Anthony's prick against the rounded aperture. A slight pressure then of his loins and the rubbery ring was forced, yielding to absorb the knob while Esmeralda's cries fluttered upon the air.

'Hold!', Marie instructed him, thereupon taking both his arms and bringing them up above his shoulders until she could attach his wrists to manacles which dangled from two chains that hung from the ceiling. Bending swiftly while Anthony grimaced with pleasure at the containment of his knob in his aunt's bottomhole, Marie applied clamps to his feet so that the only movements he could now make were with his loins. Face flushed, the maid straightened and received an approving nod from her mistress, who ever delighted in such libertine tableaux. Unsaddling herself from Esmeralda's bent back, she moved behind to inspect the insertion of Anthony's cock. The helmet was but just within. His aunt's anus appeared as might a baby's mouth around it. Giving his smooth buttocks a sharp little smack, Julia caused it to bury itself a farther inch within, which gesture of homage was received with a low moan from its recipient.

'STAY!', she commanded Anthony in a voice such as one would use to a gundog. 'Marie-you will see that neither moves so much as a half-inch or both will be put to the birch and worse. Contain them in this posture until I return!'.

'JUL-I-AP, came Esmeralda's pitiful cry at that, but only the opening and closing of the door made reply. Anthony's upraised, arms already ached and his cock twitched in the delicious, warm containment of his aunt's plump bottom, yet he dared not move a muscle, no more than she, for they knew that Julia's warning had been fully meant.

CHAPTER 4

Astrid awoke with a start to find Julia unwinding the rope that held her legs together. Her eyes blinked and she stared all about.

'Oh, where am I?', she asked.

'In the best of hands-one might say the most knowing, in your case', her hostess replied, making her sit up.

At this, all recollection flooded back into the young woman's mind. Such entreaties as Julia had ofttimes heard from her pupils flooded from Astrid's lips. 'Papa will seek you out and will surely punish you. He knows that I am here', Astrid trembled, but even as the words left her lips Julia, sitting upon the bed beside her, took her chin and kissed her lips.

'Let us be clear about one thing, Astrid. Your papa knows full well, though you did not, that your stay in my care would be longer than you had anticipated. He will not therefore come seeking you for he knows better than to do so. Come, move off the bed and stand up. I am about to further your education'.

Of course Astrid struggled fretfully, but with her arms bound to her sides was ill put to disagree as to what should be done with her. In a trice she was on her feet, naked to her stockings, her dismay heightened by the fact that Julia now applied a black-velvet gag to her mouth, causing Astrid's eyes to bulge and her head to shake furiously. Julia would have nothing than that her will be obeyed, and commenced urging Astrid from the boudoir and, to the young woman's apprehension, forced her to mount the stairs to the second floor.

'Have no fear, no ill is to come to you', cooed Julia, though Astrid's resistance grew at every step and Julia was once or twice forced to give her charming nether cheeks a hearty smack, making her stumble in her ascent. Tears glistened in the proud young woman's eyes, for in addition to all else she could not bring herself to believe that she had been betrayed by her own dear papa, who she had envisaged arriving in a day or two to rescue her. Some instinct, however, told her that Julia was not lying and possessed too much confidence to be doing so. Convinced that she was being led to some further punishment, though what she knew not, Astrid continued making attempts to impede her progress but was ever pushed forward until the door of the 'Attendance Room' was reached. Fully expecting Julia to open it, Astrid stood in trembling wonderment as a small piece of wood in the door was slid aside, revealing what looked like a large knot hole.

'Look-peer within-that is all you have to do', Julia murmured, keeping one hand on the back of the rope with which she had pinned the young woman's arms. At the same time, she knocked gently three times on the door in a signal that Marie well knew. Picking up the paddle that her mistress had dropped, Marie applied it smartly to Anthony's buttocks, causing him to squeal and grimace while at the same time the stinging impact of the leather made his hips jerk. Thus, to a bubbling moan from his aunt, was his fleshly peg driven another two inches into her bottom.

Her face pressed forward and one eye applied to the peephole, Astrid saw all and was transfixed. Never before had she seen even a male penis in erection, and most certainly she had never seen a nude female and a nude male in such amorous conjunction. Viewing as she did in profile the bent figure of Esmeralda, naught was hid from her, and few things are so lewd or exciting than to see a sturdy young pego in fine, erect condition, half-embedded in a lady's fulsome fundament. The deep blush that came to her cheeks invaded also her neck. A trembling seized her and she would have started back had not Julia pressed her face into the door.

'Look carefully-observe all, Astrid', Julia intoned, softly gliding the fingers of one hand under the maiden's silk round bottom and feeling her cunt.

Astrid wriggled rebelliously at that, yet had no alternative but to obey and suffer the caress. As it seemed to her at first, both participants within were being put to some dire torture, though in fact Esmeralda and her nephew were ascending the heights of pleasure with every slapping stroke of the paddle. Tight and hot as Esmeralda's bottomhole was, she by now clasped three-quarters of Anthony's weapon within,, while he-caught between heaven and hell-uttered whimpering cries of pleasure as inch by inch his pego corkscrewed in-between those luscious cheeks until his aunt's big bottom mounded into his belly. Both quivered, both shuddered divinely.

'In, out, in, out, Master Anthony!', hissed Marie, who was now according him a rhythmic slapping of the leather such as made his hips reply with febrile jerks.

'WHOOOO! No! He mustn't!', moaned Esmeralda, who of course desired nothing more than that he should and was perfectly delighted to find her plea ignored. Unable to move his feet, and with his wrists strung high, Anthony's young form was supple and the constrictions of his extremities did nothing to prevent his agile loins from working back and forth under the stimulation of the paddle. From moment to moment Astrid could see his knob emerging almost fully from Esmeralda's bottom only to piston deep within again.

Muffled by her gag, Astrid could do no other than gurgle in her throat, as now she felt the tip of Julia's forefinger insinuating itself into her own most secret orifice.

'You shall have such as she, my love, and frequently. Come, work your noble young bottom on my finger-I will have it so', said Julia, working her digit in to the first knuckle while Astrid writhed, her tummy smacking gently against the door panels, though all within the room were too absorbed to hear. While Esmeralda continued to moan, the sounds that issued from her throat were now softer, and with each inward plunge of her nephew's cock the breath hissed hotly from her nostrils for she knew no greater joy than to be bottom-warmed and corked. Even so, she knew better than to encourage Anthony other than by protruding her nether cheeks as deeply as she could into him.

He was but a young male slave providing her with such pleasure as she sought and now had truly gained. As for Anthony, this also to him represented the very pinnacle of attainment, for his adoration of older and mature women was intense and whether his virile cock was put to their cunts, their bottoms, or-most rarely-their mouths was almost a matter of indifference to him. So severely had he been warned by Julia of the sin of Onanism, that he knew pleasure only when his prick was handled by another.

His bottom-cheeks were by now a deep pink from the splatting of the leather, yet this stinging pleasured him secretly, too, and made his cock the stiffer. Sometimes when he was younger and his mama had spanked him, he had frequently rubbed it over her thighs, but she never appeared-to notice. Now that he was being made to do all these things, his heaven was complete.

Astrid, meanwhile, moaned into the velvet which covered about her mouth. Again the most unexpected sensations were assailing her. She knew that it was truly wicked to watch what was happening within, yet Julia did not need to hold her eye to the peephole now. At the same time the urging movement of the finger in her own bottom was causing her belly to melt and her cunny to moisten. Having established the latter condition by feeling under Astrid's pulpy slit, Julia was well pleased. Standing sideways to the girl, she began tickling her clitoris simultaneously, making Astrid buck her hips helplessly.

'How many males will sperm your cunt and bottom, my love', murmured Julia, knowing full well the power of erotic speech at moments such as this. For reply, Astrid gurgled deeply. Her mind swam hotly with the lewd and luscious scene before her. As Marie quickened the pace of the paddle, so Anthony whipped his loins the faster. He had felt his balls sprinkled several times on his forward strokes by his aunt's effusion and now to all his sensations was added the glorious release of shooting his come up her bottom. His knees buckled and shook, his eyes rolled.

'Spout! Spout in her!', commanded Marie, who knew all the signs of his straining neck muscles and the ever-deeper flush on his young face,

'HAAAR!', moaned Astrid in the same moment. She was coming again. The wicked woman was making her come, working both fingers back and forth until her juices rippled and spattered over Julia's hand. Simultaneously-as seemed nigh perfect for this lubricious occasion-Anthony ejected the spermatic bubblings of his joy. Every jet of his sperm was deliciously felt by his aunt, who caused her tightening bottomhole to suck so greedily on his embedded took that he, drawn in her to the root, was stilled and transfixed. It seemed to him she absorbed every ounce of his strength, leaving him weak and febrile. As indeed Astrid herself almost felt as Julia led her back down the stairs, fondling her nether cheeks as she did so.

'How you came, my dear! I am glad', Julia murmured. Once installed in the boudoir, she loosed Astrid's gag as also her bonds, allowing the young woman to sag and to sit weakly on the edge of the bed. 'We shall have wine', Julia said comfortingly, and rang for Amy by giving three tugs of the bell pull. The girl arrived in short time, bearing refreshments which she placed down, and then departed wordlessly. 'You have viewed your first entertainment, Astrid. I call them such. There will come a time when you will arrange your own'. With that, Julia poured the wine and settled some small tea cakes on a plate in the girl's lap before sitting beside her.

'Never! Oh, I could never do such horrible things!', Astrid replied. 'Those poor people-how were they made to do it I cannot imagine!'.

'Those poor people indeed! You shall meet Esmeralda-Lady of her own manor, my dear-soon enough, and, as for Anthony, whose cock you have now well viewed, he is but a puling young male who will obey whatever commands you give him. Know you not that some men are born into bondage and have little delight in anything else? No, do not interrupt me, Astrid, or I shall gag you again and you will do without your refreshments. Males are but penis bearers, my dear, though I confess that there are times when in our imperious wisdom we submit body and soul to them briefly in order to know and enjoy the experience. Likewise there are females enough whose greater pleasure is to be put to the whip and made to do all manner of things'.

'Oh, I do not understand you-I do not understand at all! I do not wish to know', moaned Astrid, her lips flecked with crumbs.

'What you believe you wish to know-which is less than little-and what you are going to know are two different things, my dear. Were you incommoded by your bonds? Was it so fearful as you thought? Come, answer me!'.

Her chin lifted by Julia's hand, and her eyes held by the woman's fierce but loving gaze, Astrid returned her stare speechlessly.

'Ha! What have you to say in all reality, Astrid! Drink your wine, girl. You came as splendidly on my finger as any have. Your excitement could not be denied, and well you know it. Your sphincter accommodated my finger more eagerly than you would have wished me to realise. The dual sensation is delicious, is it not? I have known women to faint with pleasure when put to two cocks at once, one fore and one aft. Were you have to been left in the calm and placid condition of your otherwise useless life, you would have known nothing of these things. Rather, you would have been made bitter and frigid by some cur of a husband who would fuck you once weekly and then enjoy himself better with a gay girl more knowing of his wants.

'Oh, don't, don't, don't! What horrible things you say!', sobbed Astrid, real tears upon her cheeks.

'I shall say naught nor do naught but what you should know and are to learn and experience, Astrid. What think you of the male once he has fucked and expended his sperm? That he remain an overlord-a mighty stallion still? What nonsense is that! Once his manly cock has spilled, he is as weak as a kitten. As for the woman who has lain under him and received his sperm, she herself is fit to take a dozen more. Yes, and will ripen in the process. I have known women whose skin was ever as creamy and smooth as my own by virtue of the sperm of young boys which they rub into it each morning'.

'Stop, stop! I cannot hear such hateful things!'.

'Can you not?', Julia laughed, rising and confronting Astrid, in whom a great apprehension rose. Reaching out to the bell pull, Julia drew upon it, summoning a waiting Amy within. 'Turn her about and hold her down, Amy!'.

'NO!', Astrid shrieked, but all in vain, for even as the wine spilled over her thighs and her small plate clattered to the floor, the maid pressed her back and spun her over, landing with a thump on her shoulders. From a wardrobe Julia hastened to produce a whip of many thongs, whose black-ivory handle was formed in the shape of a huge penis. 'YEEE-OW!', Astrid shrieked as within seconds the hissing thongs assailed her pouting derriere.

'You disobeyed my injunctions, girl? You will rebel?', asked Julia scornfully, sweeping in the whip once more in such wise that a thousand streaks of fire seemed to course through the girl's bottom, making it heave and writhe.

'HOO-HOO-HOOO!', Astrid sobbed, feeling more and more like a schoolgirl. 'Will you stop? Oh, stop, I cannot bear it!'.

'What a ninny she is!', Amy laughed incautiously, receiving such a glare from her mistress that she blenched and fell quiet. She was riding like a jockey on the heaving back of Astrid, whose bottom-cheeks reddened anew as the thongs bit into her as might a passing horde of bees.

'YEE-EEE-EEEK!', she screeched again and again, her cries going completely unheeded by Julia, who thoroughly adored whipping a bottom as round and desirable as Astrid's. Twisting the small whip this way and that, she ensured that not an inch of that luscious flesh was left unassailed. Spots of pink appeared on the flawless half-moons, merging them into an overall glow. 'HAAAAR! I cannot b... b... bear it!', sobbed Astrid, quite unable to unsaddle Amy. The maid's own cunny had in fact moistened much during the delightful conflict, and by positioning herself more artfully she was able to rub it through her dress against Astrid's spine.

Having at last afforded the writhing maiden a good thirty strokes, which left her bottom glowing, Julia tossed aside the whip and slid from beneath one of the pillows close to Astrid's head a slender, velvet-covered dildo, which she sprinkled with sweet oil from a little phial on the bedside cabinet. At that, Amy flung herself forward, and to Astrid's utter, screeching dismay, held the springy cheeks of her hot bottom well apart to expose the crinkled hole that was now Julia's target.

To a thin, high scream from Astrid, the smooth round knob of the enticing instrument was introduced into her virgin sphincter, its passage being so soothed by the oil that in but a few seconds it had burrowed up within. Astrid felt as if all the air were being expelled from her body. Clamping her knees on either side of the girl's waist, Amy held her firmly, watching with greedy eyes the now unimpeded progress of the imitation prick until over six inches of it were sheathed.

'NOOO-OOOH-OOOH! Take it OUT!', Astrid shrieked, as Amy's palms settled firmly down into the small of her back, forcing her bottom to orb up to the wicked offering. The slow insertion and withdrawal of the dildo burned and itched, complementing strangely the agonised burning in her cheeks and causing her belly to ripple and her mouth to sag. Such cries as she subsequently uttered in the increasingly rhythmic pumping of the luring instrument were then more muffled. Shamefully screwing up and then closing her eyes, she worked her derriere fretfully to each in-and-out motion of the dildo, now and then issuing a sob or a gasp as her sensations mounted.

Wise to every tiny movement of the girl's hips, as also to the tenor of her cries, Julia motioned with her head to Amy, who thereupon slid completely off and stood by the bedside. The maid knew, too,, that Astrid had passed the first barriers to pleasure and was now about to ride on the crest. Clawing at the bedcover in her newly found freedom, Astrid nevertheless did little enough to escape the steady pumping of the smooth, persuasive dildo which was affording her certain exquisite sensations she had never previously known. In her momentary frenzy, her teeth bit into the silk bedspread beneath her. Her nostrils flared. Breath hissed from her mouth and nose.

'She is about to come! Quickly, now!'.

Amy moved swiftly at Julia's command. It was not the first time that she would have helped her mistress accomplish such a feat as. With the dildo buried full within her sphincter, Astrid found herself twisted about until, laid on her back, her legs were slung over the shoulders of the maid, whose long, wet tongue sought the bubbling crevice of her cunt. Lying beside Astrid and holding the dildo in beneath her, Julia commenced again working it back and forth.

'WHO-OH!', Astrid moaned, assailed now in both her parts. Her face lolled sideways as Julia cupped her chin. Her lips parted, receiving Julia's tongue. Their lips meshed. Astrid's hips worked violently, seeking as though to receive as deeply as possible both tongue and dildo. Violent tremors shook her and a gurgling sounded from Amy, whose flashing tongue was of a sudden coated and splattered with a salty rain sparkling like a brook from Astrid's slit. 'B... b... b ...!', Astrid mumbled incoherently. Her legs, hooked over Amy's shoulders, jerked, her arms enfolded Julia's neck. Extreme quivers rippled through her, another salty effusion flowed into Amy's mouth, and then all was still. With a faint 'PLOP!' the dildo was slowly withdrawn. Amy rose to her feet, leaving the girl's legs to slump lazily down. Julia was kissing Astrid still. Their mouths worked dreamily together.

Closing the door quietly, Amy tripped upstairs to assist Marie.

CHAPTER 5

All seemed but a dream now to Astrid. Never had her body felt so fulfilled, though her mind continued to rebel. At one moment the two maids had assaulted her lewdly and, at another, they were assisting her to dress with all the meek subservience of servants to which she had become long accustomed.

'You have not yet been put fully to your trials, my dear, but you will not be long in doing so', Julia murmured to her once order had been restored and Astrid found herself clothed and quite pampered by Amy and Marie. Once her hair had been attended to with loving fingers, Astrid surveyed herself fretfully in the mirror, wondering with astonishment why she did not look different. Expecting her visage to look haggard, she found her reflection in the mirror a perfect picture of healthy, young womanhood.

'You will meet now Esmeralda-yes, the very one whose bottom you saw offering itself to pleasure. She is about to depart, I believe, but must truly have the pleasure of your company for a moment. Come, Astrid, accompany me down', said Julia.

'Oh, I cannot! The very thought of facing her-I beg you do not make me!'.

'Tush and nonsense, girl. She knows not that you were witness to her pleasures. She may wish to kiss you, though. She has a fondness for beautiful girls. You will not resist? It would-be unseemly were I or my maids to have to hold you-particularly in front of her nephew-would it not?'.

'Oh!', blurted Astrid. The maids had departed and they were alone. Tears sprang into her lovely eyes at the thought of further such humiliations in front of strangers. That the pair she had seen fucking together were aunt and nephew blazoned itself on her mind. I do not...w...

want....', she began weakly, but already her warm hand was taken and she was led without. Unable to deny to herself the strange sense of complicity that was already burgeoning between herself and Julia, she allowed herself to be meekly led down, there to be greeted by Esmeralda, who looked as fresh and well-coiffured again as anyone might ever have seen her.

Formal introductions being effected, Esmeralda placed herself on a chaise longue beside Astrid, who gazed with uncertain tremblings about her, though she did her best to look calm and possessed in front of Anthony. He, being fully dressed once more, sat observing her shyly, much as one might gaze on a young goddess.

'Truly beautiful!', Esmeralda murmured, passing her hand under Astrid's chin and stroking it lovingly. 'I have seen you before, my dear, I am sure. May I kiss you?'.

At that Julia joined them on the seat on the other side of Astrid, who felt the warning nudge of her elbow in her side. Moving from beneath her chin, Esmeralda's fingers caressed her peach-like cheek and, drawing Astrid a little sideways, placed her mouth on her own in so demanding a manner that the girl quivered throughout her frame. Softening her mouth while feeling her hand taken in a firm, warm clasp by Julia, Astrid submitted to the kiss which she had expected to be a brief one. Instead it endured. Slithering snake-like into her mouth, Esmeralda's tongue found her own while the weight of her body trapped Astrid's other arm behind her.

'So nice, so warm, so sweet', Esmeralda husked. Feeling down, she sought Astrid's skirt and commenced working it up fold by fold, causing Astrid to splutter as the lovely curves of her legs were inch by inch revealed to the eyes of both women, as also to Anthony.

'NOOOO!', Astrid moaned, receiving a slap from Julia, who hissed, 'Did I not warn you, Astrid?'.

While Astrid squirmed, Esmeralda's hand sought higher, slipping beneath the rucked-up skirt to taste the milky splendour of the girl's thighs, which the slow uncovering had now revealed. In a moment her fingertips touched the silk drawers that Astrid wore and moved them gently aside, there to savour the plumpness of her mount and the springy hump of curls that crowned her cunt. At that, Astrid jerked more wildly and sought to free her hands, for, as luscious as Esmeralda's ripe mouth was, she was thoroughly shamed at being exposed before such a young man, whom she knew was viewing all.

'Leave her!', snapped Julia of a sudden. 'I will not have my guests scorned so. It seems indeed that she has learned little'.

With a last regretful flurry of her hand, Esmeralda disengaged herself and sat up, leaving a flushed and trembling Astrid to do the same while quickly covering her legs.

'She should be put to him', Esmeralda said, inclining her head towards Anthony.

'No!', shrieked Astrid and covered her eyes, blushing fiercely, and little knowing with what understanding Julia was gazing down upon her.

'To such as he? He is but a whippet!', sneered Julia, casting her most fearsome gaze upon Anthony, who thereupon appeared to shrink. 'He does well enough to lubricate your bottom, my love, but is scarce fit for such a task. Astrid is to be better mounted than that'.

'Oh, how can you speak like this!', Astrid moaned behind her fingers.

'Easily enough, as you one day shall, too', Julia answered crisply. 'Esmeralda is about to depart truly wounded, as she is bound to feel'.

'Not at all, Julia. You have had them even more troublesome than this. She is in a pettish mood, the poor dear. You will soon enough get her out of it, I am sure. Get up, Anthony-UP, sir! Julia, my love, I shall return, with your permission, in a week or two'.

'Perhaps. I fear I indulge you too much, Esmeralda. I shall require more of you than this. 'Tis an amusing thing to keep this young stripling in training-and well he must be-but you have other tasks. Have I not spoken to you of his mama? There now is a quarter to which you must lend your talents, albeit that they are weaker than my own. Domestic interferences must be dispensed with. You will attend to this before I afford you any more pleasures. You know what to do. Have I not schooled you sufficiently?'.

'Yes, Julia', said Esmeralda, though doubtfully. She was one who took as much pleasure in giving as receiving yet she had never attained the masterful heights of Julia, whose power to command seemed illimitable.

'You will see to it. Let the thought grow upon you, Esmeralda. I bid you adieu. Amy will see you out. Come, Astrid!'.

Feeling curiously crestfallen rather than outraged, the girl obeyed, passing behind the departing visitors in the hall to proceed through the morning room and into the grounds. Julia stepped ever a pace in front of Astrid, thereby leading her on as though by some invisible cord.

'Where... where are we going?', Astrid asked hesitantly with a humbleness she had never previously felt.

Passing through the rose garden, Julia did not deign to reply before passing the summerhouse and entering the paddock through a gate.

'I shall say nothing of what is to happen, Astrid', she replied, passing neatly over the rough turf, where after a few minutes they approached a large stable. There Tom, the manservant, was attending to the polishing of saddles, girths, and various straps, seated upon a stool near the open door. Seeing him, Astrid wilted and would have lagged back had not Julia seized her arm and dragged her forward. Seeing this, Tom rose and came towards them, knowing well his duty in such matters. It was never often enough for him that some proud young lady was stabled. In a trice he had taken Astrid by the waist, causing her to shriek with alarm as he hoisted her off her feet and held her dangling as he might have a newborn lamb.

'Is not Alice here?', asked Julia.

'Yes, Ma'am, I be here', came a voice from within the stable. A young woman of some twenty-eight years appeared attired in a rough country dress with a cap askew on her tousled head.

'Good. You will see to this one, then bring her back within. You are happy, Alice?'.

'Oh yes, Ma'am', replied the young woman, who had been wed to Tom but three months. 'He does my bidding and I does his. We gets along well'.

'Excellent, Alice', replied Julia, who believed in the bonds of holy matrimony more literally than others. Both were of her training, and Alice was as wont to birch her husband's buttocks as he her own more attractive ones. Many nights had passed in which Julie had had them bound naked together, face to face, before they were wed, with Tom's cock throbbing hot and hard between their bellies, neither able to move. While Marie and Amy were truly Julia's house pets, as she ofttimes privately called them, she was prouder by far of these two who served her well and faultlessly in all respects. Tom's prick was by far one of the doughtiest in the county. Julia herself had tasted its pleasures on many occasions, of which Alice had frequently been witness, sometimes bound to a post in the stable at others left free standing with but a thick leather collar about her neck and tethered to the selfsame upright.

Alice it was who frequently whipped or paddled Marie and Amy. She had no fears about Astrid, though she knew her by her dress and appearance to be of the upper class. 'It matters not to me so long as they have tight, furry cunts. I loves to see 'em squeal and watch 'em wriggle when Tom puts it to them. He has a rare old pumper', Alice would say proudly. She herself fell to the services of Julia when required, licking up along her fine stockinged legs before delving into her cunt. Sometimes Julia would have Alice fucked or buggered slowly while she was doing it, by one or another of the males who were brought for training.

'Did you not have a good creaming, Alice?', Julia would say to her afterwards.

'Oh, yes, Ma'am, and I loved it', the young woman would reply fondly. Sometimes if Julia were in lust she would caress and fondle her and then take her down upon the carpet in the drawing room, there to wreak her own desires upon her. They would coo and peck as sweetly as two sisters, though Alice never forgot her place and was subservient when all was done.

'We'll have her inside then, Tom', Alice spoke now, assisting him in carrying a frantically struggling Astrid within.

'Save me! Julia, save me!', shrieked Astrid, endeavouring to cast the wildest of glances back. Julia however had already begun to depart. It were best that Astrid were left to them. Her wilfulness might then be finally overcome. 'No! What are you going to do with me!', she could hear Astrid crying from within the stable. Without further ado the young woman found herself cast face down over a bale of straw, her legs kicking in a way that troubled the pair not a whit. While Tom held her down with the least effort, Alice raised her skirt and, going 'round to the farther side of the bale, swiftly cupped Astrid's chin in both hands and brought her head firmly between her bared thighs. As Alice's legs were strong, Astrid found herself trapped as certainly as any rabbit in a snare while Tom, roughing up her skirt and petticoat, exposed her drawers to view.

'Let's see her bottom, Tom-get 'em down. My, ain't she got a lovely one, so white and round', Alice uttered to the wailing despair of Astrid, whose drawers were swiftly removed and cast to one side. 'I got her Tom-tickle her up with the strap first', chuckled his wife, who could already see his big penis straining up under his breeches at the sight of Astrid's cleft.

'No! Oh, my God, no!', screeched Astrid, her ears already burning in the masterful grip of Alice's thighs. No sooner had the cry left her throat then THWA-AAAACK! Across her yielded bottom seared a four-inch doughty strap that made her hips jerk madly. SPERLATT! THWACK! SMACK! To each one Astrid ripped out a wailing sob, tightening her defenceless cheeks as best she could while Tom sturdily wielded the strap from side to side, thumbing open the buttons of his breeches as he did so.

'Three more, Tom, and then you 'ave her!', cried Alice, who knew well enough herself the burning of that selfsame leather.

'OOOH-WAH! NO!'

'Oh, yes, my sweet young miss, you ain't the first across the bale to put it to 'im. He's got balls as big as a bullock's, my Tom 'as, and a cock fair fit to bring all the cows out of the pasture'.

'YEEE-OUCH! Stop it! Oh, you filthy beasts, how dare you do this to me! OW!'.

Her bottom thoroughly hot and rosy now and ready for a tupping, Tom laid the strap aside across the neighbouring bale and with a mighty snort produced a veritable broom handle of a prick, which stood a full nine inches up his belly. Hand-made as the bale was just for this purpose, it brought a young lady's bottom up to the height he needed. Flexing his knees, and with his heavy balls hanging out, he gripped Astrid's hips as in a clasp of steel and pronged his knob up beneath her cuntlips, the very touch of it producing from her such a scream as echoed to the roof.

'I beg you, I beg you, I beg you.... OOOOOH!'

'Now, me dear, I 'as you nice and slow as I bin taught to by the Lady Julia', Tom grunted, squeezing his swollen plum between the pouting lovelips while Alice leaned forward as far as she was able to observe the amorous event. Trapped between her legs, Astrid screeched, cried, sobbed, and pleaded while inch by inch the fleshy staff urged within the velvety sleekness of her grotto.

'Is she nice, Tom? She looks a rare 'un!'

'Luscious as a peach, me dear, though no ways a touch on yours', Tom said gallantly, though in all truth the spongy gripping of Astrid's cunt was prime and fair ready to draw him in despite her wild screechings. Half in, he held it there for a long moment just to let her feel the ticking and throbbing of it as Julia had taught him to do with young rebellious misses so that they might better get the feel of it.

'I don't want to! No!', came Astrid's cry, though the renewed insurgence of such a doughty tool was beginning to overwhelm her with the delicious sensations it brought. Her bottom waggled, causing Tom to breathe more heavily. Another couple of inches and he'd be right in, home and moist.

'Give us a kiss,- love', Alice laughed merrily, for she knew too well the ways of young women to fret about any of Astrid's pretended suffering. Come another half a minute and the girl would be panting for Tom to finish her off. Then like the little hypocrites they all were, she would dissolve into sobbing and pretend she had never had the pleasure of it.

'NAH-AH-AH!'. It was Astrid's final wail before the peg sank full within, bringing her rounded bottom-cheeks to nestle into his belly while above her came the sound of smacking kisses.

'Pump her up, Tom. Give it to her nice. Oh, she wriggles a lot, don't she! Bringing you on, is she?', Alice asked, working her tongue in and out of his mouth much as his cock was striving now in Astrid's quim.

'She's a tight 'un. Luscious, though. A fair peach, this one. Wait till I get it up her bottom-she'll wriggle proper then'.

'Oh, the beast you are! The Mistress didn't say as you could. Faster now-I'll hold her bottom!'.

Her cheeks seized by Alice, who could just manage to reach them, Astrid rocked and sobbed. With each plunge Tom seemed to be filling her up right into her belly, his big balls smacking under her bottom with every stroke and even brushing the outer lips of her cunt, which was fully stretched by his tool. Ceasing to hold her bottom, which in any event was by now unnecessary since Astrid seemed to have succumbed to the inevitable and was in the first throes of coming, Alice felt beneath the young woman's body.

'Lovely tits she's got, firm as melons. Tom. Oh, you devil, you're coming. I sees it in your face!'.

Tom indeed was. He had meant to last longer, but the luscious clinging of Astrid's cunt had overwhelmed his senses. He had never fucked a nicer one, though he wouldn't dare tell Alice that. A sporting girl she was, but liked to consider herself the best treat for him, and that was right and proper in Tom's eyes, since they were married. His neck muscles strained, his face became florid and pale by turns, his jaw sagged, and then with a rumbling groan he rammed his prick full in and gushed out his pleasure in long thick streams of sperm to the accompanying moans of Astrid who, gripping the thick root of flesh between heir lovelips, received every spurt and drop.

CHAPTER 6

Limp in the arms of Tom, who had carried her effortlessly back to the house, Astrid was laid on the chaise longue in the drawing room, her eyes closed, lips parted.

'She fainted, Ma'am, I fear, after her second', he said apologetically.

'You fucked her twice?', Julia asked, arranging Astrid's legs neatly. 'You must be in good form today, Tom. Not an hour has passed as yet'.

Tom grinned. 'She's a rare good 'un, Ma'am, if I may so say. Tight as a drum but very accommodating. I would have had it up her bottom but the missus says as how I weren't to or you might take it bad'.

'That's right, Tom. Here's a guinea for your pains- and one for Alice. See that she gets it for I shall question her on her spending of it. Tell her to buy some new stockings and some smart boots for they might be needed when I have visitors'.

The manservant departed, Julia sat herself alongside Astrid and kissed her forehead, smoothing the damp hair back there from. 'We are alone, my dear, you need not dissimulate. It did no harm for you to pretend to swoon under Tom's assault, but I doubt not that you enjoyed it. Let me feel how well he has spermed you'.

'Oh, no!'. Affecting to make a quick recovery, Astrid was too slow to seize the hand that meandered up beneath her skirt and sought her crevice. Wrinkling her nose up with pleasure, Julia found there, as she expected, a fine thick oiling both of Tom's sperm and of Astrid's own excited spillings. Her drawers had evidently been kept by Alice as a trophy, a little matter in which Julia never interfered. Alice would no doubt be wearing them herself by the morrow, priding herself on the fact that she might well be the only female servant in the county to have any, for they are scarce considered necessary for the lower classes.

'Fared you well?', Julia laughed. She had not intended Astrid to be put to the cock so quickly, but now that events had forwarded the lovely young woman's progress, she was glad. At this, tears swam in Astrid's eyes and she reached up to cast her arms about Julia who cuddled her warmly. 'There, there, my pet, you have enjoyed one of the best. Feel no shame about it nor take it too badly that you were handled as you were. A good fuck becomes a girl of your beauty. You must not make anything of it that it was a servant. They are here to serve, are they not?'.

Astrid whimpered and pressed her hot face between Julia's magnificent tits. In truth, she had taken no real fear of the matter and had secretly enjoyed the steady pumping of Tom's prick in her cunt, which continued to throb excitingly. For an encore, she had been turned about on the bale on her back while Alice uncovered her titties and laid them bare to the ravaging of her tongue and lips the while that Tom recovered his forces. Truly, Alice had been quite gentle with her and had coaxed her to keep her stockinged legs open, saying-as Julia had now done-that there was no shame in the matter and that a lady such as she was well fitted to take as many mounts as possible.

Being then in a somewhat dreamy state, Astrid had ceased to struggle and lay with closed eyes while Alice apprised her of all manner of fuckings that the noble lady visitors to Hardcastle enjoyed. Pretending petulance and making it appear all the while that she was swooning, Astrid had listened and absorbed all.

'The Mistress whips me sometimes, Ma'am, and I likes it. It stirs me up nice for what I know I'm going to get. I has whipped some of the ladies, too, for their pleasure. Were that not Lady Dunnit I saw a-visiting today? She's a rare one, she is, and that nephew of hers will be of use to many, not least yourself, My Lady. Tom's pecker will be arising again soon. He loves to see young ladies lying afore him with their skirts up, their pretty stockings on, and their thighs spread for pleasure. My dad were the same. He would go at my bottom just to have a good look at me. I were proper daft then. He would give me a spanking and then raise his nightshirt to show off his cock to me, standing stiff up it always were. I never let him, though, which the Mistress says were my mistake because I could have had him at my will if I wanted. Now, Miss, just lie still 'cos Tom's a-ready to give you another poke'..

All this, and much more having been said breathlessly and without much pause, had given Astrid such thoughts as she had never previously entertained. So long as Julia now held and stroked her fondly, she felt comforted and willing to confess all that Julia drew from her.

'Of course, my pet, she would have had her father at her will, though this seemingly is beyond your understanding. I have told you oft but shall repeat it until you comprehend. It is the very basis of our power, Astrid. Pain and pleasure lie at the root of all as does a subtle understanding between females. Do you not prefer to kiss me, Astrid, than any other-than a male?'.

'Oh, yes!', Astrid replied fervently, for she knew this now to be true. Quite of her own accord she laid her face beneath Julia's and, extending her tongue, licked slowly along her mouth to the ineffable delight of her teacher.

'You wish me to lick it?', enquired Julia teasingly.

Astrid nodded, her eyes half-closed. It was as if suddenly a dam had broken in her mind and she kept her pink tongue peeping wantonly between her lips while hearing Julia ask what else she now wanted. 'Play with my cunt', Astrid pleaded softly, bringing a pleased laugh from her companion.

'Come, let us go to bed. We shall be better accommodated for the sport there'. So saying, Julia led her up, their arms about each other's waists. In but seconds, as it seemed, they had stripped to their stockings. Julia locked the door, averring that they wanted no interruptions. Warm in each other's arms they lay, teasing with their agile fingers each other's titties and bottoms and slits. 'What a marvel you are-my prize pupil!', said Julia. 'Lie on me, darling, rub your cunt against mine while I tell you all'.

'Oh, yes!', assented Astrid, whose bubbles then bulged onto Julia's, their sleek silky bellies working sensuously together while the lips of their cunts kissed and writhed together as did their mouths. Between kisses and tonguings and many a gasp of pleasure, Julia then began to lecture her.

'Let us suppose, Astrid, that you were once as Alice was. Your papa wishes to spank you for some supposed misdeed. Despite your blushes and your febrile struggles, he ups your skirt, removes your drawers, and views all your maidenly charms. Laid across his lap, his hand descends upon your blushing bottom-cheeks. You squeal, you sob, to no avail. Artful as he is, he fondles you slyly the while, cupping your cunny while your bottom is heated by repeated smacks. You absorb the heat, your hips wriggle, your sobs subside into moans. He knows well your condition and feels the stiffening of your nipples through your dress'.

Astrid hid her face in Julia's neck, laving the white skin with kisses and moving her hips in the most supple fashion as their tingling clitorises rubbed.

'But I could never have let Papa take my drawers off', she murmured.

'Shush, girl. 'Tis but an example. Alice was put to such feverish play, was she not? Many a young girl is rodded in her bed by her sire after a good bottom-warming. She learns to absorb the cock and its juices, for a good spanking makes the bottom wriggle for it and urges the lusting male on. Soon enough he has her at His will. Each spanking is followed by ever-more passionate embraces, for the spankings stir her as equally to lust as it does her sire. She becomes but a houri for his pleasure. Yet it need not be so'.

'She need not let herself be spanked at all and thus avoid such naughtiness?', asked Astrid dreamily. She had already twice come, as had Julia, yet their cunts continued rubbing together, seeking even more appeasement.

'Indeed, she should let herself be spanked, Astrid, and, the first time, should affect even more excitement than she feels. That she cannot help writhing her hot bottom about is all to the good. Her eyes blurred with tears, her titties uncovered, and her nether cheeks stinging from the many slaps of his palm, she scarce knows what she is about when first he mounts her. Let her enjoy the good fuck, as well she will, but then must feminine cunning take hold upon her desires. She may yield perhaps a second time and permit him an even more luscious shafting of her cunny. Upon the third occasion, however, she should take command. Her thighs clip close together, her fingers clasp his rampant prick in such wise that he cannot remove it from her grasp without dire injury to himself. Her free hand takes his balls and squeezes. Her voice that previously had implored him to spill his sperm in her pussy now hisses to him to be still. Should he attempt to strike her or to fend her off, she will grip his balls the harder. To his astonishment he is then told that if he lies still she might pleasure him, otherwise she will raise the household.

'His mood changes. He becomes craven, Astrid, for as painful as her grip is, it is also pleasurable. He assents, believing perhaps that this unexpected turnabout will dissolve and that all will be as it was. Straddling his prone form and pushing her bottom a little into his face, she milks him quickly, by which of course I mean she draws forth his sperm. Being above him then and possessing more of her senses, she sees well how this weakens him to such extent that she is then able to rub her bottom all over his face while he can but splutter weakly. He is then her prize, rather than she his. All that follows from that night on may hence be at her bidding, for I need not tell you what wiles she will use to accomplish her ends'.

'AH!', shuddered Astrid, whose orgasmic bliss had been doubled by Julia's account. She quivered and lay still. The two continued pecking at each other's lips like doves. 'If all men should be at our command... .', she began and then added pettishly, 'Oh, but I do not understand. Why have I then been used so and put so crudely to Tom?'.

'It is necessary for all females to pass through fire, my pet, particularly if they would have it that others must do so in turn. The male must rut in you-before you comprehend all. The act is, in any event, divine and should be enjoyed as such. Many a girl will pant and cry more than you when she is first shafted or corked, but she will soon enough learn the pleasure of it. As to males, while they should in last event be subservient to us-and some may be used solely to pleasure us, as Anthony is-there are no firm rules to this delightful game. Males and females may take turn and turn about-provided ever that the men know their final place. Tuition is all, Astrid, the dull and the unknowingly go their ways and know not whit of the delights of this. Every woman has a secret desire to be taken by force just as every male aspires to return to his mother's lap and there be spanked for his misdeeds'.

'And mayhap to have his cock handled the while?', sparkled Astrid.

'How quickly you learn! Thus truly are the associations of pain and pleasure made. Need I whip you again, my pet?'.

'Only at my pleasure, Julia! What of Tom, though, or indeed Alice? I know not how to face them now'.

'This very day, Astrid, you will approach them with calm and stately mien. Upbraid Tom for his wickedness and he will cringe. Order him to lick the toes of your boots and he will droolingly oblige. For whatever his lustful pleasure in making your pretty bottom buck to his will, he senses within you the power of Woman, that ultimate power which rules all. Observe the stupid grin upon his face when you tell him that he has been wicked. He will long for punishment'.

'As sometimes I shall?'. Astrid uttered a giggle and concealed her expression.

'Of course. You will enjoy the selfsame bonds into which you put others-though of occasion they have no need to know that. You must judge your attitudes carefully in respect of each individual'.

'Yet they have seen me humiliated-your servants, I mean'.

'As to that, my pet, 'tis all of a muchness. Marie and Amy knew well enough to what end you were being driven and that they themselves are as likely to come under the lash of your whip as any. I permit them many mischiefs, as I do Alice and Tom, yet all remain finally under my heel as now they shall under yours'.

'I am free?', asked Astrid in a timid voice.

'Free enough even to deny yourself freedom, if you will', Julia sighed. 'The child or young person who would free itself from its mother's will yet longs equally to be held in her firm embrace. Who then is free? Before I know it, you will be bringing the martinet to my bottom while holding me bound'.

'I would love to!', exclaimed Astrid excitedly. 'But I would also like you to do the same to me'.

'What else then can I teach you, save the many little tricks we indulge in? Let me rise, my sweet, for I am now about to show you something'. With that, Julia slid from the bed and took from an armoire the very letter she had received from Astrid's mother. Never before had she put such a privilege to a pupil, but with Astrid all was other than had ever been before. Unfolding the letter, she returned to the bed and laid it before her.

Astrid's hand trembled visibly as she clutched the pages and read them.

'Oh, what of THIS!', she exclaimed in wonderment.

'What indeed! I receive many such missives in advance of receiving a newcomer to the fold, but none has been permitted to indulge in their secrets as you. Judge well the situation now, as your dear mama intends you to, for it is clearly her intention that you should lead the household in all your ways and so establish your reign. Before you do, however, I must teach you all such little tricks as I have spoken of. You will come more quickly to them than others, for you have the spirit for the thing. I have this very day a gentleman coming for what are best termed "correctional exercises". In this you will assist'.

'I? But I will not know what to do!'.

'You will learn soon enough-by precept and by instinct. This one is surely easy for you, Astrid. He will cringe and fawn at the very sight of your bared thighs'.

'Julia, must I uncover myself to him?'

'As you will, my dear. Speak as little as is needful. Your moments of silence alone will fill him with awe. Should you wish him to kneel before you, indicate by gestures of your hand toward the floor. If he fails to abase himself sufficiently to your liking, place the heel of your shoe on the back of his neck and hold it there firmly. In doing so, admonish him quietly'.

Astrid's hands worked agitatedly together. 'I do not believe I could-not as yet. May I not commence with a female, for surely you have other subjects of your will such as I. Once I know that I can in some wise command another, then 'twill be easier for me'.

'Very well, my dear, it shall be so. Your wisdom pleases me. Had you failed with the gentleman concerned, I would have had perforce to punish you severely, and that I do not wish to do. Let me apprise you of his identity. He is the Hon. Wilberforce Markings, aged twenty-five, an orphan who has lived in fair comfort with his sister, Harriet, these last six years or more. Harriet is his senior by three years. She is minded to marry yet cannot bring herself to cast off her brother as easily as most would. He fawns upon her, having known little other feminine company, or having perhaps made sure that he did not. I am known to Harriet but vaguely by reputation. There has been correspondence between us-more guarded on her side than I would have wished. Her belief is that I might take Will, as she calls him, into my fold and treat him as a distressed relative who could in part act as servant'.

'Then she is not herself a subject?', Astrid asked with a twinge of disappointment.

'As yet? No. Not as yet', Julia responded, whereat a smile of complicity spread over both their faces. Bending over her companion, who lay still upon the bed, Julia kissed her. 'You see, I replace one difficult task for you with another', she purred.

'I think not, Julia. Would you deal, please, with Will while I take Harriet up to the Attendance Room? It would be as well for her to inspect the means of persuasion thoroughly, and perhaps even to taste them, if I can so persuade her. I may need the assistance of Marie and Amy, or I may not. They will be on call?'.

'Of course. How admirable your ideas are already! Come, let us dress, for our guests will be here soon and we would not wish to disappoint them'.

Tea was indeed ready to be served upon the arrival of Harriet and Will, neither of whom disappointed Astrid in their appearance. Harriet was of middle height and comely of looks, her face being roundish, her mouth small, her nose of pleasing proportions. Firmly held beneath a tight corsage, her breasts were exceedingly plump, while her bottom gave promise of admirable curvature and weight. As to her brother, he looked not as unmanly as Astrid thought he might. His moustache was trim, his skin smooth. His physique did not betoken a weakling, being seemingly well formed and muscled beneath his formal attire. This at first puzzled Astrid not a little, for all her views on the submissive-ness of males were formed upon the impression she had gained of Anthony.

Tea having been taken with such decorum and polite conversation as would have passed in a vicarage, Julia indicated her desire to speak with Will alone. This intelligence caused him first to blush and then to grow a trifle pale, which spectacle did much to reassure Astrid that all was not as it first seemed. If she had any apprehensions at all, it was how to deal with Harriet, or rather whether she would be able to deal with her. Even so, these vagrant fears diminished upon inviting the young woman to accompany her upstairs.

Harriet was not displeased to leave the drawing room, and she had begun to entertain doubts as to whether she should have persuaded Will to accompany her here. 'Will she be strict with him?', she asked Astrid, upon going upstairs. For in truth she had little enough idea of Julia's purpose in the matter save that the lady had a reputation for 'settling' people.

'It may be', Astrid replied carefully.

'You assist her?'

'Frequently. But at times I serve to settle those who accompany our guests here. I inculcate them with our precepts', Astrid said glibly enough. It would be nice to take Harriet into the bedroom, but even nicer, she decided, to have her in what she personally now preferred to call the discipline room. And there indeed she led Harriet, who was all of a wonder as to where they were going to settle and how long the whole business would take. Upon the door opening, she made-as did many-to step back, but Astrid urged her firmly within and closed the door. Quite amused, she watched Harriet gaze with wild dismay about the room and the various 'persuaders' that dangled from the walls.

'Oh, dear Will is not to be whipped surely!', Harriet gasped.

'It depends on how naughty he may have been. Has he been naughty?', Astrid asked, guiding her intended victim to the couch, where she sat heavily. 'You must tell me all', she urged. 'Your letters lacked a certain explicitness, Harriet. Tell me first of his fawning over you'.

'Oh, that!', Harriet exclaimed uncomfortably and rather wished she had never come. Astrid's eyes seemed to be fixed on her rather severely.

'Yes, indeed, THAT, my dear. Come, you must not be coy, for is this not the sole purpose of your visit? Will is not the only one, you know, whom we have reason to correct or train. Some young men are brought by their mothers, others by their aunts or elder sisters or their guardians. Then there are girls and young women-some indeed of the same age as yourself. They, too, require attendance'.

'Girls? Young women?', Harriet echoed in astonishment. 'What then is the purpose of these horrible whips and straps and chains? Is this not a cruelty?'.

'Oh, pouf, as to cruelty, my dear. We know not its name. None who departs these walls does so without being deeply satisfied at his or her lot. But, come, you have not answered my question!', Astrid insisted, placing her arm about Harriet's shoulders while recalling well enough all that had been done to herself.

'It will be a secret?', Harriet pleaded.

'Of course. Naught that passes here shall be known to the world', Astrid replied, taking advantage of the young woman's upturned face to kiss her prettily upon her rosebud mouth, much to Harriet's disturbed surprise. Tear not what you say to me-use any words you wish. We are not shocked', Astrid pursued.

Harriet twisted her fingers together in some agitation, 'We live alone, as you may have gathered. Our parents left us well provided for. We have ever been close, yet Will is given to such strange habits that I know not what to do about it. I have come upon him often enough sniffing at my shoes and boots, which he insists upon cleaning even though we have servants to do such things'.

'Why, my dear, that is but a mark of adoration', exclaimed Astrid. 'A woman's body holds many odours that attract the male, whether it be the scent of your feet, the milkiness of your breasts, or the delicious perfumes of your drawers'.

'Oh!', exclaimed Harriet in much confusion, for she had never expected another woman to speak thus.

'How adorable you look in moments of surprise! The pouting of your lips becomes you. Kiss me, for in furthering our intimacy you will be better prepared to divulge all. Has he attempted your drawers?'.

'Ah, no! How can you speak thus?', quavered Harriet, whose mouth had surrendered itself more sweetly than she had intended. 'I am his sister!'.

'Which is precisely why he may wish to nuzzle your crotch, Harriet. Raise your legs and turn about. Lie down. You will be better accommodated thus'.

'No! I do not wish! Oh, what are you at!'

Having listened at the door by virtue of uncovering the peephole, Marie and Amy entered at that moment, having been apprised by Astrid that their services might be required. A merry tussle was ensuing on the couch, for Harriet proved stronger than Astrid had expected. Her cries rent the air upon finding herself placed fully on her back while Astrid held her shoulders.

'Remove her drawers, Marie, and take them down to your mistress!'.

CHAPTER 7

In the drawing room, where Julia had long sat regarding him silently, Will was in a state of mystery and apprehension. Harriet had told him nothing of the purpose of their visit save that there was a lady she wished him to see. Never before had he been alone with a strange woman and he felt distinctly in awe of his hostess, who appeared so commanding and beautiful. Even so, he wished that his sister were there, for he felt most safe with her.

At the opening of the door, he jumped visibly and saw that it was one of the maids. That which she carried in her hand brought a distinct blush to his cheeks, as Julia could not fail to notice.

'Miss Astrid says as I was to bring these down, Ma'am'.

'Thank you, Marie. Rather plain, are they not?', said Julia, examining the white drawers the maid handed her. Running her fingers through the material and testing the tightness of the elastic that but moments before had encompassed Harriet's waist and thighs, Julia rose and stepped towards Will's chair, the drawers dangling from her fingers.

'Have you ever worn these, Will?'.

The young man's jaw dropped. His eyes obtained a glassy look. The blush on his face was as deep as a red, red rose. He knew them well enough, as he did all of Harriet's drawers, whether white, blue, or pink. She had many times caught him peeping through her bedroom door when she was in a state of delightful dishabille and had admonished him severely, for the door would frequently creak as he clutched it nervously, peering through the jamb. But a week before she had caught him thus. She was deliriously attired in her black lace-up boots, white-silk stockings, these selfsame drawers, and a chemise that left half-naked the large, milky gourds of her breasts.

'Is that you, Will? Oh, what are you at?', Harriet had exclaimed whereupon, unable to contain himself, Will had entered her hallowed boudoir and had cast himself at her feet, inhaling the scent of the leather of her boots while his hands clasped her ankles so imploringly that Harriet had been unable to move.

'Do not, Will! How dare you enter when I am unclothed! Desist, Sir!'.

Such a rage of desire had seized him that, while Harriet rocked and struggled to release herself, he had licked slavishly all around her boots and then ascended his lips to the glorious roundness of her knees. But then, seeming to become aware of the enormity of what he was doing, Will had risen and fled, pursued by Harriet's sobs. That selfsame night, when Harriet was otherwise occupied, he had stolen into her room and filched the very pair of drawers that Julia was now dangling before him. In bed he had worn them, envisaging his sister's bottom where his own pressed, though it was not so ample as hers, and rubbing his cock through the cotton where her cunt had nestled.

'Well, Sir?', Julia demanded. 'Take his wrists, Marie!'.

Frozen in his attitude, Will limply let his arms be taken. That Harriet had told them all he did not now doubt, nor that he was to be punished for his secret lusts. Above where he sat, Julia fluffed out the drawers, expanding the waistband, and in a flash drew it down over his head so that Will found himself neatly enveloped in the intimate garment which fully covered his head and face. Breathing excitedly, he inhaled the most intoxicating of scents, for the drawers were naturally still warm from enfolding Harriet's cunt and bottom. Something stirred about his wrists and he jerked. A laugh came to his ears.

'He is well manacled, Ma'am', Marie announced.

'Bring him to his feet and loose his trousers, Marie'.

Mouth open in astonishment in the veiled darkness of the drawers, Will felt deft fingers laying open the front of his trousers and drawing them down until his cock and balls were denuded.

'He's coming up, Ma'am. He likes the smell of them all right!'

'I don't doubt it, Marie. Bring him forward a little and then make him stand still. The crop to his buttocks if he will not!'.

'Yes, Ma'am. He's got a real corker, if you'll forgive the term. It's right up and a-quivering now, as you can see'.

Will's prick indeed was. The rubicund knob glowed, the veins stood all about on it. Wildly did he nuzzle as best he could the divine scents that the cotton drawers contained, even to the faint aroma of urine that met his nostrils.

'Her effluvia pleases you, does it not, Will?', Julia asked. Brushing her maid aside, she cupped his balls firmly, though taking care not to brush her fingers against the rigid stem of his weapon. Like huge plums, they nestled in her palm. With every intake of breath the cotton of the drawers sucked inwards to his mouth, causing him to groan, for he could not dare bring himself to reply. 'You are to lie down, Sir! Sink first onto your knees and then arrange yourself perfectly still on your back, legs together!'.

Guided down by Marie, he lay in a moment as commanded, his quivering tool seeming to be trying to reach to the ceiling, on which, most appropriately, white-plaster Cupids played. Knowing well what was to follow, Marie stepped behind her mistress and drew up the folds of her skirt at the back until the glorious orb of her bottom was revealed in her tight, silk drawers. Then, taking up her stance with her feet splayed on either side of his body, Julia slowly lowered herself until, facing Will's feet, the plump cheeks of her moon impressed their fleshy weight full over his covered face.

'PMFFFF!', Will gasped. Not only were his mouth and nose squashed, but the most ultimate scents of his sister and of Julia's bottom now mingled. Hot already in the enclosure of Harriet's drawers, his face suffused, he fought for breath while Julia languidly settled herself even more firmly and regarded her nails.

'You may return upstairs, Marie. I will bring him up in due course'.

'Yes, Ma'am'.

Save for the extraordinary tableau which now showed itself on the carpet, the drawing room was empty. Julia gloried in this queenly posture, which is indeed known to aficionados as 'queening' a male. Many were the men who had gone under her thus and had adored her for ever after, taking whatever opportunity thereafter came to them to sniff at her skirts. Her rump squirmed a little until she had satisfied herself that Will's nose poked up between her nether cheeks, whose plumpness was splurged over him. Hearing a gurgling croak, Julia lifted herself a little then settled back again. He had tune to suck in breath for a moment through Harriet's drawers. It would be little enough but it would have to suffice until she lifted again. Resting her knees firmly on either side of his body, she patted her coiffure and gazed with pleasure at the fine erection Will was haplessly displaying to her. It was more than possible that it had never been milked save by his own quavering hand.

In the long minute that then passed, an almost suffocated Will grew dizzy. His ears roared, his breast heaved. Heated by his out bursting of breath, the effluvia in both Harriet's drawers, and Julia's grew stronger. His wrists strove at the cuffs, which encircled them. Agitatedly they shook. Regarding the movement with distant amusement, Julia raised her bottom anew, listening to his snuffling as trickles of air once more reached his lungs. To tease him further now could do no other than enflame his desires. Bending forward as his shrouded nose buried itself once more into her cleft, she delicately ringed his throbbing pego with thumb and finger and allowed her mouth to absorb the juicy knob but lightly.

Will's legs trembled visibly as she did so. Julia's mouth was warm and moist and he could not resist drawing up his knees a little to endeavour to engage a farther inch or two of his engine twixt the clasping of her lips. No mouth had ever touched his yearning cock before, nor even a feminine hand, much as he had longed for Harriet to so caress him. To invite her to have done so would have horrified her, for, refulgent as were her curves, she was also prim and had only once let him touch her bottom with his hand. Frustrated beyond endurance, he felt Julia's mouth withdraw at the first pleading jerk of his loins, as also did her derriere from his face.

Then came the rustling of her skirts as once more she stood over him, having turned about so that her feet placed themselves on either side of his hips.

'Oh!', groaned Will from beneath his hood while Julia silently contemplated him. It would have amused her to queen him for a full half-hour as many of her male subjects cravenly sought her to do. But it was a full week since she had taken a prick in her cunt, and Will's would suffice her well. In a trice, Julia knelt facing his head and wreathed her drawers down to her ankles. His cock was so stiff and well poised that she had no need to position it. Instead, she reached under herself and with both hands parted the richly gleaming lips of her slit. She manoeuvred gently onto him until, with an ardent, muffled gasp, Will felt the crest of his charger absorbed between her cuntlips.

Leaning forward over him, Julia pressed her hands down on either side of the drawers so that they were tightly stretched over his face, outlining his not unhandsome features. Now more than ever he would experience the headiness of so being covered, and would veritably swim in the nostalgic scents in Harriet's drawers while he was being ridden. Controlling her every movement, Julia sank her hips down little by little, the clinging, spongy walls of her vagina parting like reluctant waves to receive the horny shaft.

In the sweet agony of that delirious moment, Will curled his toes in delight but no longer dared to move his legs lest she unhorse him. Much as Julia had suspected, this was the first time his cock had entered a woman's dell. Feeling his swollen knob nuzzle up within, Will all but swooned with pleasure while the tip of his tongue licked avidly against the crotch of Harriet's drawers. Pulsing mightily, his prick was at last fully received, and with a sigh of pleasure Julia rested her bottom on his thighs. The St George was one of her favoured positions, though in her lewder moments she preferred being plugged from the rear. Divine tremors coursed through her form while she sustained the throbbing and ticking of Will's pego within her honey pot. In unspoken concert with Astrid, Julia's first thoughts were that Will should be brought to mount his sister, for she ever held in suspicion those females who wished their male kin trained and knew best whose bellies it should be upon. The suction of her cunt being strong, every quiver of Will's body conveyed itself to her as she rose and fell with the majestic action of a mistress who means to extol the juice from her lover's loins in the most imperious way.

Puffing and groaning each tune that Julia lifted and the sank down again, Will could feel the sperm curdling and bubbling already in his testicles. Warm and juicy, her naked bottom-cheeks settled alluringly on his thighs before lifting again.

'Do not come yet-I forbid you!', Julia husked, even as her first exquisite seizure sprinkled his cock and balls. 'I forbid!', she repeated, hearing the answering groan from his lips, all but outlined under the veiling drawers.

'HAAAAR!', Will sobbed, for at any second now he felt that the liquid treasures of his balls would erupt. He strained, groaned, gasped, nipping the cotton between his teeth while he endeavoured to control the outpouring of his lust. Her pubic hairs tickled amid his own, the gentle smacking sound of her bottom-cheeks meeting his thighs sounded to his ears the most heavenly music. Julia's own breathing quickened, though he knew it not, for it was never her custom to reveal her pleasures to a slave during his initiation periods. Pursing her ruby lips in a soundless moan of pleasure, she expelled again her salty spurtings of joy while Will, totally dominated by her, strained every sinew not to return the compliment. His teeth chattered, the veins on his neck swelled, and then to his vast relief he heard her imperative, 'NOW!'.

'HAAAR!', he shuddered again under the bubbling cotton. But this time the sound conveyed his uttermost limits of sensual delight as the spongy gripping of Julia's cunt tightened, her bottom falling SMACK! onto his thighs. The fierce jets of his spermaceous outpourings flooded her being on and on in a swimmy haze of pleasure until their glutinaceous parts stilled themselves. Like a velvet vice Julia drew from him the last pearly drops.

Resting only momentarily, she then uncorked her well-soaped slit and rose to cover herself.

'UP! Up now, quickly', she commanded, which effort caused Will great pains since his bound wrists permitted him little to lever himself to a standing posture. The last seeping of sperm emitted itself like a tear from the crest of his half-limp tool. Therewith, Julia whipped the drawers from his head and regarded him distantly. What a pathetic object he looked, still fully dressed and with his trousers at his ankles! Men looked ever thus after they had been put to a lusty female. Deftly she unfastened his wrist cuffs and tossed them onto the sofa before taking her seat there.

'You are fit at least to service females. Tell me how you have comported yourself with Harriet these past months. Omit nothing, for I shall gain the truth from her', came Julia's voice coldly while Will turned about to face her as he knew he must.

Julia listened to his halting recital, threadbare as it was of lascivious details. He had seen Harriet's thighs, her knickered bottom, often in his peepings. He had espied several times her breasts naked when she thought herself not observed. Yes, he had worn her drawers, and licked and sniffed her shoes and boots.

'That is all? You have never put this instrument of yours into her hand, even?'.

Will shook his head dumbly. Such a dream had occurred to him often, but he had never dared. Yet frequently Harriet's eyes had passed across his trousers when the nearness of her voluptuous form made his prick erect itself.

'What dullards you are, to be sure', Julia sighed. Divest yourself of your attire. Do you not know how stupid you look? Quickly now-I have not time to waste!'.

Hollow-eyed as he felt from the suction she had applied to his fervent pego in the first fuck he had ever experienced, Will obeyed, though totally convinced that he must be dreaming all this. Meek as he was before females, he was no dullard. If such were to be his training he would enter into it gladly, though Julia's oft cold expression conveyed to him that not all would be pleasure. That there would be pain and sweetness in the denials of his desires he had no doubt. Awkwardly removing his boots, and conscious of the fact that Julia's eyes were mingled with amusement and interest upon his cock and his dangling balls, he stood at last naked. 'Good', Julia said simply, and rose. 'Whatever happens now you will remain silent. That is to be understood. Your buttocks will be mightily burnished with a birch if you are not. Come!'.

Taking his thick but now limp prick, she led him out. As she expected, there was a silence about the house, a muteness that seemed to float from above the stairs like a cloud. Longing to ask, to speak, and yet not having the courage to, Will could but allow himself to be taken up, much as a dog might be led by its lead. Conscious of this, he yet felt neither shame nor embarrassment but only a strange sense of pride that a woman should so handle him. The rolling of Julia's hips attracted his eyes as they ascended. The stairs echoed the quietness. Upon reaching the second floor, Julia entered where Harriet lay, drawing Will with her.

Happily, from Julia's point of view, Harriet was gagged. Too much noise was unseemly on such an occasion. Her skirt and petticoat tightly wreathed up about her curving hips, Harriet lay in an extraordinary posture. Her wrists were tied to her ankles, which thus forced her to hold her legs back so far that the whole of her furry quim and the cleft of her bottom were displayed. At her brother's entrance her eyes grew wild, her head twisted from side to side as if a fit had taken her. Will, for his part, appeared mesmerised by the lewd and totally revealing posture in which she was placed. His lips grew dry, his eyes bulged. Nudged and pushed by Julia, he was made to stand in a corner, facing his sister, who from the hue in her cheeks appeared about to have apoplexy.

The maids, having helped to secure Harriet, had gone. Astrid stood expectantly, her eyes dwelling slyly on Will's penis. 'You will STAY! Move, Sir, at your peril!', Julia snapped, and then-somewhat to Astrid's astonishment-motioned her out and closed the door.

But a minute passed-one might have counted indeed scarce fifty-five seconds. Upon the re-opening of the door, Will, though still immobile, was seen to be hot-cheeked, with his cock again as rampant as when he had first indulged himself in Harriet's drawers.

'It will be for the best', Julia murmured. Seating herself down beside the frantically squirming Harriet, she placed one hand firmly beneath her chin and so held her while Astrid untied the cords that allowed the young woman's legs to fall. To fall and kick wildly indeed, until a sharp SMACK! across her bared thighs caused Harriet to try to double herself up as she sobbed mournfully under her gag. Julia, however, would not have it so. Another sharp slap brought Harriet to stretch her legs once more, albeit that she kept them tightly together, thus displaying only her dark bush to her brother's eyes.

'Hold still, Harriet, for no good shall come of your struggling!', hissed Julia. 'Will, you come here! Lie upon her!'.

Had Harriet's gag not impeded her from screaming, her voice might have carried across the surrounding acres as the hardened cock of her brother pronged down upon her bared belly and his thighs settled heavily upon her own. Obeying then the wiser counsels of Julia, which had been swiftly conveyed to her outside the door. Astrid commenced binding the pair together, first their thighs and then their waists until they were trussed so securely that neither could move any part of his body save toes and heads.

'We will so leave then', Julia said. 'Remove first her gag, Astrid. I think Harriet will know better than to scream full in his face, and to no avail whatever. You hear me, Harriet? I will have no disobedience!'.

Utterly red in face, and with her eyes totally wild, Harriet stared up at her while Will, either from intense excitement or embarrassment or a mixture of the two, hid his face in his sister's neck.

'I believe you understand, Harriet', Julia continued quietly. 'Neither of you shall be freed until I have obtained from you a full half-hour of silence. I am quite capable of keeping you both tied together for the rest of the day and all night if necessary. Very well, Astrid!'.

Bending over the pair, who moved not a muscle, Astrid slipped the gag slowly and drew it away from Harriet's mouth. 'I beg-oh, I beg you, how can you so shame me!', Harriet moaned. With that, however, Julia turned about and led Astrid out with her, closing the door quietly and turning the key in the lock.

'You understand?', she asked her companion softly, whereupon Astrid shook her head. 'You would have had him fuck her, would you not, my dear? That would not be the way with such a pair as this, Astrid. The bonds that hold them will scarce melt her heart, but truly they will stir her emotions. With each second that Will's cock ticks and throbs on her belly, so she will come closer to her desires and his. In such cases patience is called for. One must employ that divine instinct that women possess in far greater abundance than men'.

'What shall you do then when they are untied?'.

'Send them home', Julia responded, as if surprised by the question. They may need some refreshment, of course. He will have come over her belly before that. She will know the power of his effusion. His sperm will warm her skin. What a glorious body she has-such thighs, such breasts! She will be a sister unto us-a sister in sin!'.

'I am still bemused, though'.

doubt it not. Be not disappointed that you are, my dear Astrid. You were put through your courses more swiftly and successfully than any I have known. Therein is a certain victory for you, yet you have scarce had time to reflect upon it all and certainly not to absorb all you have learned. You have yet to take up the finer strands. Harriet will not rise like a tigress, as you suspect, but will be as bemused as yourself. Never again will she see her brother other than a male animal whose cock becomes fiercely erect for her. Let it be so. She is one who will fulfil her most secret desires by being forced to indulge them. In essence, that is true of us all. We are all children who wish to be made to be naughty and then, in addition, desire to be punished for it'.

Had I then put him to her, I would have spoiled it?'.

'I do not know Harriet deeply enough yet to say so, but that is indeed possible. She is like one who must be teased by the sight and smell of food before she is allowed to taste it. Saw you how sweetly rolled and closely clipped together the lips of her cunny are? She will be a superbly tight fuck for her brother, but she must be allowed to moisten slowly first'.

'As she will be doing now, I am sure', Astrid laughed as they entered the drawing room. Her eyes were hot, her hips rolled, the fragrant dew upon her lips pleaded for a kiss, which Julia all too tauntingly gave her.

'Ah, Astrid, how you are going to be fucked! But you must learn to monitor your desires!' averred Julia fondly. 'Now above all is such a moment when your loins are hot. I shall bring Tom to you'.

'Oh, no, I could not! I do not wish to be held!'.

'You will not be. Therein shall lie your trial of strength. I vow that if you do not come through it I shall truly whip you soundly and have the maids hold you firmly the while. You are to receive Tom's cock as any lady might her serfs. He will be put to you dutifully, for he will know well enough your station now. From you I require nothing but imperious silence, to be broken only by such curt words of instruction as you give him. Whatever the excitement that his ploughing of your furrow gives you, you will evince no pleasure save perhaps by some urging, some sensuous wriggling of your bottom, to draw him one. He will perform the service that you require and demand. This shall be so with all males in future, Astrid'.

'Always? Oh, but I do not think I could always so control myself.

Julia smiled. 'You may permit yourself certain dispensations, my pet, but not with servants. Only with those of equal rank will you fully sport, and even so you must then show that a certain distance obtains between you. For though there may be moments when you will wax hot and when your tongue answers the call of your writhing bottom, there will be yet many more when your cold disdain shows. However much you may desire a second course after you have been well threaded, never toy with a man's cock when it is soiled by your combined spendings. Order him first to wash and prepare himself for a further bout. Thus you do not become his puppet. Rather he will go in awe of you'.

'Shall it be so also for Harriet, then?', asked Astrid.

'Perhaps, at some future date. But for the nonce, no. Despite her pretence of arrogance, she is made from different stuff. You, Astrid, are of the highest female rank. Once her cunt has been juiced by her brother's cock, she will become somnolent and lustful, obedient to his whims'.

'As he to hers?'.

There speaks my Astrid! Precisely! I will appoint you their visitor, and in so doing I accord you a rare honour'.

Their visitor?'.

To their home. You will monitor all-their actions, then: desires, even such frustrations as it amuses you to put upon them from time to time, as for instance binding them naked back to back. The heat of her bottom will invite, yet he will not be able to reach it. You may toy with them, erecting his cock, twiddling her quim. You may make lewd suggestions to them that they must obey. Bound to each other, they yet shall be bound to you also'.

'Then I may join with them in their lusts? Must I not show coldness?'.

'Such shall become the finer strands of your understanding, Astrid. These are not as others. Pairs may be handled differently than single persons, in particular when they are of different sexes and have been already joined. These nuances will grow upon you. There is scarce a wish that you may not indulge. Prepare yourself now. Remove all save your stockings, shoes, and chemise. I shall fetch Tom to you. Here, yes, upon the sofa. You will present yourself to his doughty standard with your bottom well raised. He is permitted now no kisses or caresses other than you instruct. I doubt that they will be many. You desire him only to pleasure your loins. Upon reaming you for as long as you wish, he will expel his sperm and then withdraw not only his steaming prick but his person-unless you wish him afterwards to kneel in obeisance to you'.

'I may!'. Astrid's eyes sparkled merrily, her trembling fingers endeavouring to control themselves as she commenced unfastening her gown. 'Bring him to me!'.

CHAPTER 8

'NO, WILL, NO!'

The plaintive moan came oft from Harriet's mouth as she strove to avoid the seeking of her brother's lips. Poised almost exactly upon her whorled navel, the swollen crest of his charger pulsed and throbbed, communicating to both their bodies an intensity of excitement that could not long be suppressed. Beneath the weight of his tightly clasped body, Harriet's rolled-up skirt rustled with every tiny movement that obtained between them. Most alluringly, from Will's point of view, his balls nudged up against the moist peach of his sister's slit, the lips of which had parted haplessly.

'Let me but kiss you, dearest!', Will husked.

Harriet's lips were particularly full and richly curved. Several times his own had brushed them feverishly, only to have them escape as her neck twisted this way and that. Her richly fleshed thighs were warm and plump beneath his own, and the ridging of her stocking tops and garters tingled under him madly. After long minutes, and unable to thresh her face from side to side any longer, Harriet surrendered the sweet wetness of her lips with a sigh.

'Do not, Will', she murmured more faintly, yet the words being said against his mouth served only to stir him the more. Savaged by his lips, she began to sob quietly, yet the sound was as much a measure of her erotic arousal as despair.

'What a glorious cluster of brown curls you have around your cunt, what a plump arse you have, what magnificent thighs! Ah, had they but bared your tits to me, Harriet!'.

'Do not speak thus-ah, no, do not! Grab!', choked Harriet, as now her brother's tongue intruded in-between her teeth and dived so deeply within that it met her own. Then did the red mists of lewd desire cloud upon Harriet for the first time, as Will mounded his testicles in closer to her cunt. 'AAAARGH', she choked the while that their tongues met and fought as merry a dance as ever a man's and woman's did.

'I have seen you in your drawers and kissed your thighs. Now, divested of the cotton that has veiled your cheeks, I have seen the magnificence of your bottom-cheeks. How proudly they jut! Promise me that I may fondle them and kiss your divine nipples when we are alone!', Will groaned.

'You... you m... m... must not speak thus, Will. Ooooh! Ah! Yes! Suck my tongue! Darling, I can feel your thing throbbing all the time! How naughty you are!'.

Silkily Harriet's belly rippled, causing her brother's prick to throb faster. Her upper lip rolled back as each sucked in turn greedily upon the other's saliva.

'Let me come, Harriet!'.

'You bad thing, yes, if you want to. Oh, you are flooding me! How warm and sticky it is! You must never put it in me, Will, your promise? Promise you will not!'.

So gabbled Harriet on and on, as with every word a fresh jet of spermatic bliss issued from Will's prick until a veritable pool of gruelly delight swam between his pulsing organ and her body. Unable to contain himself, Will covered her mouth completely with his own and issued another fierce jet that caused Harriet to tremble with delight throughout her ripe and nubile form.

Astrid, meanwhile, was sustaining an even greater pleasure. Naked to her shoes, stockings, and chemise, which was turned up above her hips, she received passively the grunting thrust of Tom's big prick, his hands being permitted to cup the creamy globe of her bottom as he did so. Kneeling as she was upon the edge of the sofa, Astrid rested her cheek and forearms as calmly as she could upon the rolled back of the seat, her low posture causing Tom to keep his knees well bent while he laboured valiantly in her honey pot. That he knew her stature now, she proudly had no doubt. Julia had led him in by his cock, his trousers so rolled down that he was forced to shuffle awkwardly. Closing her eyes briefly in that moment, Astrid had waited quiveringly upon his approach.

'The lady requires you, Tom. Bend your knees, man, cup her bottom for purchase and enter your knob just between her lovelips. You will hold it there until you receive her assent!'.

It was to Astrid as if she had waited long for such a moment. The plum having nosed within her was held. Thus was a servile male exercised, she thought, and moved her would-be ardent hips not a whit, while Julia, taking a seat to the rear of them, placidly took up a book and sat as if nothing were happening. Only then by an assenting wiggle of her bottom did Astrid invite the sheathing of Tom's organ, which fumed and throbbed mightily as it surged in-between the velvety walls. At the first nestling of his huge balls to her bottom, Astrid uttered coldly, 'Hold!', the command bringing a discreet smile from Julia, whose eyes engaged themselves with the page beneath her. A full two minutes passed while Tom snorted occasionally but dared not move, the silken, hot orb of Astrid's bottom almost making him come then and there.

'Continue!', came Astrid's voice at last. Peeping up slyly, Julia observed the trembling of his trunk-like thighs as he drew the knob down almost to the pouting of Astrid's cunt and then pistoned it again within. Dizzy with the pleasure that she could now thus command and obtain, Astrid churned her luscious derriere a little and then so tightened the walls of her slit that his thick, stiff penis was held as within a velvet vice. 'Be still now!', came her clear command, much to the fond amusement of Julia, who saw her pupil progressing mightily by the hour. For Astrid alone had decided upon this form of entertaining herself. She now slew her hips back and forth so that she it was who drew with her cuntlips and the interior of her grotto upon Tom's motionless rod.

But softly did Astrid's breathing sound as she continued the motion, glorying in the revelation that Tom dared not move or urge his cock an inch, his knees quivering and straining as he sought to maintain his awkward posture. With every forward motion of her hips, his gnarled staff was seen to be glistening with her juices, the emission of which in little sprinkling spurts caused Astrid to bite upon her lip and hide her face the more so that he might not know of her outward signs of pleasure.

Julia spoke not, though she dearly wished that Astrid would also roll her bottom. No doubt she would learn to rotate her hips soon enough. The minx meant the bout to last, and well she might, for thrice and four times did Astrid come, her body rich with pleasure, before she began pumping her bottom faster.

Tom's eyes were glazed. He longed to accompany her movements with his own, but to do so now would put him in dire disgrace with both his mistress and with Astrid, and would cause Alice to scold him severely, not to say to bring a horsewhip to his buttocks were she to learn about it. From victorious stallion, he had become again but a serf, yet both roles pleased him. And, if all were known, perhaps the latter more than the first. Frequently he had fucked Julia in this wise, and almost always in the silence that now obtained. Groan after groan escaped him, though he tried to mute the sounds.

It mattered little to Julia that males should grunt at such tunes, though they could well be taught not to. Astrid for the moment accepted it as homage and mewed softly in her throat. At any moment she would come again and-ah, yes-Tom then must. The rivulets of bliss must combine, their spendings must swirl together. 'Now, Tom, now!', Astrid gritted, regretting only the slight note of supplication in her voice. Then did his hips move, bottom and belly meeting in a resounding smack as he injected her with cannonade upon cannonade of his spermatic offering while his balls, wet with Astrid's fine salty sprinklings, slapped beneath her bulge. Compressing her lips anew for fear that she might cry out with pleasure, Astrid received her stallion's offering, clenching his rampant tool deep within her sodden grotto until the last thick pearls were expended. Even then she continued to grip upon him tightly until she was satisfied that every drop had been spent. Gesturing pettishly with her arm, she caused his cock to withdraw, glistening and fuming as it did so.

Straightening up his aching back, Tom then stood in waiting as he knew he must. Riven with pleasure in every limb and nerve and sinew, Astrid remained silent and unmoving for a long moment, the lips of her cunt literally frothing with his sperm. Tremulous that for some reason he had not fully satisfied her, Tom made as if to turn his head to gaze upon his mistress, but thought better of it. In this moment she whom he had pleasured was the female who obtained immediate power over him. Cock drooping but slowly until it resembled an enormous slug, he waited, still.

'Go! You are dismissed', Astrid murmured. She sensed a sweet apprehension in herself as Tom's sluggish footsteps took him out. Julia advanced upon her even as she curled up upon the seat, her features with deliriously flushed.

'My dear, you are indeed worthy. I now give Harriet and Will into your care', Mia breathed. Seating herself on the sofa and passing her hand under Astrid's cunt, she smiled appreciatively at the vibrant pulpiness she felt there.

'On

my own-you so trust me?', sparkled Astrid. I have little more to teach you now, my pet. What has taken weeks with others has taken but hours with you. They must first be chastised, of course, then you will escort them home. I will send a carriage for you later. Dress now, for you are in the full bloom of a woman who has been well fucked and yet is ready for another'.

'Shall we then chastise them here?'

'Why not? I vow they are deserving of it', responded Julia, who had a distinct penchant for chastising male and female bottoms together. Having seen to Astrid's coiffure when she was again dressed, the two took themselves upstairs. Within the room where Harriet and Will lay was a silence broken only by faint murmurs from the pair, their faces shiny with perspiration as they lay together in their unsought bonds. Such a silence, however, was broken immediately Julia and Astrid entered. Harriet shrieked and then moaned, averting her eyes as best she could to the wall. Will, too, uttered a cry but then lay still, a vibrant trembling coursing through him as he felt Astrid's fingers at the knots of the ropes.

When the couple was drawn apart, as Astrid then did, the drying pool of their pleasure was seen glistening on the belly of Harriet, who with an alarmed shriek interspersed with shamed sobs endeavoured to thrust down her skirt.

'No, my dear, you do NOT!', snapped Julia, catching the young woman as she made totteringly to rise. As for Will, he sat upon the divan in a daze, thus impeding his sister's efforts to escape.

'Will! Save me!', Harriet screamed. Her limbs being a trifle stiff, she was unable to evade being dragged up and turned about, thereby providing all three with a perfect view of her large and well-fleshed bottom, the cleft of which added a slight gingery tinge to the otherwise dazzling whiteness of the cheeks. Simultaneously, Will had his ear seized like a schoolboy. Uttering a yelp in Astrid's firm-fingered grasp, he found himself perforce made to bend over in turn so that the tautness of his naked buttocks complemented the more voluptuous roundness of his sister's.

'What are you at? Oh, my God, let me get UP!', cried Harriet, whose knees were firmly planted on the edge of the couch alongside Will's. Swiftly accommodating herself in front of them by virtue of mounting the erstwhile bed of sin, and with her back to the wall as she knelt, Astrid took purchase with each of her hands on the backs of their necks, so forcing their faces down.

So rapidly was all effected that only a few seconds passed before the alarmed and outraged cries of Harriet sounded as a martinet in Julia's hand scorched across her bulbous bottom.

'Hold her well-take her hair, Astrid! Will does not dare to rise or I shall put him to greater punishment, as well he knows'.

'You beasts! AH! It stings! How dare you, how dare you! OW! Do not!', came in frantic screeches from Harriet, whose thick, dark hair then was wreathed in Astrid's palms, effectively forcing her to remain bent over so that she could but writhe her reddening derriere madly.

'Be QUIET!', Julia thundered, 'or I shall put you to several score,

Harriet. 'Tis you, my dear, who holds the guilt for not acceding to your brother's desires before this. Hold your bottom up, woman!'.

'SWEEE-ISH! SWEEE-ISSSH! HOOO-ITTTTT!', the martinet sounded to the impassioned delight of Astrid who, having tasted it herself, felt more fondly now for the luring heat it induced in female bottoms in particular, though one would not have thought so to hear Harriet's rending sobs and heartfelt cries. Never before had she received so much as a slap on her bottom and, now that the thongs of Julia's disciplinary instrument were whistling and burning across her outstretched nether cheeks, it was as though she had been cast into hell. Her mouth hung lax with her repeated sobs and down her attractive cheeks fell a veritable waterfall of tears.

As for Will, he could feel his sister's bared hip bumping against his own the while that her stockinged leg also rubbed his. Both fearful and excited that he was to be next, he sought her hand blindly and clasped it, making them appear very much as two children who have been caught stealing from the pantry or scrumping in a neighbour's orchard.

'WHOO-HOOO-HOOO!', Harriet moaned, her gleaming derriere now fully streaked with wavering pink lines while the fig of her cunt, couched in its thick nest of dark-brown curls, showed clearly to Julia's excited eyes. To finger her now would be delicious, for the lips glistened with dew. Yet to do so meant she would not be able to attend upon Will. Stepping then farther back, Julia next brought the whip across his upturned bottom which then smacked sideways against his sister's, causing both to cry out.

'HUI-ITTTT! SWEEE-ISSSSH! 'Ouch!', cried Will aloud to his shamed dismay, his balls swinging. That he deserved it he did not doubt. He had sinned wickedly with Harriet, whose first signs of sensual awakening had fully aroused his lust. His sperm had not only flooded her belly but had trickled and meandered down to nestle in the springy hairs of her mount, where he had felt it wet beneath him. Delirium was his, as equally now was the stinging admonition of the martinet. Gritting his teeth, he succeeded in muffling his cries, though it appeared that Harriet was uttering them for him since she ceased not to sob and yelp each time he received the bite of it.

'NOOO-NOOO-NOO! Will you not stop!', Harriet cried, quite beside herself not only from the searing of the martinet, which spread licking tongues of fire into her most secret orifices, but also because she felt all too strangely stirred by the untoward lewdness of all that was happening. Every slight flinching of her brother's buttocks made their bodies squirm and rub intimately together while the tight clenching of their left and right hands together on the seat of the divan betokened both acceptance and rejection of the miasma of sensations into which they had been thrust together.

'Have them dressed and tidied. I will send Will's garments up', announced Julia at last, her breasts heaving, her face full flushed from her endeavours as she surveyed the brightly pink orbs of their bottoms. Releasing Harriet's hair, Astrid permitted the young woman to fall forward, her fingers clenching and unclenching as she strove to tighten her outraged nether cheeks against the insurgent heat, much also as did Will, who had by then received as round a score of strokes as she. Tumbled and dismayed, they lay in positive confusion and bottom-tightening while Julia, calling to Amy for Will's clothes, strode out, leaving the martinet most visibly on the floor.

'No, no! Let me cover myself!', Harriet howled then, being drawn up by Astrid. Her cheeks were smeared with tears, her hair awry, her eyes as wild as any gypsy's. The hem of her dress being caught up still, the fullness of her legs showed above her stocking tops. As for poor Will, he displayed perforce another erection, the stimulation of the whip being such that it had both stimulated and stung him.

'I will see to you! Leave your drawers, you will not need them', Astrid said crisply. Thereupon she spun Harriet 'round towards Will who, having risen and teetering about on his feet in the aftermath of bottom-burning, as was his sister, could not help but again display the lewdness of his risen cock to her.

'NO!', Harriet shrieked and covered her eyes the while that Astrid bent and smoothed her dress down at last, patting it around her legs and ensuring herself a generous feel of the young woman's glowing derriere as she did so. Upon that, Amy entered with an armful of Will's clothes, which she thrust upon him with a big grin at his glowing state.

'You have been told to be quiet-be QUIET, Harriet!', Astrid said, echoing her mentor, who evidently meant to take no further part in these particular proceedings. Between herself and Amy, the sobbing young woman was then hustled down to a bedroom and sat firmly upon a stool before a dressing table while incoherent sounds of apparent grief and horror issued from her lips. Quite ignoring these, Amy set to dressing Harriet's hair. Taking up a sponge from the marble top of a washstand, Astrid lifted Harriet's chin and wiped her face. 'You have been well served for your sins, Harriet. Let us hear no more from you for the nonce. I shall escort you both home', she uttered firmly.

This intelligence brought a further wail. 'No, no! I cannot face anyone! Do not let me face Will again! Oh, the shame of this! I shall report you to the authorities!'.

'You will do nothing of the sort, Harriet. I shall have no such nonsense. You were caught in flagrante delicto with your brother while guests were here. Sufficient punishment-though many might think it not enough- has been meted out to you both. You will attend now in future to what I have to tell you. Very well, Amy, her hair is tidied nicely. Fetch some wine and biscuits'.

'I can never eat nor drink again, I can never!', Harriet sobbed, cupping her face in her hands.

'What nonsense! You are going to eat and drink exceedingly well, my pet. I have a certain hunger myself. We shall see to ourselves well in that respect-as to several others-when we arrive chez vous. Come, sit upon the bed, you will be more comfortable. Did you come much?'.

'WHA-AAAAT! Oh! The horror of things that are said and done here! What devils you are!', moaned Harriet, whose shoulders shook anew as limply she allowed herself to be re-seated, her hands twisting all about each other.

Undisturbed by this display, Astrid placed her arm about Harriet's shoulders and said no more until Amy entered, bearing a silver tray. 'Mr. Will is dressed now, Miss. Shall I bring him in?'.

'NO!', Harriet shrieked from behind the hands that once more cupped her face.

'He may take refreshments where he is, Amy. See to it that their carriage is ready. Your mistress has no doubt seen to other things'.

'Oh, yes, Miss, she has. She has had several things you might need put in there'.

'Good', replied Astrid while the maid bubbled wine into two tall glasses. She took one and, pinching Harriet's nostrils after brushing the young woman's hands aside, poured a generous libation down her throat. Spluttering and choking, Harriet endeavoured to struggle but, having Astrid's other hand firmly gripping the nape of her neck, subsided again into little wailing cries while Amy made her exit. 'Drink slowly now of your own accord. Here-take the glass. Take it! You prefer to go under the whip again, Harriet? No, I thought not. We are in no hurry. Finish the glass and I will pour another. You are in need of it'.

'You... you... you do not understand! I came here to... .'.

'To receive correction, Harriet', Astrid interrupted. 'You knew it not? Very well, I accept that. You are all the better for the surprise of it. It was timely that Will should impel his sperm upon your belly if nowhere else. What a luscious form you have, such divine curves, my dear! Put them not to waste or you will rue it. Will is a fine manly figure despite his slavish ways. You have not known how to wend them to your mutual benefit. It shall be quite other now, for I deem you will much like him beneath the skin'.

'Oh! I c... c... cannot believe what you are saying! You have caused me to sin beyond redemption! What am I to do!'.

'Oh, pouf! What stuff and nonsense, Harriet! Your initiation into the true realm of womanhood has now begun. Your tears have dried. Your bottom no longer stings but glows. May we not be friends? May I kiss you?'.

This being said with such grace and ingenuousness, Harriet could only stare bemused, bringing a sparkle of amusement to Astrid's face. Instead now of gripping Harriet's neck, she began stroking it lovingly, causing the young woman to shiver. Therewith Astrid removed the wine glass from her hand and, placing it upon a side table, enfolded the bewildered Harriet in her arms. For Astrid had already learned that much instruction and delight could be gained from alternately cozening and admonishing those who tended to submissive ways as instinctively as she divined that Harriet did. Laying her back upon the bed amid febrile struggles, she laid her moist lips warmly upon those of the young woman.

'Wh... wh... what are you at now?', flustered Harriet, utterly bewildered by all these turns of events, as well she was meant to be. Consequent upon the kiss which was of the tenderest and lightest, she felt Astrid's hand engage itself beneath her skirt, where it sought and fondled first her warm, lush thighs.

'How adorable you are going to be when I make you naughty, Harriet', Astrid breathed, quite ignoring the petulant movements of the young woman's hand as she strove to fend off the insidious upward creeping of Astrid's slim fingers, which moved suavely to caress with butterfly touch the engagingly moist lips of her cunt. Clipping her thighs together, Harriet succeeded only in trapping Astrid's hand.

'Do not, do not! I do not wish to!', Harriet moaned even as a thumb brushed its smooth surface over her clitoris.

'But you do, you do, my pet. Too long have you held yourself within, too long have you veiled this hallowed nest from love's seeking. How ardently Will spouted upon you, did he not? There is no denying it, Harriet, for the traces of his manly effusion were all about your silken skin. Did you not kiss divinely while he did so. Come, dear, part your thighs'.

'Ah! Ooooh! What are you d... d... doing to me!'

'A little more, Harriet, a little more-open them wider. There! Oh, you good girl! Is it not nice? I can see by your eyes that you are coming. Did not first his balls and then the martinet bring you on? Your tongue, darling, come, lick it in my mouth! Yield to the divine pleasure I am about to bring you. Work your bottom, Harriet! More of your tongue-more!'.

'HOOOOO!', Harriet moaned. Quite beside herself now, she had widened her legs wantonly, urging her plump buttocks as the long licking flames of pleasure spread through her. Her arms wound about Astrid's neck, drawing her mouth more fully upon her own. Ecstatic shivers coursed through her heaving loins and breasts. Careless of all, she sought Astrid's hand and caused it to rub faster around her cunt. Electric thrills coursed through both as the warm slivers of their leaping tongues coiled together. 'AAAARGH!', gurgled Harriet. She was coming, coming as she had secretly wished to do when she had felt Will's balls against her. Her offering spurted, leapt, dousing Astrid's fingers as from a bright fountain. Her eyes rolled, her legs straightening. Another spasm shook her, causing further rivulets to trickle down upon Astrid's fingers. Words of erotic fervour that she had never thought to hear flowed about her ears from Astrid's lips. Then she was still, her quivering thighs glistening with the abundance of her effusion, her eyelashes fluttering upon her cheeks.

Rising, Astrid gazed down upon her recumbent form with victorious glance. While Harriet stirred but faintly, she carefully unbuttoned the young woman's corsage and laid bare at last to her view the magnificent gourds of her breasts, which rose as two mounds of snow upon which her brown nipples stood erect. Incoherent moans issued from Harriet's lips as Astrid bent to suck the yearning points.

'You will listen to me now, Harriet, for I shall instruct you further. Do you hear me?'. Raising her own skirt and so allowing her thighs to rest upon Harriet's, Astrid teased her little finger tenderly along the young woman's lips.

'I have n... n... never thought to do such things before! Oh, how have I come to this?'.

'By guidance and precept, Harriet, yet you still have much to learn. That to which you are brought is that which you most secretly desired and yet perhaps knew it not. Being brought by force and persuasion to enjoy yourself, you will do so now again many times. For your sins you shall be punished and yet to your sins you shall be returned, there to wallow in the delight of doing things you are forced to do and to which you will gladly yield. The path is now taken-the fields of delight lie before you'.

. 'I am wicked-you have made me wicked-and yet how pleasurable it is! I know no longer what I am at! Oh, do not let Will see me thus! Where is he?'.

'Awaiting your pleasure-your mutual pleasure, my pet. Come, let us rise, for I must return you to your fold. We shall breach further the floodgates of desire, Harriet'.

'Do not make me do things!'. Harriet's haunted eyes were wide open, her swollen breasts soothed and fondled by Astrid's nimble fingers the while that she re-buttoned her corsage. Harriet's lips trembled. Her voice was that of a younger girl. 'Will you make me do things?', she asked querulously.

'We shall do what we shall do, Harriet, as you know well enough'.

'You will bind us again! I know it!'

'Is that what you wish? There is a strange comfort therein, is there not? The helplessness of yielding is quite divine, Harriet, yet it is but one of many sensations you will come to know. There is the waiting, also.'

'The... the w... waiting? Oh, Astrid, I do not understand you.'.

'Precisely because you do not, I shall not tell you. Therein will be your waiting before you discover it. Come, Harriet. How far is it to your house?'.

'F... f... five miles or thereabouts, but I do now... w... want... .'.

'Come, Harriet!'

CHAPTER 9

The hon. Ralph Cane, M.P., gazed sombrely about his study, which he meant frequently to tidy up but never did. No servants were permitted to enter this particular domain, for here within he guarded secrets that were to be seen by no eyes other than his own. In his duties as a Member of Parliament, he was naturally privy to State papers and memoranda of a confidential nature that even his departed wife had never gazed upon. More importantly for him, she had certainly never settled her eyes upon a most interesting collection of books, which he had acquired in London's Holywell Street during his various visits there. They included such niceties as Miss Coote's Confession, The Rod, Venus in the Country, and Pretty Little Games.

Such erotic delicacies, enlivened as some were by coloured plates, amused him from time to time. But like many secret seekers after pleasure, Ralph Cane had never quite obtained what he most wanted, despite his urgent seekings among the shelves of bookshops of ill repute. For while he presented a manly aspect to the world and was still reasonably firm of form in his maturing years, the deserted father of Astrid hungered for experiences he had never enjoyed since his late youth.

Then it was that he had first been whipped by his Aunt Claudia, who prided herself somewhat on the taming of would-be boisterous young men. Enjoying as he had been a summer holiday on his aunt's estate, Ralph had indeed been boisterous to such an extent that he had upped the skirts of several of the farm girls, had fondled their cunts, seen their naked bottoms, and given himself many an erection thereby. Curiously enough-as had often occurred to him then and since-he had sought not to fuck them but rather to observe such underwear as they wore and to thrill to the shapeliness of the bottoms and thighs that the raising of their skirts revealed.

It was in such a moment, close to one of the cowsheds, that his aunt had come upon him feasting his eyes upon a particularly fulsome quim of a young woman whom he had paid five shillings to see it. Her skirt and her chemise, as well as her boots were, however, exceedingly grubby. And though his cock had stirred up well, it did not then present the proud proportions that, unknown to Ralph, it was soon to do.

The farm girl, shrieking, had run off, while Ralph had stood hot-cheeked in the face of discovery by his aunt, who wore a black riding outfit and somewhat menacingly, as it seemed to him, carried a silver-handled crop. Expecting her to upbraid him then and there, his momentary relief dwindled into apprehension when he was told briefly to follow her into the house, being bidden at the same time to walk three paces behind her. This, as it happened, gave Ralph more tune and opportunity than he had ever had before to observe the rolling of his aunt's bottom-cheeks, which were rather closely sheathed by her skirt, fashionably designed to pay homage to her posterior. Perspiring not a little, he could almost feel the heavenly weight of those firmly jellied hemispheres, which displayed themselves so boldly with each sway of her hips.

Consequently, and to his increased dismay, Ralph's cock was well up and prodding through his trousers upon entry to the house, where he was led silently up to his aunt's boudoir and his condition fully seen. Causing him to stand still while removing her gloves and a rather fetching tricorne hat she had worn while riding, his aunt took up the crop again in a manner that made Ralph blench and start.

'Remove your boots, your socks, and your trousers, and bend over the bed, Sir!', she proclaimed. He was in such a dither to obey her that he quite forgot the rampant display of his upstanding penis, which in a trice was revealed to her in all nakedness. Such a lewd display appeared not however to dismay her. Rather, she caused him to tuck his skirt up farther so that, to Ralph's mingled embarrassment and excitement, his most virile possession was totally on show. Indeed, she stood before him, examining it quizzically for a moment and then licking her lips before motioning him to the bed. There bending, Ralph offered his naked buttocks to her.

In the moments that followed, Ralph remembered little other at first than that the crop was slinging him so mightily that his yelps might well have been heard in the servants' hall had he not been sternly bid to quiet himself. His bottom reddened by a dozen quick, smart strokes, of which both nether cheeks took the full impact, Ralph howled more softly and bit his knuckles, not unaware meanwhile that his cock was throbbing all the more.

'Turn about now, Sir, and kneel!', commanded his aunt, who, in consequence, stood majestically above him as he acceded with sobs to the humble position. Finding no words to excuse himself he could say nothing and wondered what next was to happen.

Not long was Ralph kept in ignorance. Of a sudden he felt a flurry of his aunt's long, black pleated skirt as it was drawn up. Before his bemused and heated eyes appeared the full majesty of her silk-sheathed legs, banded at the thighs by resetted garters, which bit into the fulsome columns of ivory. Scarce had he had time to absorb this pulse-beating view than the selfsame skirt descended over his head, enveloping him in darkness and yet also in a haven of mingling scents such as made his senses reel. Covered right down to his burning buttocks by the long fall of her skirt, his ears were clipped between her thighs. A musky odour assailed his nostrils. The crotch of her silk drawers brushed his nose. No word being uttered, his aunt's hand then pressed the hidden bulge of his head upwards until in pure ecstasy Ralph felt his mouth rammed against her silk-sheathed cunt.

'Lick, you little beast, is that not what you want?', she hissed, ramming his mouth in farther so that his lips splurged against those of her slit through the thin material. Having oozed her secretions there during the bouncing heat of riding, she gave him much to taste- so much so that Ralph grew heady and dizzy and all but fainted in the joy of it. Gone were the grubby chemises of the farm girls and their often mud-spattered bottoms, for few wore any drawers. Here he was in a veritable haven of delights, of fresh linen, of sheer silk stockings, of a soft, spotless chemise, that fell about his face as did her skirt. Above all, and with all, he was able to lick and inhale the exquisite, pungent odours that emanated from her. Licking amorously, he felt her large, firm bottom quiver, the vast cheeks tightening as a spasm shook her and her fine, salty rain of pleasure filtered slowly through the silk to ooze upon his tongue.

Then suddenly came daylight as again she raised her skirt and so nudged him with her booted foot that Ralph fell backwards with a cry of anguish and dismay that so soon had he been robbed of the hidden treasures.

'Up with you, on your back, on the bed-lie over the edge!', she hissed.

Quite uncomprehending, Ralph scuffled up to obey, his cock waggling fiercely. Nor would she have it that he might settle himself comfortably. He was to poise indeed on the small of his back so that his bare buttocks protruded over the edge, and he was forced to support himself in great part by the pressure of his feet on the floor, a posture he found most uncomfortable since there was naught but air to rest his bottom on.

Thus did he stay, his hot-flushed eyes staring wildly up at the ceiling, towards which his cock also pointed. While he did so, his aunt, moving to the other side of the bed out of sight of him, divested herself of all save her waist corset, her stockings, and boots. Being of above medium stature, she presented to Ralph's gaze a figure of statuesque glory upon appearing once more before him. The glimpses he had up to now had of girl's bottoms, cunts, and thighs were as nothing to the mature, ripe curves his aunt presented to him. Her slit, being particularly hairy, had a bush that sprouted boldly upon the plump curving of her mount while her pale breasts, adorned with two ruby nipples, jiggled like blancmanges. Having already experienced the clamping of her thighs, Ralph knew their majestic fullness well, the rich creamy columns flowing up on their outer surfaces to blend into the firm rump of her bottom and the weighty flowing of her hips.

'You will remain still, arms at your sides!', she breathed, whereupon, spreading her thighs, she drew them up on either side of his own and so positioned her avid bower that but a second sufficed to take and position Ralph's prick. A gasp escaped his lips upon feeling his knob brushed against her waiting cuntlips, for he had never known such a thing before. Disregarding his fleeting expressions completely, and being minded only to pleasure herself, his aunt steadied herself by placing the tips of her fingers on either side of his hips, and then she lowered her humid honey pot down around his prick.

Ralph remembered forever that first ride she had taken upon him, exhorting him fiercely not to move his arms and to control the shooting of his sperm until she bid him release it. This, of course, Ralph was quite unable to do the first time and so suffered for his sins by receiving afterwards a fierce bottom-smacking from her hand for having released his juices even as she was about to come for the first time.

'Little beast, little beast-you will learn to obey!', she had admonished him during his spanking while he howled and cried with his cock still dripping. Thrice weekly after that for the rest of his holiday Ralph was called to his aunt's room. Not always did she crop or spank him, though he was never sure when she would and so was ever kept on tenterhooks. Sometimes, having brought him to strip and having erected his cock, she would tie a cord about it and lead him all about the boudoir until she deemed him ready to service her. Thus did he enjoy some momentously splendid fucks, sometimes even being allowed to approach her from the rear and so engage his cock in her slit that way. This he delighted in, for his aunt's big bottom-cheeks would smack juicily against his belly, though he ever had to guard himself against injecting his sperm before being told to.

Thus Ralph came to the knowledge that women were Nature's most glorious creatures and ever to be obeyed. Even so, it puzzled him greatly that his aunt toyed also with her female slaves, among whom were counted two of the prettiest farm girls who had never let him raise their skirts. Therefore it seemed to him that while all women were glorious and commanding, some were more so than others. But all were to be venerated. This, however, he had never been able to convey to his departed wife, who had scorned him as a weakling and seemingly not even fit to be put into slavery to her.

As to his daughters, Jemima and Patricia, it seemed to Ralph as though they inhabited a different world. Of occasion he had wondered what might happen if he birched or spanked them, though he could not imagine such a thing, for in some ways it seemed a desecration. At other moments he longed to see beneath their skirts, particularly that of Patricia, who was nigh on nineteen now and as fulsome and curvaceous of form as any man could wish. Long had his eyes dwelt furtively on the slenderness of her waist, the promising curves of her hips, the protrusion of her breasts, and the impudent thrust of her bottom. Jemima, on the other hand, was but sixteen yet possessed already such a cherubic figure as sometimes made his cock stir guiltily.

Alas, thought he, that he had not been able to engage with his aunt for longer, for he would have learned more of the secret ways of the world. Several times she had bound him tightly with cords and made him lie beside her naked body all night, his cock fiercely prodding up the sheet. Yet he was unable to move limb or muscle until his aching arms and legs were freed, though that was seldom before morning.

'Such exercises are good for you', his aunt would say simply. 'They help to fire your loins and to teach you humbleness'.

To return to such a world, Ralph ever yearned, and he fretted much that the licentious volumes he obtained-while often including merry tales of birchings and such-gave him no instruction upon that which he most sought. Might a man bind a woman for his pleasure? The idea frequently distracted and taunted him. It would be devilish wrong yet great fun to do so, though he might be punished for it afterwards. That it was the punishment he sought, he had no doubt, though, like many, he found it hard to confess it to himself.

Now his musings and memories interrupted as a knock came upon the study door.

'Come in', he mumbled ungraciously, not wishing to be disturbed at all. He found himself in the presence of Patricia, who looked at her most desirable in a cream summer dress prettily adorned with blue ribbons.

'Papa, shall Astrid be long in returning?'.

'A few days, my dear-a week, perhaps-I know not. Do you then fret for her?'.

'Oh, no, Papa, not especially, for it will be a short time, will it not? I came only to enquire of news of her. Shall you be down soon?'.

'I think not, for I have much work to do', sighed her father, who found himself seeking solitude more and more.

'Very well, dear Papa, then we shall see you at dinner', enjoined Patricia, who in turning away wore upon her lips a most secretive smile. Whether her papa stayed in the study or not she did not normally care a jot, but on this occasion she had reason for seeking a privacy that he would not interrupt. Unchaperoned as she had been of late in her mother's absence, Patricia had made the acquaintance at an afternoon reception of a gentleman she much fancied, for his tastes, though a trifle peculiar, suited her livesome nature. Hands trembling not a little with excitement, she made her way unseen into the garden and from there to a rustic hut her father had once had caused to erect on the edge of a neighbouring field.

This being the place she had chosen for a secret tryst, Patricia hastened there as well as the sweeping folds of her dress would allow and was delighted to see that the door stood ajar, thus betokening that her in amorato had already arrived. Her heart somewhat in her mouth, she entered and found him sitting there, smoking a cigar and waiting.

Major Hopstone, as he was known, was a much-travelled man who could engage ladies by the dozen with accounts of his military and other adventures in India and elsewhere. It was the 'other' adventures that particularly intrigued Patricia, for he had spoken to her rather boldly of them already and had considerably stirred her senses. So much so that, although twenty-five years of age divided them, she felt more womanly than ever before in his presence.

Rising gravely, the Major bowed and kissed her hand. The hut was a poor enough place, containing only a table, two chairs, and an old couch. Yet it seemed to both to suit the mysteriousness of their tryst, as did the dim light within.

'What shall I recount to you then today, my dear?', asked he jovially.

'Oh, I know not, for I blush to hear much of it', replied Patricia coyly. 'I am much shyer, I fear, than those dusky maidens of whom you have spoken. Much that you have told me is indeed so strange that it is plain to me it could never happen in England. Oh, but do not look at me when you speak or I shall blush!', 'For that, my dear, there is a most intriguing cure', averred the Major. 'Will you permit me to show it to you?'.

'I know not. What is it?', flustered Patricia, who had seated herself at the small table. Tray, Sir, what are you at?'.

'This, my pet, is but an ordinary handkerchief, though being of a dark colour it serves the purpose well. I place it so about your eyes and then tie a knot behind your pretty head. Enclosing you as it does in darkness, you have no other eyes to meet and thus have no conscience in the matter'.

'But I cannot see! Ah, what are you doing now!'

'Furthering your education, Patricia. A little lifting of your skirt suffices to display your beautiful limbs. No, my dear, you must not struggle or it will spoil the game. I mean not to harm you but merely to titillate. Now- what was it you wished me to tell you?'.

'How you have uncovered me! For shame-no one save my sisters have ever seen my thighs before! Ah! I cannot pull my skirt back down-you have tucked it too tightly under my bottom. No! AH! What are you doing with my hands!'.

Tying them behind the back of the chair, as well you can feel. The cord hurts you not? I trust it does not', murmured the Major solicitously while surveying Patricia's long, slender legs with considerable pleasure. Her stockings being of white silk gave her an air of added purity while the sauciness of her frilly white drawers drew his pecker to a fine stand. Adorning all at the very tops of her taut stockings were pink, rosette garters which he longed to twang with his fingers but decided to wait upon it.

'Let me go! What have you done to me!', Patricia moaned, though in truth she felt no real fear, only a trickling apprehension that something very wicked was to take place. What it would be she had little idea, for her knowledge about such matters was as yet somewhat rudimentary, as befits some well brought up young ladies.

'I told you, did I not, of Semira', replied the Major, who drew his chair up closer to hers while Patricia rather wildly pressed her elegant legs together. 'You have no cause to blush now at my recital, for you cannot see me and hence may well pretend that you are in hiding and overhearing a conversation. Neither can you fidget since your hands are tied behind you. No-pray, do not interrupt or you will spoil the narrative. As I recall, you much enjoyed my introduction to it on our last encounter. Semira, who lived in Delhi, was but a year older than yourself yet she obtained the wisdom of the ages in all matters appertaining to the amorous delights of men and women. Her body, my dear Patricia, was a pure symphony of curves just as your own is. Her tits were high-placed and firm and her bottom as round as an apple.

No doubt yours will prove the same and mayhap superior even, but we have yet to come to them'.

'Oh! But... OH! Take your hand away!'

Rising from his chair and lifting her chin, the Major had planted a single kiss firmly upon her mouth while at the same time levering her thighs apart to permit him to cup the warm nest of her quim through her drawers. To this, Patricia squealed and struggled, the colour rising high in her cheeks.

'You dare, Sir, oh, you dare!'

'Dare indeed I shall, my pet, if you interrupt me further. What a lovely warm, furry cunt you have under your drawers', chuckled he, returning to his chair. 'Now I shall proceed for you are well warned. Semira was such a one as you in the beginning. Wearing as she did a sari with precious little beneath, she was quickly denuded. This of course occurred in my bungalow, to which I had enticed her. What glittering earrings she wore and what a richness of gold bangles! Deliciously indeed did they compliment the dusky hue of her skin. Her nipples were finely pointed, her muff jet black and forming a perfect triangle at the base of her belly. The cheeks of her adorable bottom were as proudly jutting and as velvety to the touch as the skin of a peach. Being held as she was by my servants... .'.

'No! I do not wish to hear-this is too naughty! AAAARGH!'.

With a shrill cry of alarm, Patricia felt the crotch of her drawers being fumbled aside by the Major's ready hand. In so doing, he uncovered a fine fluff of dark curls and the upper part of her slit.

'Do-oh-on't!', she moaned, while his fingertip gently foraged between her juicy lovelips.

'I have warned you, Patricia. On the next occasion- the slightest interruption save if you wish to ask a question-I shall have your drawers off, my girl. Listen closely now. I, believing Semira to be but an ordinary albeit lovely nubile girl fit only to be mounted, knew little of her ways, as shall be seen. Hence you may feel yourself privileged to hear this narrative, for I have told it to no other. While then she was being held in her seductive state of nakedness, I prepared myself for the divine assault by stripping off my clothes and presenting my stiff pego to her outraged eyes. With what lightning and fire they flashed! Her cries rent the roof, struggling as she was against the arms of my two female servants, whom I had paid well for this moment. Her legs, twisting this way and that, served only to excite my senses. Her belly button was twinkling, her silky belly rippling, and the lips of her quim became visible in her squirmings.

'Commanding that she should be placed down on the carpet with a cushion beneath the small of her back to raise her belly up, I fell to my knees while she was so held. Her nails would have clawed me had they been disengaged, and well I knew it. Lusting upon the blissful moment, I sank upon her delicious form and inserted the crest of my charger in her dell. What further screams she then uttered! All was as velvet within. Inch by inch my cock inserted itself, ever driving upwards until all was firmly ensconced and my balls nestled warmly beneath her bottom. The wild arching of her back and the twisting of her arms which were held back behind her by my servants served only to increase my desire to empty my plunger in her pot and then again repeat the operation. Holding her thighs flat down with the palms of my hands I began to piston my prick, very slowly, of course, for I wished to give her the pleasure of it... .'.

'But you did not!', sneered suddenly a female voice from behind him, which caused him to start up so suddenly that his chair fell back while Patricia uttered a rending scream.

'Julia!', stammered the Major, whose face had first gone beetroot and had then paled.

'Indeed, yes. I followed you here, and not for the first time. Have I not told you often enough that there may be no entertainments without my presence? To whom do you owe allegiance?'.

'T... t... to you, my love, my adored, my mistress, my... .'.

'Oh, be quiet, you oaf, and still this stupid girl's screams. Here-put this gag on her. I will not have this noise. You know that well enough'.

'GOOO-AAAARGH!', gurgled Patricia then, for quick as a flash a broad band of velvet was fastened securely around her mouth and hastily tied in a knot under her hair. Thus immobile, dumb and sightless, she waited in great apprehension and wonder as to who this visitor could be.

CHAPTER 10

'How fared you then?', Julia asked upon Astrid's return. Dinner being about to be served, they seated themselves at a table while Marie and Amy scurried back and forth to serve them.

A fault flush of pleasure stole across Astrid's cheeks. The entirety of her previous life now seemed to lie far behind her. In a short space of tune she had entered a realm of such amorous excitement, intrigue, and adventure that there could be no turning back to the dull and conventional ways of the past.

'Uneasiness, of course, overtook them both on the journey back. They sat silent, sometimes stealing quick glances at one another and then at me as though in awe of what had happened. Of the two I suppose that Will seemed the more nervous, though this was due in great part of his state of excitement. The poor young man's cock was almost bursting his breeches, though, unlike his sister, he knew not what was to befall.

'Their house is pleasantly commodious though not as large as your own. There is one maidservant of about forty and a gardener who does odd jobs about the place. He himself in his in thirties, unlettered but strong. He cast a glance of fearful surprise upon me that I do not doubt in all modesty was tinged with admiration. He would appear to be a fit subject, I believe. I have told Harriet such, though she is not yet ready to advance herself in other directions. The maid will have to go. In such a small entourage a younger girl will be more suitable'.

'Most wise of you, Astrid. I will arrange for one of my maids to seek out someone. They know exactly the type of girl to look for-one who is a little forward but who can also be trained. It is something they can well undertake themselves by now and will much enjoy. Harriet will need the comfort occasionally of feminine arms about her and a fine long tongue to lick her cunny in a way that no mere man can do. But tell me all!'

'Shortly after our arrival we took a repast, which gave me longer time to assess them further. As you did warn me, Julia, I was well aware that both or either could retreat within themselves, yet at the same time I did not wish to hurry matters. Having already lectured Harriet somewhat in the bedroom here, I turned my main attention to Will, who sat blushing and silent throughout my discourse. He was, I said, to continue to treat his sister with reverence while at the same time she must in future show as much obedience to his occasional desires as he to her. Such ideas of mutuality surprised them greatly. Harriet sought objections which of course she could scarce express without indelicacy. The maid being at that stage dismissed, I made plain to her that all matter of things would in future be spoken of openly. "Will has a good cock, has he not?", I asked, whereat she knew not whether to laugh or cry, I swear.

'Being seated then in the drawing room, we were more at our ease than at the dining table, where one's posture is necessarily restricted. "Answer, Harriet!", I commanded her. Dropping her face she mumbled, "Yes , but then added in great confusion that she was shortly to be married and that such things could neither be spoken of nor thought of. At that I told her abruptly that her marriage plans were to be terminated for the present. There would be no bar on wedlock, but she must put off the day until I knew her better and could put greater trust in her. To this she replied that she did not understand at all what I was at, which was such great nonsense that I grew angry with her. Rebellion was clearly rising in her, she having the temerity to tell me that she did not like what she called "these ideas '.

'You whipped her, I trust?', Julia asked merrily, seeing to it that both were well served with liqueurs.

'The moment was not right for it. Between the two of us Will was truly like the ass between two bales of straw and knew not which way to turn his mind. I pretended then to be tired of her and told her that she had best retire, a suggestion to which she acceded all too easily, being perhaps convinced that I would leave. Upon her departing upstairs, I turned my attention to Will. Alone with me he was as putty in my hands, tremblingly eager to obey. I counted much upon Harriet doing as ladies often do-that is to say, divesting herself at least of her outer dress and lying down upon her bed. I knew her mind better than she thought. I knew she was fully prepared to let Will fuck her once I had departed.

'Naturally I did not make it so easy for her. How well I acted in all this only you can judge, Julia. My preliminary seduction of Will was easy enough. Displaying myself to him in my drawers and stockings, I soon had him naked and with a fine upstanding cock for his task. Obedient to a degree, since all was utterly new to him, he was made to temper his desires by standing upright and still while I handled his prick and balls gently and told him firmly what was to be. He trembled mightily and made several times to touch my near-naked form, for which he received several not ungentle smacks and several tugs on his stiff prick, which caused him to blink and wince. He knew better after that than to move without permission.

'His surprise and delight were great when I apprised him that I was acting out the future role of his sister, who at other times must be put into a frame of mind to obey his whims in turn, so that each acted upon one another to their perfect delight. To this he naturally stammered that Harriet would never obey him, while I replied that I would see to it that she did. Acting as I had to, solely upon my instincts, I told him that I would next see to Harriet and that he must be prepared upon my call to do his duty to her. I minced not my words on this, telling him frankly that he was first to whip her and then put his cock to her, thereby fulfilling the manly duty she expected of him.

'His astonishment and disbelief at this was great, but so well had I tuned his rigid cock that he was ready to dare all. Leaving him then in the drawing room and warning him not to stir until I bid him to, I attended to Harriet. By great fortune I found her not only as I wished her to be-attired in but her chemise and stockings-but fallen into a doze on her bed.

'She was easily surprised. Giving her no time to gather her senses, I fastened her wrists with the cuffs you had given me, upped her chemise so that her fine round bottom was bared, and, by the severest of slaps and warnings, brought her up on to her hands and knees on the bed in good posture for what she was to receive. Then I called Will, who naturally hastened up naked as the day and with Ms prick as high as a flagpole. Such cries of alarm as his sister uttered were quickly stilled by my severe warnings that if she continued in this path of conduct I would whip her myself and more severely than had already been done.

'"Come, Will, you will give your sister a dozen good strokes. I want her bottom well heated , I told him. Harriet screamed and rolled onto her hip, which did her no good at all for, by taking purchase on her hair as you had previously shown me, I soon had her up again, her bottom bulging. Seeing then that there was no help for it, and being naturally aroused to the task, Will treated her well enough with the thongs until she shrieked, sobbed, and sought for mercy. 'I had intended him then to poke her without delay, but a better idea occurred to me'.

'You caused her to ride St George upon him?', interjected Julia.

'Oh! You guessed! But of course you would. Indeed, yes. Her resentment that he had carried out my wishes upon her and scorched her bottom was more than sufficiently strong for her to take the upper role. Releasing her, I cast the cuffs upon Will, much to his dismay! Writhing and sobbing as she still was, Harriet began to beat him and upbraid him the moment that he was laid in her place upon his back.

'"Be not a fool, Harriet, mount him, put him now to your will. Weaken him, my dear. Come, do as you are told and you will both take the benefit of it , I told her. Being stirred more than she would ever confess by the luring of the whip, she obeyed with some assistance from myself, straddling his hips to find that my hand was already guiding his prick towards the mouth of her cunt. Ah, Julia, what a sight that was! Once saddled, she wanted no other, and stemmed his throbbing cock full within. Her sobs of outrage and pain turned to pleasure, indeed she all but swooned with the sensation. As for Will, he bucked his loins, madly seeking to work his prick within her sheath while her bare bottom rested heavily on his thighs.

'"Keep him still, Harriet!", I said, much to her delight, for she then gave him a sharp slap and with real mischief sparkling through her tears kept him firmly down while her eyes seemed then to appeal to me. Being much of a mind to join with them, as you can well imagine, I took my turn upon the bed and knelt over Will's head while facing her. He thus had my knickered bottom to look up into. "Oh, squash, him, Astrid!", Harriet exclaimed, her excitement truly at a peak. Lowering my bottom fully on his face, I embraced and kissed her. Poor Will was truly squashed beneath us both and groaned as best he could under the muffling of my knickered bottom.

'"Will you not fuck together freely now, Harriet?", I asked. Her assent came in the dipping of her tongue into my mouth. She was well on heat and more fully understood then the pleasures of the game. "He shall fuck you dog-wise, then, for you must now once more be the obedient one , I said. To this she replied, "Yes , in a thick, excited voice. Will, being released, was uncuffed, I having moved off him. Harriet, however, could not wait. Flinging herself down upon him, she began to pump her hips excitedly. Their arms clasped one another, their mouths joined. Oh, what a pretty sight it was! I went all around the bed, having a full view of it and with quite a delirious excitement watched the fleshy staff of his prick slewing up and down in her cunny as her bottom rose and fell.

'How they panted and threshed, exchanging such wicked and pretty words of desire! All was soon enough over, of course, for neither could restrain himself. Will's come pumped up into her, her own effusion wetted his pubic hairs. Draining his cock to the last drop, Harriet fell full upon him and lay heaving with his face pressed between her tits, where I had drawn her chemise up.

'A trifle later, when he had recovered his forces, I had her put Will to me. We ran a delicious course, she laughing and holding his wrists so that he could not caress me the while. I left them both somewhat exhausted but contented, Harriet declaring that she loved me to distraction and had never known such pleasure. To this I replied with many kisses between us that they must not simply fuck wantonly together but must manage all sorts of tricks between them, the one to be bound and toyed with on occasion, and then the other. As to the future roles the gardener and their new maid would play, I said nothing, feeling it were best left to a future occasion. Did I do wisely?'.

The slight anxiety in Astrid's voice caused Julia to smile and kiss her. 'Exceedingly so, my dear, on your first adventure. You have ensured your future visits that I wished you to undertake, I see! What mean you to do with the gardener?'.

'I shall put him to her, for she must learn to take more than one cock, and this besides will excite Will's jealousy. They will punish each other for that most prettily, I think'.

'Splendid. But there are occasions when you must be stricter with them. You were perfectly right to take the course you did, for the sooner Harriet was pronged by her brother and knew the pleasure of it the better. Even so they must learn their disciplines. You must put the gardener's prick to her bottom'.

'Oh! Is that then a punishment?'.

'It may be either a punishment or a pleasure, dependent upon the female subject or one's personal whims. A lusty woman will take it as a pleasure, as you will-indeed, a demanding one so far as the captive male is concerned, for the suction of your bottomhole is much stronger than that of your quim, Astrid. The eventual superiority of Harriet must not be put in doubt, though Will has yet to learn it fully. In order to know it herself she must pass through fire, as we say. She will see the entry of the gardener's prick into her bottom as a punishment and yet eventually will understand it. He must be severely monitored during the act of buggery, of course, and not merely permitted to indulge his lusts'.

'Is not a man's prick too big to go in there, though?', Astrid asked, wriggling her bottom a little as she spoke.

'Consider, my dear, what comes out and therefore what may go within', replied Julia, eyeing her carefully. 'An enema is an excellent method of preparing a female for the lubricious assault, but I employ it infrequently. The anus lubricates itself sufficiently when a woman is brought on heat to entertain a cock there. The strap, the birch, or the martinet suffice, as a rule, to bring her on in this respect, as you well know. Your own adorable bottomhole, my love, will entertain such a prick as you may first wish it to, for I intend not to force you in that matter'.

'As you have perhaps other girls here?'.

'Undoubtedly. Some young ladies who are sent to me have already known the excitation of the birch or cane but have yet refused with silly giggles and struggles- and perhaps even calling out for their mamas-the manly offering of Priapus. Neither have they been fucked by the normal route, for it is often thought wisest to take the safer one. They can be pumped more frequently in their bottoms without the tiresome interference of Nature swelling their bellies. I find no cause or excuse to delay the progress of the silly, simpering ones. I birch or strap them and soon enough put a knob to their rosy orifices. Being well-held, they cannot refuse the majestic entry of the cock between their heated bottom-cheeks and are soon enough given their first lubrication there'.

'I am honoured then if I am to make my own choice upon it', murmured Astrid.

'Honoured, perhaps, but not yet completely trained', Julia responded to Astrid's surprise. Her eyes widened as she was drawn up from the sofa on which they sat.

'Wh... what will you do to me?', she asked.

'Have you forgotten so soon that all is in the waiting, Astrid? I think not, for I advised you to inculcate Harriet with that rule. It is better to stand in wonderment than to know, for then the senses are quickened and the body pulses excitedly for what is to happen. Is that not so? Did you riot first learn that when I caused you to be bound and left in waiting upstairs?'.

Indeed-I quivered and could not control the trembling of my limbs. I felt apprehension and excitement in equal measure'.

'As you shall now, Astrid. Stand in the centre of the floor, raise your dress to your hips, and lower your drawers to your knees. It is, designedly, the pose of a naughty girl who waits to be spanked or birched. Do it! Silence now, or I shall have to be stern with you. I mean not to whip you. Have no fear of that, though I suspect that your saucy bottom would now happily withstand a spanking. What I bring you shall be even more pleasurable!'.

With that Julia swept from the room and closed the door, thus surrounding Astrid in a silence that was broken only by the quiet ticking of an ormolu clock upon the marble mantelpiece. Licking her lower lip furtively, she held herself exposed, finding a curious excitement in doing so even though she was unobserved. Her mind implored Julia to return as the minutes ticked away, first five, then ten, then fifteen, until Astrid began swaying gently on her feet, her cunny moistening with excitement. What Julia intended she had no idea and felt both chastened and yet strangely pleased that she still found herself in training even after her adventure with Harriet and Will.

When the door finally opened, she started. Julia entered in concert with Marie, who held in her hand a small black bag. Unspeaking, Julia advanced upon Astrid and tucked her skirt and chemise more firmly up so that they formed a tight ring about her waist. Astrid's drawers slipped down a little and wreathed themselves at her knees, which could not help but tremble. Marie then stepped immediately behind her and waited.

'There are two things you will ensure, Astrid. The first is complete silence. You are to control yourself to a point where you do not even utter a whimper, though a tiny sound through your teeth might occasionally be permitted. The other is that you hold your knees apart as far as your drawers will allow and remain still. Now, Marie, the feather!'.

At that, Astrid's eyes dropped furtively and quickly, though sufficiently to see that the long quail's feather which Julia took from her maid had a well-pointed tip. Pursing her lips in a perfect agony of waiting, she parted her pale and lovely thighs in a posture that forced her knees to bend about an inch and made her feel exceedingly lewd. From the bag which she held behind Astrid, the maid then drew out a slender, velvet-covered dildo. At one end was a knob which she could clasp. At the other extremity-the device being some seven inches long-was a prominence that well resembled a man's knob and was of highly polished ebony that emerged from the sheathing velvet.

'Be still now, Astrid', murmured Julia. 'Look into my eyes and nowhere else!'.

With that she placed herself within two feet of the beautiful subject of her desires and training and, extending her arm down, brushed the tip of the feather lightly under the lips of Astrid's cunt, causing her jaw to sag momentarily. The tickling sensation, intense as it was, repeated itself. Every muscle in her body strove then not to stir, as simultaneously she felt Marie slyly part the springy cheeks of her bulging bottom and insert the polished crest of the slim dildo against her crinkled orifice.

'NEEE-YNNNNNG!', Astrid gritted between her teeth. The feather rolled, twirled, and moved back and forth, seeking to part her lips with its tickling persuasion and then circling around the pink bud of her clitoris, which erected itself like a tiny penis. Humming distractedly in her throat as she endeavoured to restrain her cries, Astrid felt the dildo force the rubbery ring of her bottomhole and ooze upwards within her, causing her legs to strain. Tears sprang into her lambent eyes, her cheeks puffed.

'Control, Astrid-this is what you must be taught- control. The dildo is but a path opener to your own private pleasures, my sweet. Is it well up, Marie?'.

'Almost half so, Ma'am, but she is tight'.

'WHOOOOO!', Astrid moaned, despite Julia's warning, though Julia knew well enough that she could not sustain this first dual assault without making some noise and hence did not upbraid her for it.

'Urge it up slowly, Marie. She must learn to take it. The pleasure of it will be upon her soon enough. She will come in a moment'.

'THOOOOO!', Astrid gritted. The beautiful sensation was swirling already in her belly. With a muffled gasp she received the whole seven inches of the slender, imitation prick in her bottom, causing her to clench upon it so tightly that Marie had difficulty in withdrawing it and urging it in again within. Sensibly the dear girl suavely caressed Astrid's quivering bottom-cheeks with her free hand at the same time, savouring the gleaming firmness of them and their springy jutting.

'Come, Astrid, come. You wish to but you are withholding it, girl. Imagine that there is a real cock up your bottom ready to sperm you there. How you will feel it pulsing!'.

'Oh, Julia! AH!'.

'Quietly, quietly, darling. You must learn to control your expressions of pleasure, in particular in the presence of an enslaved male. With women you may do as you wish, whether they are submissive or not. You are listening, are you not?'.

Astrid nodded. By punching her now occasionally, Marie was forcing her to work her bottom to the motions of the dildo, which second by second moved more easily in her until the sensation became less stinging and more pleasurable. Her long eyelashes fluttered.

'One prick in your cunt and another up your bottom-would you not like that?', Julia purred. Her eyes narrowed to a slit as she watched the girl's face, then with a quick gesture of her hand she thrust Astrid's looped drawers farther down so that they slid to her ankles, permitting her to open her thighs wider.

'Work your bottom now Astrid. A lovely sensation, is it not? A thick, warm prick will suit you even better there'.

'D... d... d... d...!', Astrid stuttered wildly, though she knew not whether she wanted to say, Do it!' or 'Don't!'. Quite miraculously she realised that she was controlling the otherwise natural out bursting of her orgasm, the fiercer and more abundant to make it when she did come. A divine shudder ran through her form, her clitoris peaking and quivering to the never-ending tickling of the tip of the feather. Her eyes beseeched. Her arms flung themselves about Julia's neck, the latter smiling and straining back so that Astrid all but toppled. In that moment Marie urged the full length of the dildo up into her bottom, causing her to jerk back on her toes. 'AAAAARGH!', she gasped, and was received into Julia's arms, their lips meshing rapturously as spurt upon spurt of pleasure liquid spouted from within Astrid's cunt, her belly seeming to be invaded by a thousand tiny rockets.

Long moments passed while Astrid quivered and came. The silky inner surfaces of her thighs were oiled with her juices right down to her stocking tops. Much more gently then was the dildo worked in and out, and then, as if with infinite regret, withdrawn. Weak and sobbing with the rapture of her pleasure, Astrid was led back to the sofa, on which she collapsed bare-bottomed while Julia soothed her brow and kissed her lips.

'A few more steps of training, my love, and you could have sustained all with scarce a murmur-but no matter. You have passed your trial exceedingly well', observed Julia while Marie departed silently.

'Oh, Julia, I never thought to experience such! I will be quieter, I will!'.

'I need put you to no further trials, for I am sure of it. Roll onto your hip towards me a little that I may feel you. How warm and moist your bottomhole is now! You are truly ready to receive there now, are you not?'.

'Yes', responded Astrid breathlessly. Her bottom squirmed as Julia's fingertip scouted the crinkled ring of her rosehole and then dipped mischievously within as their tongues met.

'Whose shall it be?', Astrid asked, almost as if to herself.

'You witch! You really look forward to it! It is an arcane pleasure, Astrid, that not all women allow themselves to succumb to. Those who refuse it are therefore best put to it by force. They learn soon enough that they can best feel the sperm pumping and bubbling there within. There is one, though, who has known the pleasure of it already. One quite close to you'.

'One close to ME? Oh, who? How can you know?'.

'I have been a little naughty, my dear, in your absence. Prepare yourself for an undoubted surprise. Your dear sister Patricia was the very one I put to it!'.

CHAPTER 11

For a moment Astrid could not bring herself to speak. Her lips parted from Julia's and appeared to remain frozen.

'P... P... Patricia?'.

The same, my dear. I shall not take it badly if you decide to whip me for it but hear my tale first. There is a certain gentleman of my acquaintance, a major, who is wont to enjoy little games on his own without my permission. I will not have this, of course. Secrecy may be occasionally amusing but is not to be carried to excess. A particular penchant of his is to entertain young ladies with accounts of his adventures. The susceptible cannot help but listen. He has a way with him-an avuncular way, one might say-that teases their imaginations further. Perhaps they feel safe with him, believing him only to be a wicked story teller. Little by little he overcomes their prejudices with his lewd tales and puts them soon enough to his cock'.

'But men may do this of occasion, surely? You see, I am still confused a little'.

'Indeed they may, but I, being his true mistress and having well trained him through the years, expect him to first come into my confidence. It is a great pleasure for me to be present on such occasions and, moreover, the rascal misses his own punishments with such young fillies who, having been birched, believe that is all there is to it'.

'But how could Patricia? She is so demure!'

Ha! You are a fine one to speak, my girl! So indeed were you, yet you were soon enough converted and brought to it. I had decided, you see, upon a ride in your absence, and took my way along the lanes. There I encountered the Major, though from the rear, and hence he knew it not for I kept a fair distance to see what he was at. A trifle undignified as it was, I was later forced to follow him on foot across some fields which neighbour upon your house. Thus did I come upon them in a hut which they had chosen for a trysting place. The rascal had already tied her to a chair and blindfolded her. Having then upped her skirts so that he could see her thighs and drawers, he began-as he imagined-titillating her by recounting one of his partly invented tales of India. Upon my approach to the hut I heard him speaking of Semira, who indeed was entertained at my house a year before. She is a beautiful young Indian girl whose father is a Commissioner in London. To what purpose he had sent her to me, I leave you to guess. Upon her departing from the course through which I put her, she waggled as naughty a pair of hips as ever you might see and was as fully lusting for her nightly fill of cock as you or I.

'The Major of course adorned his story to Patricia and would have had it that he alone arranged her seduction in the far-off land of her birth. What nonsense! I saw to all, as is my wont. Indeed, he fucked her well and with my whip at his buttocks the while. Such details he would have omitted from his story to your sister in order to engorge his ego. Naturally enough I could not let this pass. I therefore entered and surprised them'.

Astrid put her hand to her mouth and said, 'Oh!'.

'Oh, indeed, Astrid. I should perhaps have made play of rescuing Patricia, but one must judge the situation as one finds it and, besides, I thought it might make it a trifle easier for you on your return'.

'Easier? But I would have never...!'

'You fool, of course you must. Would you see her pass along forever on the path of dullness and convention? And what of Jemima? You must see to them, Astrid. The household must be brought under your control. You cannot ever run to me. You must have your own domain'.

'Yes, but Papa... .'

'ALL, Astrid, ALL'.

'I w... w... would not know how!'. For a moment all confidence appeared to drain from Astrid.

'You will know. Instinct will drive you to it, for you must I do not permit furtive behaviour, Astrid. The strength to command is yours. Were you any other than I already know, I would demand your word upon it. I do not need to. Once beyond my influence, you will be as unbounded as you were with Harriet and Will'.

'Oh, but I do not wish to desert you! You have taught me all!'

'No more you shall, foolish one. We shall engage ourselves in many delights, not least of all some orgies, for we may permit ourselves those occasionally in our own circles. However, I must continue my narrative. Patricia was already in that state of apprehension and excitement that we both well know. Upon my entry- unexpected as it was-her screams were such as you can imagine. I was forced to gag her. What should I have then done, Astrid?', Julia asked cunningly.

'Er... ah... you should have whipped him soundly for being so naughty with Patricia'.

'Yes, quite. What of Patricia, though? I induced from her, you see, the confession that she had listened freely to him twice before without being bound and had been much excited thereby'.

'Oh, the bad girl!', exclaimed Astrid.

'Precisely. So you see, all was not as simple as first seemed. He had not merely leapt upon her and bound her as a complete innocent. Naturally, however, I dealt with the Major first. He is thoroughly craven in my presence and bared his buttocks timidly for my crop, though not before I had removed your sister's blindfold. Her astonishment that I did not first release her was obviously great, but I fear that the gag gave her little chance to express herself. Making him bend over the table but somewhat away from it so that his cock was well exposed, I gave him quite a severe cropping, which caused him to moan and grant and bellow no end. Her eyes uncovered, Patricia had full sight of his penis which, being already upstanding, was kept so by the stinging of my crop. Then, bidding him sternly to remain as he was, I took Patricia up and forced her to assume the same posture beside him but with her drawers down.

'Fear not, Astrid, for I afforded her only a little cropping. Quite a light one, to bring her up a little. She sobbed and wriggled exceedingly. I had removed her gag while warning her that any undue noise would result in my informing her papa of my discovery. Some fine pink streaks lay across her lovely bottom-cheeks, I can tell you, by the time I had finished. She has a delicious cunny, but I did not want it breached by one as churlish as he. The Major knows my signals well enough by now. While Patricia howled and cried, expecting me to swish her bottom more, I clicked my fingers, causing him to rise quickly and present himself to her. Ah, what a shriek as he bent over her and got his prick in-into her bottom, yes! I permitted him however but one long, slow thrust until all was sheathed within, then made him hold it there.

'Such cries from Patricia you would never believe! There was no help for it, however. She could not get up. His weight was upon her and her rosy hole had already contained his prick to the root. I made him hold it there an entire two minutes, at the end of which Patricia had ceased to cry out and had dissolved into softer moans which betokened, I thought, some enjoyment of the naughty engagement of her bottom to his cock. However, the entire punishment was not really to be hers. Imagine his dismay when I commanded him to draw out and stand to attention! Had I not moved aside quickly when he did so, his sperm would have splashed all over my skirt. Ugh! Her bottom was so warm and tight that he could not contain himself, you see. Quite briefly then I dismissed Patricia, telling her that she had learned as fine a lesson as ever she might be taught. Pretending to tears again, she covered herself and ran out, being as well aware as I that there was no one to whom she could confess the matter since the original sin was hers'.

'Oh, then you achieved all! She has had a prick up her bottom. She has not been ridden, but was taught a fine lesson, as you say! How marvellously you accomplished it! What a perfect balance of events!'.

'You are not displeased, then? I am glad. I have prepared the route, as I told you, and caused her to think much about it. She will have felt his cock a-throbbing in her bottom all day'.

'How restless she will be, the dear girl!', murmured Astrid pensively.

'The rest is for you to accomplish, my sweet. You are as one who may play chess now with your subjects. You will bring them all to love one another even more fiercely in the bondage of obedience'.

'May I? Oh yes, of course I may!', Astrid said excitedly, but then to Julia's pleasure controlled her expression. 'Am I to be as cold with them as you first were with me?'.

'As you will, my pet. You are young, strong, and beautiful. The fire of it will lick through your veins. Thoughts more wicked than ever you could have thought to entertain will be translated into reality. What of your servants now, for you must have true servitors as I have Marie and Amy-not to say Tom and Alice!'.

Astrid pondered a moment. 'There is John, the valet. He is strong and not displeasing of face. I feel certain that in my new mood I could bring him well to heel. He has cast sly eyes upon me often enough. As to the maids, there is Crissie. She is but nineteen, quite pert if one lets her be, smallish of stature but strong from her work, I suspect. Her ankles are slender, her breasts full. I have seen not much of her yet in her physical aspects, but shall do so now'.

'They will do for the moment', Julia interrupted her. 'Bear in mind at all times the necessary hierarchy, for apart from being important of itself it maintains the balance of things that you must ever watch with care. It must be much as you have witnessed here. At the uppermost rank and mistress of all will be you. Your papa and your sisters will occupy the middle ground, so to speak. The servants remain ever such and must be trained to know it. Consider Tom and how I had you put to him, yet well he knew your rank and that in all his actions he was but a male serf acting upon my pleasure-as also yours. But this you know already, for you performed magnificently with him in this very room. Upon this very sofa, indeed. Had you told him to withdraw his cock at the very moment of his orgasm, he would have obeyed'.

'That is true. I might then put Patricia to John in the same wise, but as to Jemima she is a little young as yet'.

'Tush and nonsense! She is ripe for it. More than you know, perhaps. In India, and in other Far Eastern climes, girls of but fifteen prove the most adept of houris, for their tits are already as polished and firm as their adorable bottoms. Have no fear of it but that she will enjoy her pumpings. Of course, you must spank her first!'.

'Oh, I shall! And afterwards, too, perhaps', laughed Astrid, to whom all things now seemed possible. Rising, she drew up her knickers and smiled at her apparent awkwardness in doing so. 'I may go then? Shall I?'.

'With less mischief and excitement in your voice, my sweet, yes. That you may reserve for me and, later, for Patricia and Jemima, once they are fully inducted into our pleasures. How quick it has all been!'.

'Yes, has it not? But I would never have learned without you. I thought you so hateful and cruel when first I arrived'.

'At which moment, then, did you think other?'.

'When I was first bound. Indeed, I screamed and cried still, yet all the while I knew myself drifting into a world of pleasure and... oh, how strange it is to say it... of safety!'

In saying such you have learned all', Julia sighed. 'The baby is tightly swaddled and can scarce move its little limbs. But then being so, it is cuddled and kissed by its mama and so already learns the pleasures of both conditions. Thus to our origins do we endeavour to return. What are you smiling at?'.

'The thought of having a prick in my bottom. How wicked I am, and yet not. I wonder much at Patricia's reactions in the matter'.

'Those you will learn soon enough. I will have a carriage called for you, my dear. Your cunny is still a little on fire, I imagine. Your bottomhole veritably winked upon my finger when I put it in! This is all to the good. Imbued with desires, you will be impelled to act as you instinctively wish, yet all that I have taught you will control your actions when the moment comes. Is there anything else you would have wished here?'.

'I would love to have whipped Marie and Amy!'

'That, my love, you shall do on your next visit, and more, for they are such delightful minxes that you will not wish to stop at that, I know. As to your accoutrements, you will need a martinet, some cuffs, a tawse, and, let me see, what else?'.

'Determination?', sparkled Astrid with a silvery laugh.

'Your very manner of using the word betokens that you have it. Come, let us see to your departure'.

With that, and amid many kisses and fervent promises, Astrid finally departed, little able to believe that she had been different on her arrival than now. Thoughts brooded in her darkly to the swaying of the carriage, as its sides occasionally brushed the hedges of the narrow lanes. Then, lifting her face and gazing out upon the verdant fields, the trees, and the herds of cows, she smiled at the thought of Patricia receiving her due. It was surely a sign that she had done so, and under the aegis of Julia. The best was yet to be. With that thought, she at last arrived. She entered the house to the great surprise and delight of her sisters. Coming downstairs later, for he knew not the reason for the commotion and was quite put out by it, Astrid's father drew upon his face a pleased look and made to kiss her cheek.

Astrid however avoided his touch. 'No, Papa, not now, for I am a little weary', she said, adding much to his surprise. 'I will see you later. You are working in your study?'.

'Why, yes', he exclaimed awkwardly, bemused to find that a flush had appeared upon his cheeks. What a strangeness of behaviour had seized his elder daughter, he could not imagine.

'Good. I trust you will remain there, for your work is no doubt important, Papa', Astrid rejoined languidly while Patricia and Jemima positively gaped at the manner in which she had spoken.

'Where have you been then?', Patricia asked with some attempt at jollity.

'I have been learning, Patricia. Do we not all sometimes-whether here or elsewhere?', asked Astrid in a voice so lightly cutting that Patricia bit her lip and appeared to be in great contemplation of the pattern in the carpet.

'I do not know what you mean, Astrid'.

'Ha! As to that, you know more in one respect than I, my sweet. Where is John now?'.

'In the pantry, I do believe. Why do you ask?'.

'I have some matters to discuss with him-household affairs, you might say. Have Crissie lay out my black-silk dress. I have a fancy to wear it tonight'.

Sweeping out before Patricia could reply, but having left her on a purpose with a simple duty to perform, Astrid sought out the valet, whom she found idling through a copy of Sporting Life.

Well, John, what are you at? Is there not silver to be polished and my boots perhaps to be cleaned?'.

'Oh, lord, Miss, I didn't hear you coming. You could have rung and I would have attended on you'.

'You will do that soon enough, John, in many respects. How impudently you gaze upon me sometimes! Do you like what you see?'. Quite amused at the reddening-up of his face, Astrid eyed him carefully for a long moment, not failing to espy a certain growth in the front of his plush breeches. 'Well, John, I asked you something!'.

'Oh, yes, Miss, you are very beautiful. The pride of the county, I reckon. Such a... .'.

'Nice bottom, John? Here, you may feel it. Come, don't be shy. I shall tell no one. Put your hand all around and under it for a moment. Does it feel firm and round?'.

'Lovely, Miss. Can I keep my hand there! Ain't you lovely and warm, full solid flesh, as they say, but it gives to my fingers a bit, as it should'.

'Really, you must be an expert, John. Your cock has risen, I see. No, do not try to hide it with your jacket, man. I want to see. Feel right under my bottom, John, for the moment will be brief enough, but you may have your pleasure of it. What would you not do to get this truncheon of yours up between my legs, say?'.

'Oh, I couldn't never imagine such a thing! I would faint, Miss, I think it would be so nice. Especially with your stockings on, for I likes a woman who rubs her stockings under you'.

'You do, do you? Quite a connoisseur! That pleases me. Take your hand away now, you have had a good feel of it. I intend to ask you something, John, something that is not to be put around either in the house or in the servants' quarters, upon pain of your immediate dismissal and my informing all the households in the county that you are a useless servant'.

'No, Miss, I wouldn't say nothing, I promise. God's honour on it, no matter if it were tried to be beaten out of me'.

'That is the talk I like to hear. Stick well by that, for you will have need to. My requirements-indeed my demands-are very simple. You will obey unquestioningly all that I tell you to do in future. No more, no less than that. No harm will come to you and you will have much enjoyment of it. Have you worked your cock often in a woman, John?'.

'Not as much as I would wish, Miss, and hereabouts there's not much chance. The old pecker comes up stiff for it as soon as I wakes'.

'Let me feel it, John. Open your breeches, I want to see the size of it. My goodness, it's a fair one, isn't it, and such a glowing head! No, do not move, John. Attempt to touch me and I shall scream and there will be a rare scandal of it which would surely end with you in prison'.

'Oh, Miss, you are torturing me like this-your hand is so soft and warm. I don't know as if I can hold it back from coming, it's that excited. Push your fingers along it a little more!'.

'No, John. Did I not tell you that you are to obey? Listen to me carefully, arms at your sides! Think only of this: that, provided you control yourself now and do not come, I shall let you put it in me tonight. There is another condition, though. You will enter my room quietly after midnight. You will not speak. I shall bind your wrists first, for at present I have no desire for you to touch me otherwise. Your prick will then be inserted and you will be given forty strokes in and forty out eighty in all, John!-before you spill your sperm. I shall then untie you and you will return to your quarters. Do other than this and I shall tell Papa you have attempted to rape me'.

'Oh, Miss, yes I'll do it! I never thought to hear the like of this coming from you. I'm trying to hold back now, but it's that excited. Will you be naked, Miss?'.

'I shall wear my boots and stockings only. We shall have a good fuck, John, but forget not that all such matters will be under my control. Put it away now and keep it fit for a long pumping tonight. If you come before I tell you to, it will not happen again. I have a lovely, tight cunt, John, I promise you that'.

CHAPTER 12

Returning to the drawing room, Astrid found only Jemima there, curled up in a chair and looking somewhat fretful. Concerned lest her pretty little sister should be of dull spirits, Astrid sat on the arm of her chair and kissed her fondly.

'Are you well, Jemima? You look a little peaked'.

'I am well, really, Astrid, but life is so boring, isn't it? Scarce anyone comes to call, and Papa seems especially broody so that there is nothing to be got out of him at all'.

'Well, darling, I intend to see that changes are made about the house now and that we shall indeed have a merrier life. As for Papa, you may be sure that we shall get plenty out of him. I mean to make it my duty to see so. Did Patricia tell Crissie about my dress?'.

'No, she didn't. She is all of a mood, too, and said she did not see why she should have to do it for you'.

'Not to fret, Jemima, I will ensure that she is put into a better frame of mind. Be a good girl and go and tell Crissie for me. Before you do, there is a package I hid behind the stand in the hall. Will you fetch it?'.

'Are there presents in it?', Jemima asked excitedly, but before Astrid could reply she had run into the hall and returned carrying a small, black-leather valise. 'What is in it-oh, do tell me! Is it a secret?'.

'It is rather one, pet, but I will show you first. Come, let us go up to your room for we shall be more private there and need have no fear of interruptions'.

All aglow with interest, Jemima followed her sister upstairs. Having entered the bedroom and locked the door, to the great intrigue of Jemima, the bag was opened and its contents laid out. Jemima's expression took on one of astonishment. 'Oh, what funny, horrid looking things!', she exclaimed.

'Really, Jemima, they are not horrid at all. Come, sit with me and I will explain. First we have these two pairs of leather cuffs, which fit closely but comfortably around the wrists or ankles. Then we have this broad leather strap, which is called a tawse. The end is split into two, and makes a fine slapping noise. There are several lengths of cord, as you can see, some longer straps for the body, and finally this little whip, which has a full twenty thongs, all very slim, with the ends are tied in a knot'.

'Oh, Astrid, are they for naughty girls?'.

'For naughty girls and naughty boys, dear. Have you been naughty while I've been away? I'm sure you have a little. Let's pretend you have and play a game. I will just slip these cuffs around your wrists, so. No, don't struggle, silly, or it will spoil things'.

'Really, what are you doing! I don't want to! Why are you pulling my dress up? Oh, stop!'.

'Shush, Jemima! You must not make so much noise-that is one of the rules of the game. If you struggle so hard I shall really spank you. I am just getting your drawers down for a moment. There! What an adorable bottom! To think that Papa has never so much as smacked it'.

'OUCH! What are you doing? How hateful you are, Astrid! I shall tell Papa of this, and Patricia, too!', squealed Jemima, as Astrid drew her across her lap and gave her two quite light smacks landed on the resilient cheeks of her chubby bottom. The cheeks were prettily dimpled and of perfect whiteness. Beneath the cleft orb showed an already promising fluff of curls, the whole seeming to invite such titillation as Astrid intended to give it. SMACK! fell her palm again, the impress of her hand leaving a most attractive imprint upon the plump little half-moons. This brought a further yelp from Jemima, who wriggled madly, though, her wrists being bound behind her back, she could little to effect her escape. 'BOO-HOO!', she sobbed, and would have rolled off Astrid's lap had Astrid not caught her. 'If you don't st... st... stop, I shall scream and scream!';

'Very well, Miss, if that is to be the case I shall have to dun your cries, will I not?'. With that, Astrid took a black cloth from the valise, which lay open at her side, and promptly gagged Jemima, rolled her upon the bed, and made her draw up her knees.

'No, no, NO!', her sister endeavoured to screech but only a thin sound came from behind the gag while her dress and chemise were drawn up high over her hips and her bottom more fully bared. With that, Astrid reached for the little whip of many thongs and began swishing it quite gently across Jemima's bottom, for she had no desire whatever to cause her pain but only to let her feel the first urging of the burning tips, the tiny knots at the ends ensuring that they nipped like bees.

'OOOOH-WAH!'. Jemima could hear her own voice echoing in her ears. Her back being clamped down firmly by her sister's hand, her bottom squirmed and bounced while the tips seemed to seek between her cheeks and even occasionally beneath, to tickle her cunny. It did not hurt her half as much as she thought it would, but it was a most funny sensation, and made her nether cheeks grow hot all over as again and again- and now and then with a little more force-the thongs swirled like striking snakes all about her delightful posterior.

'Now, Miss, I propose to give you a fine sixer to polish you off', declared Astrid, who was delighted to see what charming hues of strawberries and cream her efforts were producing. It would do no harm at all for Jemima to be well heated, she decided suddenly, and by no means against her better judgement, for she knew she could wield the thongs as delicately as any or as strongly as might be wished.

'NEEE-YNNNNG!', came Jemima's muffled cry. SWEEE-ISSSH! came the thongs again and again, causing Jemima hips to rotate delightfully while all over her bottom appeared splotches of pink. Her knees jerked, her face grew ever more flushed, and her bubbles seemed to swell until the sharp tips of her nipples pressed through the cotton of her dress. SWEE-ISSSH! WEEEE-ISSSH! SWEE-ISSSSH!.

'Up with it, Miss-come on-two more!', Astrid sang with a most bewitching smile playing about her lips. No sooner had she accorded them, and brought her sister's bottom to a full, rosy glow, then she acted with all such speed as she knew was required. Slipping a sobbing Jemima's gag, she fell on the bed beside her which, being narrow, caused them to lie closely together.

'OH-WOH-WOH!', Jemima blubbered, while Astrid, cupping her hot bottom firmly, held her tight against her so that their titties bulbed together and her mouth softly silenced her sister's cries. Feeling smothered and squirming still from the stinging, Jemima sobbed into Astrid's mouth the while that Astrid reached far under her bottom to tickle and tease her cunny.

'BLUB!', mouthed Jemima, who was now seized by so many different sensations at once that she felt even hotter and headier. Little by little as Astrid's persuasive finger moved and, while her tongue twirled all about in Jemima's mouth, her sister quivered, gasped, and then began to cling to her as with her free hand Astrid loosed the cuffs.

'There, darling, there-does it not feel nice now?', Astrid soothed. 'Lift your leg up, darling, so that I can feel your pussy better. There! Ooooh, how moist it is! Don't be afraid for I am going to make something very nice happen. Ah, now I can feel your clitty. What an adorable little bud it is! Shall I rub it more while I hold your bottom?'.

'NOOOO! Y... yes... yes! Oh! I feel I'm melting!'.

'You are coming, pet, you are coming. Lie on your back now and open your legs well. There's a good girl! Give me your tongue now! Ah, how you are gushing! How lovely and sticky-wicky it feels all over my fingers'.

'GOOOOO!', quivered Jemima. The hot stinging of the thong tips made her bottom bounce still, which of course is exactly what that instrument is designed to do, so that the maiden is brought to respond to the delights that follow. Her legs, held wide open, straightened, and her toes curled while Astrid so artfully kept on brushing her clitty with the lightest of fingertips. Jemima once more spurted and then again until, with a huge contented sigh, she lay still, her eyes wide open in an expression of innocent delight.

'You see? Was it not nice? Keep squirming your bottom, dear, for you may come again, if you wish. Come-tell me that you liked it, for I know you did'.

'It st... st... stung me-oh!', replied Jemima, blushing but at the same time keeping her pretty legs apart.

'It is meant to, for it brings you on. What a delicious little mouth you have-fresh as a peach. Confess to me, you little minx, that you enjoyed it despite all'.

Jemima giggled and hid her face, for she felt both naughty and excited at the same time. 'Yeth!', she lisped, and gurgled quite happily as Astrid passed her lips suavely across her own while feeling the straining of her nipples through her dress. 'You must not do it again though, Astrid, must you?', Jemima asked naively.

'If I do not, darling, you will only wish that I had. I have lots to teach you and you will find it very exciting, I do promise. Let us keep it a secret, shall we? Papa has never spanked you, which is very remiss of him'.

'Ooooh, but I don't want him to!'

'We shall see, Jemima. Now pull your knickers up and change your dress, for I want you to look at your prettiest always. I shall see to it that Papa buys you many new things this very week and I shall help you choose them myself. A little corset will draw your slender waist in even more and make your hips flare. Indeed, you look womanly already. A perfect little Venus, as they say'.

'Papa will never buy me new things-I know he won't', pouted Jemima, rising from the bed and almost tripping over her drawers which had been worked down to her ankles.

'Papa will do as I say and so will you', Astrid replied firmly to the great astonishment of Jemima, whose navel twinkled as she covered herself. Obey me in all things henceforth, my sweet, and you shall have your heart's desire'.

'Oh, do you mean it? There is such a change in you I know not what to think!'.

'What one thinks and what one does are occasionally two different things, as I have been surprised to learn myself. But all this you will know also in due course. Your prefect obedience is all I seek now, Jemima', Astrid said, lifting her sister's chin.

'I promise-oh, I do!', Jemima replied breathlessly.

'Very well, dear, and I shall keep you to it. Attend to your appearance now, for, whatever befalls, a woman must always look at her best'.

With that, Astrid departed and went straight to Patricia's room, where she found her sitting hunched up in a chair. At her entrance, Patricia glared at her and looked away, pretending to be much busied with her contemplation of the sky through the leaded panes of the window. In truth, though, she sensed that Astrid was going to upbraid her for not having given her message to Crissie. Moreover, Patricia was exceedingly restless. Her apprehensions as to the identity of the woman who had interrupted her tete-a-tete with the Major had not lessened, and she feared lest she might appear at the house and reveal all. At the same time, the sensation of having the Major's cock in her bottom was also ever present. At some moments it filled her with shame and yet at others it excited her.

'You did not then give Crissie my message', Astrid said, placing herself before Patricia and thus effectively forcing her to look at her.

'No, I did not, Astrid. What a bothersome, silly thing for me to have to do when you could perfectly well do it yourself.

'You have much to learn', Astrid sighed. 'Perhaps your amorous occupations in my absence have befuddled your mind a little'.

At this Patricia naturally displayed great dismay and wonder. Her hand flew to her mouth, her eyes opened wide. 'What? I do not know what you mean!', she stammered.

'Patricia, you know perfectly well what I am about, though you have no need to fear that I shall divulge your escapade in the hut. Neither have I any wish to make the Major's acquaintance. He is not the type I wish you to consort with'.

'You know of this? Oh, my God, how do you know? Who has told you? Have you seen him?'.

'A good stiff cock up your bottom, indeed! Well, I am sure it benefited you, and is as good an introduction to the amorous arts as any young lady might have. How did it feel? You must tell me', Astrid said in her softest voice while quite ignoring her sister's questions. So saying, she stepped back and allowed Patricia to spring up.

'You will tell no one, Astrid-I beg you!'

'What have you to fear, my dear? All men are possessed of cocks and all women with the appropriate apertures for them to poke', laughed Astrid, turning her back on her and surveying the placid gardens beyond. Feeling Patricia's hand imploringly upon her shoulder, she stiffened, much as if to brush it away.

'I beg you, please-promise me, Astrid! Oh, the shame of it-I would die of it! That dreadful woman who forced me to the act-do you know her?'.

'Tut, tut, so many questions. Patricia! Let it suffice that you have at least been rodded at last and in a perfectly appropriate place. Sit down on the bed, for I wish to speak to you'.

'I cannot, I cannot! Oh, you will tell Papa-I know it! What am I to do?', wailed Patricia, wringing her hands and looking much more pitiful than Astrid knew she really felt. Amid then such agonies of remorse as she was endeavouring to confess, she found herself pushed backwards by Astrid who, having turned, pressed her down upon the edge of the bed which. 'I will never do it again, I promise!', she declared wildly.

'You will not? Of course you will-and much more pleasurably, I trust Indeed, I shall see to it that you do. Listen to me carefully, Patricia, for I shall not repeat myself. Should I be forced to, you will find yourself in quite an inescapable position in which you will have no help but to listen. I give you my word that Papa shall hear naught about this, nor Jemima either-provided only that you do as I say.

'Oh, yes, I will promise anything! Papa would surely cast me out were he to know!'.

'Papa will do nothing of the sort, my pet. Come, dry your tears, for they quite spoil the natural beauty of your eyes. There is much to be changed here. I count you a sensible girl, whose acquiescence I will not find it hard to obtain. However, we must have a little honesty first. My decisions will rest much upon your confessions. How was it then when you were put to him? Delay not your reply, Patricia!'.

'Oh, must you know? Do you not know the shame of it? My drawers were removed and I was thrust beneath the weight of Mm. He had been whipped soundly, I can tell you. But to my infinite astonishment that seemed only to serve to increase the length and girth of his... his big thing'.

'His cock, darling. Be not shy to use the word'.

'I screamed, I cried, I struggled-truly I did Astrid, but there was no one to come to my aid. That awful woman commanded him in all he did. He held my b... b... bottom-cheeks and parted them. My shame was too intense to describe. I felt the hot glowing of his... his cock... and then it was pushed in. Ah! I could not get my breath-I was being split in twain. I cried for mercy but to no avail. Spurred on by her crop he pushed it up me inch by inch until-I know not how-I contained it all'.

'Fiercely throbbing, was it not?'.

'It pulsed, it burned, it tickled-I could feel every inch of it and every vein upon it. How long he held it in I do not know, for I had all but fainted. The woman lifted his shirt front to ensure that my poor bottom was well pressed into his belly. "Remain!", she instructed him, and so I was held'.

'You were bottom-corked', Astrid smiled. 'Tell me truly, for we are sisters and can divulge all manner of secrets to one another, was it awful or did you not have some pleasure from it once your bottomhole has eased?'.

'Oh, how can you say that!'

'Did you not, Patricia? Remember what I told you. Truthfulness is all-not to say, obedience to my wishes, which I desire most'.

'Perhaps a trifle. Pleasure, that is to say. OH!', exclaimed Patricia at making such a confession, and hid her burning face against Astrid's breasts.

Smiling to herself, Astrid stroked her hair and soothed her. Her arms tightening about her sister's shoulders, she held her firmly and began to whisper to her. Now and then Patricia uttered gasps and wildly shook her head. All these gestures and exclamations Astrid ignored.

'You have been initiated-in small part, at least. That is the strength of it. Such delights we occasionally call "exercising , though the term applies more to males than females. The fearsome lady you encountered is none other than a dear friend of mine, who chanced upon you by accident while grazing her horse. Knowing the excited condition in which you were, she saw to it that you were at least briefly accommodated. Oh, yes, you need not look surprised. Being well aware of who you are, she was mindful to see that you were not as thoroughly and crudely pumped as the Major would have wished. Indeed, she saved you from that, remember. Had you been less than you are-and, indeed, not as beautiful, as she observed to me-he would have been allowed to spout in you at his will. As it was, she afforded you but a glimpse of the pleasures that now await you'.

Even in her confusion, Patricia could not hide a quick smile of pleasure as Astrid brought her face up to the light. 'She said that of me? Oh, but, Astrid, what a change has come over you!'.

'Do you think it for the worse? I do not! In your womanly heart, Patricia, the image of that yearning prick rises ever before your eyes, and indeed you can feel the probing of it at your nether cheeks, which are full ripe for such an adventure. Let us refresh ourselves with some tea, for I have much to talk to you about. I have but to ring and Crissie will bring it up. She is a pretty girl, is she not?'.

'Yes, I had not thought of it overmuch, but now that you say so there is a great attractiveness about her. Why did you say that? I cannot keep up with your thoughts!'.

'There is a reason for it, as you shall discover. There is great innocence in you but, now that your bottom has been breached, it will quickly dissolve into a much more exciting vista'.

'Oh, what words you use, Astrid! I never thought to hear you speak such!'

'What a perfect silliness we have about words which are merely to describe that which we may see before our eyes! To deny the words is not to deny the existence of the objects. A man's cock and balls are the very pride of his being. They seek the orifices that we females alone possess. Therein lies the secret of many a pretty game that may be played, as I intend that we shall play them. Your thoughts are already much changed, as mine are. Have you not wondered now about having a man's stiff prick in your cunny?'.

'No-yes-oh, I have, though I should not say it'.

'Stuff and nonsense. I intend to make you as bold as possible in such matters. Suppose I presented Papa's cock to you, as ruddy and stiff as well it might be. Supposing, too, I were tickling your quim at the same time and that your legs were open'.

'Ah, you must not say such things! How wicked! OUCH!'.

'I shall smack you again, Patricia, and much harder if you interrupt me with such silliness. Ah, here is Crissie. Fetch tea and cakes, Crissie, and be not long about it. Miss Patricia and I will be staying in her room a while'.

'Yes, Miss, I'll get it on the double'.

'Get up and pull the curtains, Patricia. The sun is too strong across my eyes. Draw them more tightly together. That's it. What a pleasant gloom there is. How nice and secretive. Come, lie down with me'.

'What a strange mood you are in, Astrid! Crissie will wonder what we are at'.

'There is no strangeness about pleasure, Patricia, as Crissie herself is shortly due to discover. I mean to unveil her bottom and give her a fine whipping this evening, as I shall you, my pet, if you prove obstinate. Yes, you may well look astonished, but I mean to have all things as I intend. Stop fluttering your hands, you silly, for I am only caressing your legs a little. What beautiful smooth thighs you have! I must have Papa buy you some prettier garters. Blue upon white stockings would suit you best. I may allow him to put them on your for a treat'.

'Oh, Astrid, stop it-you are tickling me-don't say such things!'

'Very well-you insist upon such attitudes? What a little hypocrite you are! Julia did not fail to observe, you know, that you wriggled your bottom quite a lot when the Major's cock was plugging you. Crissie? Yes, you may enter. Put the tray down and go immediately to Miss Jemima's room. You will find a black valise there. Fetch it on the instant!'.

'Oh, my goodness, yes, Miss!'.

Eyes wide, Crissie scurried forth, not believing quite that she had seen what she had seen-Miss Patricia with her dress up and Miss Astrid's hand held under her drawers. Scurrying like one possessed, she found the valise in the bedroom, that Jemima had vacated, and returned holding it.

'Now, Crissie, I mean to punish Miss Patricia for her naughtiness. Give me the whip from the bag and then come and sit upon her shoulders when I turn her over. Hurry, girl, for I mean it!'.

'Oh, Miss!'.

Pealing forth cries and screams of outrage, Patricia was firmly held

131

down while Crissie's trembling fingers drew out the black menace, whose thongs hung limp about her wrist. From his study, Ralph Cane heard the screeches that then ensued and pursed his lips. The girls were forever playing about. He would have to summon up the courage to put a stop to it.

CHAPTER 13

'Whoo-hooo-hooo!', Patricia screeched. Hung over the side of the bed with her drawers forcibly taken off and her bottom jutting out as Crissie sat astride her back, she received again and again the stinging sweeps of the thong. Astrid spared her not. Whereas she had merely toyed playfully with Jemima, the slightly larger bottom of Patricia was made to squirm and squirm. Again and again and again the hissing thong tips bit into her richly fleshed posterior, which in but a dozen strokes had already assumed a rosy hue. Crissie, open-mouthed and with her knees clamped excitedly against Patricia's hips, felt her awe of the occasion turn to excitement. How lovely it was, she thought, to see the naked bottom of such a proud Miss wriggle and rotate each time the thongs fanned across it. A warmth made itself felt in her loins and her cunny tingled.

'NOO-OOOH-OOOH! Astrid, don't, DON'T!', Patricia howled.

'At the end of this, my dear, you will listen better', Astrid declared, underlining her promise with an even fiercer HUI-ITTTT! of the whip, which brought a shrill, moaning cry from her sister.

Alas, or not, it was at this juncture that their father decided to intervene. He had heard oft enough cries and giggles coming from one or other of the girls' rooms, but never such as these. Striding from the study on the floor above, he made his way quickly down and thrust open the door from behind which the beseeching wails came.

Astrid it was who shrieked first, though not in fear but as one highly disturbed by any interruption. 'Father! Out! Go!', she cried. Crissie yelled and fell back, daring not to be seen by her master in such a position upon one of his daughters. As for Patricia, whose bottom was fully on view to him, not to say her long stockinged legs, which had parted haplessly to show the peeping of her cunt, her shriek was the loudest. Freed of Crissie's weight, she rolled frantically first one way and then the other, betraying the whole of her treasures to his dazed eyes before slumping backwards onto the carpet, where she made the most frantic efforts to veil her charms.

In contrast then to the sudden cries that had rent the air came a curious silence. It was as if all were momentarily frozen in their attitudes while an extremely pink flush stole over Mr. Cane's features. Had he wished perhaps then to recover both his wits and his authority, it was not to be. Advancing upon him with panther-like steps and with her eyes blazing, Astrid all but prodded the black handle of her whip into him, which threatening motion caused him to step back hastily.

'What is the meaning of all this, Astrid, eh?', he endeavoured to demand while Patricia crouched upon the floor and sobbed, and Crissie hid behind the farther side of the bed. Alas, the tone in which he intended to utter his question was not the one he would have sought, and became unaccountably a veritable croak.

'We will go to your study, Father. Come, please, let us not have a scene!', Astrid uttered coldly while ever crowding him through the doorway until, to the vast relief of Patricia and Crissie, he was no longer immediately visible to them. To their ears came a mumbling and then the sound of retreating footsteps. Taking swift advantage of the situation, Crissie removed herself from hiding, skirted nervously the slowly uprising figure of Patricia, and skipped through the door, there to see her master and Astrid going slowly upstairs. Half-closing her eyes ostrich-like fashion that she might not be seen, Crissie made to descend but was brought to a sudden standstill by the whiplash voice of Astrid.

'CRISSIE! You will go to my room and stay there until I come down. This instant!'.

'Yes, Miss, yes-oh, dear!'

'Astrid, my dear, what am I to do? If this were some game, I apprehend that your poor sister was the loser of it. What means this whip you are carrying? I demand an explanation!', declared her father as soon as the study door had closed upon them. Leaning against it, thereupon, in a manner which was far from that of the demure young lady he had so recently known, Astrid withheld a reply for a long moment. Julia had advised her never to speak in such moments but always to leave the questioner hanging upon a silence. Such would invariably discomfort them, Julia had said, and in this case her prophecy proved correct. Most uncomfortably-indeed, to in horrified dismay-Mr. Cane became aware that his daughter's eyes were running searchingly over the front of his trousers, where a very distinct hump had appeared.

'Punishments are deemed appropriate on occasions, Papa', Astrid said slowly at last. 'The pity of it is that their bottoms-and I refer to Jemima also-have gone neglected'.

'N... n... neglected? What talk is this? Have you left your senses?', demanded her father, who under her gaze had begun to edge towards his desk. He hoped, by taking his seat, to conceal the evidence of his erection, which Astrid's revelations of desirable flesh had occasioned. Taking note of his intentions, however, Astrid moved the swifter, and with feline steps intruded herself between his person and his intended retreat,

'No, Papa, I have not left my senses, but rather I have gained them. A young woman's bottom needs occasional attention, though you have no thought fit to see to it. The flesh grows plumper and richer under the stimulation it requires. Patricia's bottom is already superb, yet it will improve now a little more under my ministrations, as also will Jemima's. You had cause to see Patricia's well. Do you not agree with me? Her cleft is tight and will become even more so with a slight swelling of her cheeks'.

'My God, Astrid, how can you speak thus? I have never heard such talk!'.

'Better than to hide in the darkness of one's mind, Papa. The evidence of your own thoughts shows clearly enough. Pray, let us have no more hypocrisy. Your prick hardened at the first sight of your daughter's delightful derriere. I blame you not. This is Nature's way. She is ripe for attention. My presence has but excited you the more. I think it best that you remain in here, Papa, until I call you'.

A croaking gurgle came from Ralph Cane's throat. That he would wake in a moment to discover this a vivid dream he had scarcely no doubt. Such things could not be, nor could such words be spoken. All the worse, his cock had failed to subside. Indeed, the very words be spoken. All the worse, his cock had failed to subside. Indeed, the very words that Astrid had uttered had caused it to stiffen the more so that the shape of his knob was all but visible through the dark cloth of his trousers. Incomprehension and dire embarrassment mingled in his mind amid the chucklings of the devils of guilt.

'I have NEVER in all my life!', he began portentously.

That I do not doubt, Papa, but it maybe that you are about to. I shall give the matter thought. Pray, do not attempt to follow me for I intend to lock the door. I do not wish either Patricia or Jemima to see you as yet in this condition'.

So saying, Astrid swept out, neatly removing the key from inside the door ha her passing and thereupon locking it from the outside as she closed it. With that, she could not help letting a mischievous smile flit across her richly curving mouth. All too unexpectedly her dear Papa had cast himself willy-nilly into her net. That which she had deemed would be her hardest task had been presented to her by fate. Passing down, she made for her own room, where Crissie sat huddled but started up at her entrance. The whip that Astrid still held swished against the side of her skirt.

'Oh, Miss, I ain't done nothing-nothing save what you told me to do! You'll all whip me now, I knows you will!'

'Not all, Crissie, just I. And I will be quicker about it than I presently mean to be if I don't have you doing exactly as I say. If but one word passes your lips about this to the other servants, I promise you triple the whipping that Miss Patricia received. That she required it is obviously not your concern', Astrid added carefully, mindful of the hierarchy that Julia had spoken of.

'Miss, you mean she wanted us to do it?', squeaked Crissie.

'Have you never been spanked, Crissie?', Astrid responded, moving toward her.

'Yes, Miss, I have-that's the truth of it. I didn't like it-not the way it were done. His hand were real heavy and blasted me proper'.

'Really? How crude! Nevertheless, you got some pleasure, I trust, from the outcome of it? What need have you to blush? Were you not pleasantly fucked afterwards? As I thought, for I can read it in your face'.

'I never meant him to, Miss, but I never wore no drawers so that made it easier for him. None of us could afford drawers, we couldn't. He got rare excited. I tell you, I got spanked more than I deserved and then he would put it in me while I was a-howling still'.

'Well, then, you are at least in good part converted, Crissie, which is all for the better. Here's a sovereign for your pains today, but think not that it will excuse you from a whipping if it so pleases me. How much does Papa pay you? Ten pounds a year and all found? I think I may find it possible to improve on that, but you will be paid upon performance. No, you silly girl, not your domestic duties. I have things more favourable in view for you. Attend upon me here in my room immediately after dinner'.

'You are still going to whip me though, Miss. I can see you are!'.

'Good instincts become an attractive young woman, Crissie. We shall say nine o'clock sharp. Go now'.

Upon the maid's departure, Astrid repaired to the room of Patricia, who had not only got upon the bed, but within it, her face being hidden beneath the sheet. Upon Astrid's entrance she huddled up tighter and was completely invisible, forming a shapely hump beneath the covers. Seeing not who it was but sensing that it was her older sister, Patricia remained still while uttering a little cry as she sheet was drawn down to reveal her flushed face.

'I am disgraced forever! What am I to do now that Papa has seen me!'

'Consider yourself well looked upon and some benefit perhaps to come from it. All is well now, Patricia. You have taken your punishment and I have no doubt are all the better for it'.

'Why did you whip me? Oh, that I should be held down by a common servant!'.

'Hush! We will have no more questions nor remonstrances nor objections. These are three rules by which you are to abide, Patricia. Come, let us lie together as we were doing before I had to correct your rebellious behaviour. Place yourself on your back with your arms behind your head. There, now, you are more acquiescent, are you not?'.

Patricia's eyes blinked. Relentlessly once more her dress was being drawn up to her hips until, still without her drawers, she lay naked from her navel down. Feeling the tip of Astrid's forefinger brushing about her clitty, she wriggled but did not otherwise move. Her lips pursed together, a soft whistling sound emitted as by hazard from them as the finger teased. Caressing her fondly, Astrid passed her free hand beneath her sister's bottom and felt its throbbing warmth. Thereat, Patricia jerked and would have brought her arms down but was stayed by a warning murmur.

'D... d... d...! You are p... putting your finger in there!', came a stutter.

'Yes, my darling, where the Major put his prick. Do not pretend to me any longer that it is not to your liking. Roll upon your hip now and pass your upper leg over mine that I can attend to you. Wind your arms about my neck but loosely and pass your tongue between my lips. Your bottom is pleasantly hot for the exercise, my love'.

Hissing through her nostrils with an excitement she could no longer deny herself, Patricia kissed, tongued, and worked her hips lewdly as simultaneously Astrid's fingers inserted themselves, the one in her bottom and the other in her slit. Warmly their breaths flowed together, the moisture from their lips and mouths sweet to one another's.

'Papa had his cock well up for you, my sweet. It is the best of signs'.

'Astrid! Nooooo! Oh, do not speak of... AAAH! OOOOH!'

'His eyes were languid with desire, his balls full. He spoke of your bottom, your cunt, your thighs. Had I remained in the study a moment longer with him he would have delved into my drawers. How wicked of him! I have locked him in'.

'HAAAAAR!', Patricia sobbed. Her legs straightened full down, her toes straining. She held Astrid's finger in her rosehole full to the second knuckle while her sister's other hand beneath her quim brought her to the very peak of fulfilment. Just as it is said that a drowning person sees his whole life flash before him, so Patricia obtained the most vivid glimpses of the licentious behaviour into which she had been driven with the Major. All now had changed in her life and to nothing but the present could she retreat. Licking the pink, wet tip of her tongue against Astrid's, she released the spilling flow of her juices with utter abandon, heated the more by the insensate whisperings of her sister into her pleasure-wobbling mouth.

When quiet then reigned, and knowing her sister to be in a thoroughly receptive state, Astrid spoke quietly to Patricia of all those things she had never thought to think. Murmuring impulsively from time to time, and uttering soft exclamations of surprise, Patricia imbibed all.

'But what if ...?', she interrupted again and again, or posed her questions in other ways. But all this time were answered. Not until the early evening came did they rise, Patricia revealing the most thoughtful cast upon her fine features. 'Shall it then be so-really so- all of that which you have spoken, Astrid? What of Papa?'.

'The fault is mine, darling. You have been too flushed with excitement and pleasure this past hour to absorb all that I have said. Papa shall play his role as surely as any male must. The erection of his penis at the sight of your naked bottom was truly impressive. You have yet to know the power and the pleasure of such an engine. Even his balls showed clearly through his trousers. A female tongue and fingers will delight you in a thousand ways, but you must surrender more fully to the cock than you have yet been brought to'.

Patricia paled, then flushed, for she no longer had the will to oppose her sister. The whip lay ever as a reminder at the foot of her bed. Even so, the thought of what was to be made her tremble.

'Astrid, there are matters of which you do not know!', she exclaimed impulsively, while at the dressing table her sister toyed with a brush and comb.

'You cannot avoid the issue so, Patricia. Come, embrace me, you are all of a tremble. It is natural that you should be so. You have yet to be mounted, darling, and well fucked. The moment you feel the divine throbbing of the prick and absorb its gushing juices, you will be as eager to toy with Papa's as any. Say no more of it, for I know how best to bring you to it. You are a sensible girl. Your cunny hungers for a lewd encounter'.

'No, Astrid, you fail to understand. Papa has a lady friend. I am much afeared on the outcome of it'.

'A woman friend? Tell me all. Who is she, what is her name?'.

'It is Lady Belinda Smithers. She is widowed, as you know. Jemima and I believe her truly to have designs upon Papa, for she has been here several times, though not to your knowing. Upon your absence, Papa hied himself to her, for I so gathered this from the coachman. They were long engaged together. It was midnight before he returned'.

'This is the selfsame one whose daughter I have always so disliked?'.

'Clara-indeed, yes. The son is foppish and takes on airs, as you know. It is said that they have dismissed two of their servants due to certain economies. I fear then you see the nature of Lady Smithers' designs, for she knows well enough that Papa lacks not money'.

'How right you are, Patricia. It alters my plans a little, but not so that they are finally disturbed. Indeed, they might benefit from it. She would dispossess us if she could, I do not doubt that for a moment!'.

'I know, Astrid, I know. What are we to do?'.

'All the more reason you have for obeying me now, Patricia. Have I not been wise to act as I have?'.

'Oh, yes, you must be strong! Dear Papa is in the best of health, yet what if under her designs he were to alter his will in her favour?'.

'Precisely, my pet. It shall not be. I will contrive to alter her plans, though I need a little time to think about the matter. I shall need your assistance, as also perhaps that of another. By the morning I shall have found a solution'.

'You will speak to Papa? Oh, do not tell him that I told you!'.

'What silly fears you obtain still! It is he who shall be servitor to you in many respects, though at tunes I will put him on a longer leash if it amuses me to do so. Papa need no nothing of my intentions, nor of your complicity. We shall engage his senses in ways that will divert and utterly confound him. Have I not brought him already a little to heel? He remains locked in his study until it pleases me to release him. This you may pretend to know nothing of for the nonce. However, I do see that I must forward your initiation, else you will be in even greater wonder than you are. Come to my room tonight after Papa and Jemima have retired. I must see at present to Papa's well being, though I am not sure that he deserves it'.

Leaving thus her sister to endeavour to collect her raging thoughts, Astrid repaired to the study and opened the door. At her entrance, her father sprang up and look utterly bemused.

'We shall see you at dinner, Pap, but not before. It would not be seemly, and neither do I wish it. I see that you have been comforting yourself with port. That will do you no harm. Dinner will be at eight, for I have things to do afterwards. I will see you at table. We shall have no matters to discuss there save trivial ones'.

'But, Astrid...!', came her father's cry, as then once more she closed and locked the door.

'My plans, John, are a little altered', she was saying to the valet but a few minutes later. 'You will attend upon me as instructed. That which you may then discover before you may occasion you some surprise, but you will utter not a word or the most severe retribution will fall upon you'.

'I shall do as you say, Miss, like I said. You have my word on it'.

'Make sure that I do, John, for it is not I you are going to mount, but another!'

CHAPTER 14

The most curious emotions had now seized upon Ralph Cane. Not unnaturally, it was ever his habit to take his seat first at the head of the table. Upon entering the dining room that evening he had been astonished to find Astrid already seated there and looking her most regal. Affecting a black-velvet choker in the manner of her mentor, she wore also the black dress that sheathed her inviting form most tightly. Pendant earrings, each with a single diamond, swung gently from her pretty ears, and her fingers and wrists glittered with the adornments she had favoured herself with.

'Patricia will sit upon my right, Jemima here upon my left. Father, you will take the seat next to Patricia'.

For a moment it seemed as though the pater familias might rebel, but, even as Astrid's jewels flashed, so did her eyes. Incredibly they reminded him now of his aunt's in her most imperious moods. Patricia flushed, Jemima gaped in awe, and then all was quiet as the entrees were served.

'Patricia and Jemima are to have new wardrobes, Papa. I will see as to the mode of them. Accounts will be opened at the new emporium in the town. You will see to this on the morrow, Papa, so that their desires are no longer frustrated', Astrid ordained while delicately spooning her Vichyssoise.

'Why, of course, my dear, precisely what I intended to do', mumbled her father, who knew not where to look nor how to place himself. That Astrid looked at her most beautiful he had no doubt. An amused smile played upon her lips as she surveyed him.

'Had you intended to do it, Papa, then I would have expected it to be discussed with me first', Astrid replied crisply. 'Patricia, you have to attend my room tonight. Do not forget!'.

'Why, no, Astrid', Patricia replied timidly, though she would rather have had such a command given her beyond the hearing of her sister and father. There was naught to do but obey, however. That a new era had come like a thunderclap upon them, none of the three seated beneath Astrid's gaze was in any doubt. Nor perhaps was John, who became ever more aware of the colder glances that his new mistress was casting upon him while he assisted Crissie in the serving. His heated mind had played much upon what he would do with this lissom girl, whom he was convinced had fallen at last to his manly charms. Now, however, a cold wind of doubt swept through him, for it seemed to him that her mood had changed to one of menace rather than seductiveness. Neither was this feeling dispersed when final quiet descended upon the house. Forty strokes in and forty out, she had said. That were a lot to ask of a man in prime condition who found his cock lodged in an inviting new cunt. It was the strangest order he had ever been given.

Close upon midnight, he made his final rounds and doused the lamps. The night was warm enough and yet he shivered strangely as with sweating palm he turned the door handle to Astrid's boudoir. There was illumination within when he had expected darkness. Trembling not a little with expectancy, he urged the door open with some timidity. She would be abed, half-naked, and waiting. Of that he had no doubt, yet what would her manner be? Was all to be trusted? She was in a rare, funny mood since her return.

Astrid was not abed. Whip in hand, she confronted him, legs astride. They were legs of such beauty as John had never thought to see. Sheathed in black stockings and boots, they displayed themselves to his awed gaze almost to the juncture of her thighs. Her mount was veiled, however, by the lacy hem of a dark-blue chemise. Apart from this, Astrid wore nothing.

'Come! Close the door, you dolt!', she hissed.

John saw then the bed. Upon it knelt Patricia, though he knew it not to be she for her head and shoulders were shrouded in the sheet which had been cast over them. Unable to move, and naked to her stockings as she was, Patricia was doubled up by the ropes and straps that secured her. A gag muffled the cries she had first uttered but which had long diminished into plaintive whimpers. Across the pale uprisen orb of her naked bottom showed the pink streaks of the thongs.

'M... M... Miss?', choked John, though at the first sight of Astrid's glorious legs and of Patricia's inviting globe his cock had thickened with remarkable speed.

'To the end of the bed! Lower your breeches, man, and put your hands behind your back. Will you hesitate? I shall call Papa if you do and have it that you assaulted me! You know not who this is, nor at present do you need to know. Come, display your prick and balls-she is in need of furrowing!'

Much as he had listened solemnly to Astrid's commands earlier, John had taken them but for the strange whims of a young women in heat, and he had been minded to mount her as fiercely as he liked and to bring her under the spell of his. Now most certainly he knew otherwise, for, even as Astrid spoke, the thongs licked down and forward around his calves, bringing a yelp from him and a hastening of his steps to obey.

Daring not to fall sideways upon her hip as instinct told her to do, Patricia waited and heard the muffled sounds of John's preparations. His balls were huge, as Astrid noted with pleasure, being matched by the broomstick of his prick, which she did not deign to touch, taking a greater pleasure in binding his wrists tightly behind his back.

'Now we shall see, John, the value of your services to such ladies as I shall call for you', declared Astrid, motioning him to clamber as best he could upon the end of the bed so that the rubicund knob of his stiff penis waggled menacingly close to Patricia's offered cleft.

Affecting disdain at the gesture it was then necessary for her to make, Astrid pressed down upon the springy prong of his tool so that it was better positioned to assail the moist slit of Patricia's cunt. That her dear sister would take pleasure from her first act of fucking was all that Astrid then desired.

A groan of pleasure was emitted from John's lips at the fleeting touch of her fingers, a groan that brought a twitching of displeasure to Astrid's features. She knew well enough that he could see almost the whole of the pale globes of her tits as she bent down.

'You will be quiet!', she hissed. 'Urge yourself in now and hold!'

A thin, gritting whine came from beneath the sheet then as the bulbous head of that bull-like cock effected its first entry between Patricia's lovelips. Pouting and moist as they were from the light whipping that Astrid had given her, they received the warm pear tremulously. Eyes bulging, and wishing desperately that he could but get his hands on either of their tits or bottoms, John urged his ramrod in slowly, every effort of his sturdy loins being closely observed by Astrid.

Patricia's hips waggled wildly. As big as the Major's prick had felt in her tight bottom, so John's felt in her cunny as it eased the spongy walls of her vagina apart, striving to lodge itself fully. Literally snorting, he effected his lewd entry inch by inch to the watching satisfaction of Astrid, who herself had quelled her sister's wrigglings by holding her waist so that Patricia had no chance whatever of resisting. Gasping through her gag, she felt at last the pestle enter until John's big balls hung and dangled at her bottom.

'Remain so!', commanded Astrid, who dearly wished she could cast off the sheet and see Patricia's face in this moment.

'Oh, Miss, she's tight-lovely and tight and warm!', croaked John, who in the intensity of his pleasure quite forget the vow of silence he had undertaken. He was quickly reminded of it. Quick as lightning, Astrid had straightened and taken up post to his rear, a move she celebrated by bringing the full force of the whip hissing scornfully across his manly buttocks.

'You will learn, my fellow!', she breathed, to an accompanying cry from John, whose prick jerked and throbbed in the tight clutch of Patricia's nest. 'You will learn to obey, John, implicitly and without ado! It is not your salacious nature that is being satisfied but the will of a woman-nay, two-for the one who is receiving your cock is but receiving her natural due. Fuck her now slowly while I count the strokes, and heaven help you if you come too soon!'

Upon that meritorious exercise, however, we will draw a veil. Suffice to say that Patricia was so well pumped that the sperm of her donor literally frothed all down her thighs and left the curls of her nest glistening. As her nature had by now become ardent, she assisted not a little by all sorts of devious squirmings, drawing from the last pearly drop in a manner that well pleased Astrid. John was afterwards minded, by the ever-firm display of his prick, to offer yet more. But that did not attract Astrid, who, having loosened his wrist bonds, hustled him out with his breeches still at his ankles. He made a far more comic display than he had wished, and found it needful to frig himself twice in bed that night to rid himself of the surplus that the event had aroused.

Having then untied her sister, Astrid quieted all her blatherings swiftly. 'Enough, Patricia. You will enjoy many another such cock and in attitudes more to your pleasure, though it well becomes you to be bound up for it sometimes. The matter of Lady Smithers is much upon my mind. I have hastened my thinking and my plans. Listen to me well, Patricia'.

'Oh-ho-ho, Astrid, I feel so quivery and sticky and funny!'.

'Shush, you silly, of course you do. The reason for your strangeness is not only that you were thoroughly fucked but, with all the natural desiring of your young womanhood, could be again and again this very night if the mood took you. Such will come to pass, for you are truly my darling pet, as is Jemima'.

Clutching her sister's naked form against her own, and letting their stockinged legs rub pleasurably together, Astrid then continued with the adumbration of her plans. Patricia listened in excited awe and might even have been glimpsed fingering Astrid's cunny towards the end of their discourse.

'We are settled upon it, then, for I shall need your assistance, Patricia'.

'Y... y... yes, Astrid, dear, though it is a very wicked thing'.

'What nonsense! I have no wickedness in my heart at all, no more than you. Think you it wicked that I put you to John's cock?'.

'No. Oh, I do not know, you have me so confused. I confess that his prick felt very strong and powerful, and, oh, how he doused me! Do all men come so?'.

'Provided they are well fed and housed and occasionally titillated-but not always fulfilled-yes. A male of thirty to fifty years is best in my estimation, for their parts are the most vigorous and they can be better trained than many younger striplings. The primary task of men is to pleasure the females-remember that ever, Patricia. Even so, they may be allowed their caprices sometimes. It depends much upon their temperaments, just as it is needful for a woman to be whipped sometimes upon her bottom. You will come to understand this better in due course, Patricia. Be mindful at all that you obey me, as Jemima must'.

'Will she... will she be p... put to John's thing, then?'.

'I have not decided upon that no more than I have decided upon the role that Papa will play. He will be called upon occasionally to put himself to you both'.

'OH! Oh, no, Astrid!'.

'Be quiet, child! Are you not a child still in comparison with myself? You will need your pumpings now more regularly than you think. His cock has already twitched mightily at the sight of your bare bottom. Would you prefer that I put him to Lady Smithers?'.

'No. Oh, that would spoil things! We would truly be undone!'

'The sacrifice then will be well accounted for. After a little while, though, you will no longer deem it that but will receive the salute of his prick as readily as any other. Our inheritance must not be put in jeopardy. Who commands you now?'.

'You, Astrid, no one but you', murmured Patricia, hiding her blushing face.

'Then so be it. Should there be hesitancy in you in future, I will thrash it out of your bottom. You know me well, you hear me well, do you not?'.

'Yes, Astrid'.

'You are accommodating yourself better now to my desires, I believe, though you are still a novice. Lie upon your back, dear, and part your thighs wide. So. Good. Give me your tongue. Forget that we are sisters but merely two women in the throes of desire. Ah, how your belly twitches when I tease your clitty! You must learn to control more. Retract your tongue. Lie passive-do not jerk your bottom so. Oh, you naughty girl-be still!'

'Oh, oooh! Your f... f... finger-it excites me so! Make me come!'.

'Shush! I will have quiet now. This is but one of many lessons you now have to learn, Patricia. The male must not always see you in such a state of pleasure. Your reception of his cock must be cold and demanding, yet by occasional little assenting movements of your bottom you will show silently what you require. Hold your legs straight and open now. Stir your bottom but very occasionally. Keep your lips unmoving. Ah, you little devil, you jerked your cunny again to my finger. Draw your emotions within yourself and hold them there. Try, darling. Will you not try?'.

'Y... y... yes, I will... t... try. Oh, it is hard-I want to wriggle so. It feels strange'.

'Strange indeed it feels at first, yet you will draw power from it, knowing the male subservient to the demands of your cunny. I will insert my forefinger. Use your muscles. Draw strongly upon it'.

'HAAAR! Ooooh, Astr... r... r... rid, I am coming!'

'Hush! You must not say so. Contain yourself. Let the pleasure but merely surge in waves through you. All is then yours to command. Surrender yourself to the male and all is lost. He will use your hot, moist nest merely as a sanctuary of bliss in which to deposit his sperm. Thereafter you will become but a handmaiden to him. I would do naught but scorn you for that'.

Hissing her breath through her nostrils and compressing her lips, Patricia spilled her urgent love juices upon the very finger that was enticing her. Her eyes rolled, her neck twitched the while that Astrid stroked her moist forehead.

'So, you have tried, my love, and tried well. In a moment I will make you come again and then you will do better. Understand you not the purpose to which I lead you?'.

'To... to make men obey us', stammered Patricia dreamily.

'Or, perhaps, as in due course you will further see, to make all obey one another. How else are we to manage our affairs now or to bring Papa to our will? For, if we do not, then surely he will go beyond our desires and further his closeness with this awful woman'.

Oh, I had not thought of that! But if we are always hateful and horrid and cold when we are d... d... doing it then it will not be very nice and they won't want to!'.

'They?', echoed Astrid with a silvery laugh. She cupped Patricia's fingers under her own gently throbbing quim. 'I am glad you are thinking in the plural, my sweet. Were I even more learned than I am then I could well explain all to you. Suffice it for you to know that a man who is permitted-I say, permitted-to put his cock to your nest will forever savour the mystery of your remoteness, will dwell on it in his mind, and will know that he is being strangely punished for his sinful acts to which he must ever return. So it is with a woman who is soundly smacked on her bottom and put to the male'.

'Oh, yes, I felt the same when you were making John do it to me. You were making us both do it and I knew it was very wicked. I wanted to stop and yet to continue at the same time'.

'Precisely, my pet. In time you will come to pleasure yourself only. It is in your nature, as it is in mine. It is we who shall command. Others are cast in different moulds. Even when permitted to indulge their whims, they will still be under our control, and with certain quiverings and shiverings of knowledge in them they will know this. So is the world made, as I have now discovered. Such as they will return forever to the fold-and it is we who are the fold'.

'But, when a man is upon me, how can I trust it to be so?'.

'You fear that he will ravage you, that passion itself will ravage you? By the training of mind and body, Patricia, you will escape this. Besides, you will always prepare your ground. The elements of fear that you instil in the male will both awe and excite him-as it also will some women. The sexes are not to be differentiated when one's pleasure is paramount'.

'That is why you whipped Crissie tonight? I know you did, for I could see it in the way she walked when she returned downstairs'.

'Lessons must be early taught, Patricia. Crissie knows well her place now-as well indeed as she also knows the pleasuring of my tongue, for I brought the little minx to come again and again after her bottom was well heated. She is bound to me now as surely as you. She will know no pleasure now save at my command. So it must be with all who dwell within here. But now, darling, I will give you your second exercise and then we shall discuss the downfall of Lady Smithers!'

CHAPTER 15

Lady Belinda Smithers was a lady who had lived life well. So well indeed that, with the death of her husband a year before, she now felt life's riches slipping away from her. No more the caviar and champagne, no more the hunting and shooting parties, when joy had been unalloyed and aristocratic ladies wanton in their cups. True, her bank balance would have kept many a poor labourer in bread, cheese, beef, and beer for a lifetime, but such a comparison would have shocked Belinda, who viewed all working people as entirely a different species of homo sapiens. Thus she had cast her eyes about for one who would not so much be a breadwinner, nor even a bread-and-cheese winner, but a caviar supplier and mayhap a diamond digger.

This is not to say, of course, that Belinda was any more greedy than many of her wealthy neighbours, whose Christianity was practised solely with an eye to saving their own souls and receiving therefore the approbation of the local vicar. By any standards of upper class society, Belinda was much as they, save that her hypocrisy stopped short at attending church regularly.

Moreover, both her daughter, Clara, and her son, Ronald, were an additional weight upon her, for they sought ever the same comforts as they had enjoyed since the nursery and had seemingly no idea where money came from. Hence did Belinda's not wholly unattractive eyes fall upon Ralph Cane, whose standing as a Member of Parliament impressed her even more than the occasional standing of his cock when both were in an amorous mood.

That he did not rejoice more in the ample offerings of her curves fretted Belinda a trifle, though not so much as to make her change her plans. Truly, she failed to understand him-or he failed to understand her, as she frequently conjectured. On occasion, he had tried to kiss her drawers, albeit that she was still wearing them. This she did not mind so much and was quite amused when his mouth tickled her there. But she drew a line whenever he bent-rather furtively, it is true-to kiss her boots. It was a decidedly unmanly thing to do by Belinda's standards.

Her late husband had always born a large stiff one with which he would poke her not infrequently and in a masterful fashion, a mode that Belinda most enjoyed. Occasionally he had birched her for pleasure, a sport not entirely unknown in the neighbourhood, though referred to in only the most discreet manner. He had in all senses, so far as Belinda was concerned, been a sporting gentleman, vigorous and soldierly in manner, and extolling from his better half such pleasures as he wished in return for keeping her in more than mere comfort.

Laden with many private treasures as she had been, mostly in the form of necklaces, rings, and other expensive gewgaws, Belinda had forgiven him all, even to the extent of aiding his caprices with several of the younger female servants, who came and went as fast as raindrops.

'I will have her, my dear, this evening', Lord Smithers would say languidly at dinner, indicating some fresh young country girl who had come under his eye when brought into their service.

'Yes, my dear', Belinda would answer, and would feel quite an amorous shiver run through her at the thought of her lord and master putting his manly cock to the girl. She might perhaps whimper and struggle until she took the pleasure of it, whereat she would be slipped a guinea or two by Belinda, who not infrequently watched the amorous battle, being satisfied when the girl was filled to the brim with her master's effusion. Watching her husband's gleaming shaft emerge from a clinging nest, Belinda would feel true pride, ever knowing that it would remain stiff for her afterwards when the maid was dismissed.

Not only of course were the servants served in this manner. Many aristocratic ladies who, once in their cups at some uproarious hunt ball, would doff their drawers and proceed to some merry bottom-bumping on the carpet-not seldom within sight of their spouses, who were equally occupied on some adjacent part of the floor.

Alas, such diversions were no longer part of Belinda's life, for she could no longer afford to gather around her those who were of like mind. Hence she fretted, for, while Ralph Cane possessed the monetary wealth she required, he lacked the doughtiness of purpose in making her ripe bottom move to his cock in the lordly fashion she had erstwhile enjoyed. Perhaps, so she considered to herself, it was in some wise her fault, for she tended to simper in boudoir encounters while, unknown to her, Ralph hungered for a more masterful woman. Thus in her unknowing did Belinda turn to her daughter, Clara, upon whom she had high hopes.

Alas, such hopes were not of the high moralistic stature that one might have hoped for. Indeed, there are those among you who may wish to avert their eyes from what is to follow. Such well-conducted behaviour and such altruism as Astrid intended to impose upon her kin and her eventual followers is not here to be found. In a word, Clara was to rut with Ralph and thus to provide the eventual lure that would draw him into the very centre of Belinda's web. Once achieved, the very nubile young lady could be married off and so domestically dispensed with, to the contentment of all concerned, naturally.

So it came about that Belinda made few bones about the matter when now addressing her daughter, who always listened carefully to all her dear mama had to say. That there was a reason for this shall be unfolded, for Clara-though not always of the nicest nature-was by no means unprepossessing. At the age of twenty, she displayed all of the physical attributes of her mama, which is to say that her breasts were full and firm, her waist of pleasing smallness, her thighs well fleshed, and as a bottom provocative as any demure young lady might secretly wish to possess.

Clara, however, was far from being demure in her inner nature. Outwardly, she affected a prim and petulant mien. Save for the lushness of her curves, none would have suspected her to be a secret worshipper at the altar of Priapus, as indeed she was and as Belinda well knew.

Belinda had good cause to know it. There had come a time three years before when her husband's eyes had strayed not to a new young servant but to their daughter. Belinda had at first affected not to notice this, but then, being a woman of egotistical philosophy and ever mindful of the brimming coffers, she had drawn a discreet shade over her eyes, constantly reminding herself that her husband's virile tool ever sought new pastures and stayed none in long save her own. As to Clara's seduction, it had proved an artful variation on the classical mode, and one that Belinda had discovered through her propinquity for peering in keyholes. Moreover, her suspicions had first been slightly aroused by her master's decision to install a comfortable divan in his study, an article of furniture that he had never previously found use for.

Apprised on the first occasion that Clara had misbehaved and must be given a taste of the strap-as Lord Smithers casually put it-Belinda had not only agreed that disciplinary measures were sometimes requisite but had herself scolded an apparently tearful Clara into attending upon her father in his study.

Within a minute or two of her doing so, there had come to Belinda's ears the sound of the leather being regularly applied with that particular splatting, smacking sound that a good broad strap produces. Being concerned at the time with the household accounts, Belinda absorbed these background noises casually until it distantly occurred to her that her offspring was making remarkably little noise herself. This being her papa's first attendance on her bottom, Belinda naturally expected to hear loud squeals and cries, a detail evidently forgotten by Clara in her excitement. Or perhaps the minx thought that her mama was otherwise too occupied to take notice.

Belinda was never lost in the matter of fine instincts and raised her head several times to listen. Hearing then several strange moans emanating from her daughter-though muffled by distance and the closed door of the study-she became ever more curious as to the manner of Clara's reception of the strap across her bottom. Insofar as the rhythmic slapping of the leather still sounded, and seemed to be rather prolonged even for her husband, Belinda betook herself along the upper corridor to her master's haven and applied her eye to the keyhole.

What she then saw was truly remarkable. Clara was indeed bending, though not as convention would have it, over her father's desk. With her skirts and petticoat well tucked up to her hips and her frilly white drawers at her ankles, the nature of her posture was such that she was gently manipulating the well-risen prick of her papa, who was seated comfortably on a wooden chair beside his desk. He, for his part, was fondling her naked bottom and much else while slapping the strap idly on the leather arm of another chair.

Drawing her mouth to his, Lord Smithers then proceeded to kiss it most lusciously the while that his fervent palm caressed the smooth hemispheres of Clara's chubby bottom. Moving her legs apart as far as the banding of her drawers would permit, Clara offered herself invitingly to the lewd insinuations of his fingers, which, from moment to moment, curled right under her bottom and titillated her cunny, making her hips wriggle agreeably. Her bottom was indeed somewhat pink, but whether this was from some initial ministrations of the leather or the result of the fervent caresses it was receiving, Belinda was unable to decide. This conundrum was, however, solved for her by the murmurings of conversation that then came to her ears. 'Do you not like it, my pet?'.

'Oh, yes, Papa, and how big it is! Truly it became stiff the moment I pushed my drawers down. Is it not naughty for us to do this, though?'.

'Indubitably, my darling, but that is the spice of it. What an adorable little cunny you have and how moist it is after your strapping'.

'Wicked Papa, I thought you would not leather my poor bottom. It stung me so!'

'That is its intent, my dear, to bring your bottom well up to your pap's cock, as so it did. What silky thighs you have and how plump and firm your bottom is! Rub faster, my pet. Put your tongue in my mouth and open your legs more so that I can tease your cunny all the better'.

'Ooooh, Papa! I feel so strange-my tummy is all afire!'

'You are about to come, Clara, even as I. Soon enough I shall put my cock to your cunt and we will lather one another deliciously. Ah, you minx, work your bottom and tongue more!'

Stung by jealousy, and yet not a little moved by the amorous spectacle,

Belinda would have found herself quite unable to move had it not been for the unwonted intrusion on the upper floor of one of the servants, which caused her to hasten back to her room where she sat in a frightful lather of frustration at not knowing the continuance of the affair. As luck would have it, however, the intruding maid caused her brush and pan to drop, which in turn alarmed the overheated occupants of the study and Clara in particular. Fearing that her mama was about to witness the stolen moment, she uttered a little cry of alarm and, starting back from her papa, swiftly pulled her drawers up. He, realising that the opportunity was lost, just as hastily covered himself as with a loud 'Herrumph!' he offered vocal warnings to his daughter that he prayed might be heard beyond the door and so exculpate the pair.

Within minutes then, while Clara hastened to her room, he had presented himself to his wife in such a lewd state that she, deeming it better not to confess what she had witnessed, fell back upon their bed at his gruff bidding and received within seconds the lordly offering of his bubbling sperm.

'My dear, what an excited state you were in', Belinda chided him softly, while yet his throbbing prick soaked in her then well-oiled quim.

'Indeed, it must be the heat of the day, my love', he had answered pantingly.

'Of course', her reply had come while clutching him greedily still between her thighs. For, having received such a heavenly effusion, Belinda decided to say naught-of what she had seen nor to give any hint as to her knowledge of the affair. From then on, however, she became more watchful while Clara for her part became ever more devious and frequently joined her papa in the summerhouse or some other discreet rendezvous. He rapidly introduced her to all the amorous arts, inducing her to imbibe his sperm by way of her pretty lips and her rosy bottomhole as well as her cunt.

By then Clara had attained her seventeenth birthday and was in such a glow of health that her mama renewed her suspicions, for the winsome girl had become positively smug and would frequently give her papa the most amorous looks when she thought they were not observed. Soon enough, as must occur in all such matters, carelessness intruded. Having ensured that the couple found no opportunity whatever for their illicit passions, Belinda put her vigorously equipped husband to such frustration that he was mindful to find cause to give Clara another strapping, which intent he thought it frightfully clever to avow openly.

Playing her part as well as she could, Clara sobbed and protested to no avail-as well she hoped-since she had been deprived of a lusty ramming for several weeks.

'Why, Clara, you must obey your dear papa at all times', declared Belinda, who was then careful to add that she intended to retire, which intelligence of course delighted both her husband and daughter, though they were careful not to show it. 'I am tired, my dear, so you must forgive me. Apply the strap to the naughty girl's bottom well, for I am sure she stands in need of it', she averred and then made great play of entering her boudoir and closing the door. Albeit that her heart was beating rapidly, Belinda allowed quite some minutes for passions to reach their heights and endeavoured to distract herself by disrobing to her corset and stockings and casting on a peignoir.

She had now every intention of interrupting the pair, though in truth she knew not what she was to do upon effecting her surprise entry. To her ears for several minutes came the regular smacking of the strap and the plaintive cries and moans of Clara, which her mama knew well enough by now how to interpret. With her pulse racing and her palms not a little moist, Belinda then moved quietly along the corridor in the direction of the study and silently opened the door.

Clara at first neither heard nor saw her, for she was in the very throes of pleasure. Her dress, chemise, and drawers, cast off, lay upon the floor in artful mingling with the little-used strap. Nearby, Lord Smithers' garments equally adorned the carpet together with his boots. Naked as the day, he knelt upon the divan with his stiff prick half-inserted in the moist nest of his daughter who, on hands and knees before him, looked divinely desirable in her white-silk stockings, pink garters, and nothing else save for her boots. At that very moment, her papa's cock was entering her again after several juicy thrusts, which had already churned their bellies warmly. Bowed over her, his palms fervently cupped the luscious gourds of her titties, whose creamy, swollen surfaces offered the tingling of her aroused nipples to his touch.

Murmuring incoherently but blissfully, Clara kept her flushed face resting on her forearms while moving her hips about gently as he had taught her to. Reaching his free arm under her smooth tummy, her papa caused his fingers to toy around her clitoris while his cock moved powerfully in and out between the greedily sucking walls of her cunt. Oiled as it was by her secretions-for Clara had already come once even as he had inserted his bulbous knob in her quim-his prick moved easily. Albeit that she was blissfully tight, she had learned rapidly how to apply the nutcracker action of her interior muscles to draw him on.

Thus was the lascivious spectacle that came to Belinda's eyes as she stood swaying in the doorway. Becoming aware of her presence, Clara uttered a wild cry and his her face. For his part, however, Lord Smithers seized her waggling hips and rammed his charger full into her so that her heated bottom-cheeks balled tightly into his belly. Casting out one strong arm, he seized his wife's wrist and he pulled her down beside them.

'Ah, Harold, no!', Belinda cried, finding her face adjacent to her daughter's while her robe was manfully thrust open and her own cunt offered to her husband's hand.

'Yes, Belinda ', croaked he, determined not to be deprived of his final pleasure in this ardent moment and, indeed, to add to it. His wife's sturdy, black-stockinged legs, kicking wildly, contrasted erotically with the white ones of Clara, who could do nothing but moan as his pestle continued to pound her. All was then lost in the wild passion of the moment.

Tom between outrage and arising passion, Belinda succumbed, knowing well enough that she had no other course to take anyway other than to totally disrupt the very relations that ensured her steady supply of caviar and champagne. Thus did opportunism reign. Joining mouths and tongues wildly together in the haphazard squirmings and wrigglings that ensued, all three ran a delirious course until a softly breathing quiet obtained. Continuing to soak his rammer in the frothing quim of Clara, who by then lay flat beneath him, Lord Smithers afforded his wife the most passionate of kisses and continued to caress her own pulpy slit.

'Oh, Harold, what are we at!', murmured Belinda hotly.

'Naught but pleasure, my pet, and who is to say us nay. But come, let us all to the boudoir where we may have a larger bed on which to spread ourselves'.

Withdrawing then his still-thick penis from his daughter's come-soaked nest, he aroused the pair to their trembling legs.

'Oh, Mama, what are we to do! I cannot!', Clara wailed, covering her blushing face.

'What nonsense, Clara, you have done it with Papa once and you might as well do it again', declared Belinda rather to her own surprise. Swept up in her father's arms, Clara was then carried to the nuptial bed, kicking and sobbing theatrically, as she felt it necessary to do. In this, Belinda saw well enough her opportunity for some revenge at least, and persuaded her husband to spank the wicked girl soundly in their bedroom until. If not quieted, she was at least sufficiently subdued to find a panting pleasure in his thoroughly re-aroused cock, which both mother and daughter then dutifully fondled. Thereat, their lord and master threaded them both in turn, much to their shameful delight, as each again witnessed the other in the throes of desire. By morning, indeed, Belinda had been thrice pumped and Clara twice more, so that each received their due, the sheet being much puddled with all their liquid treasures.

Not wishing however to let her daughter take an upper hand in the matter, Belinda thereafter saw to it that Clara received the parental cock much less frequently and always in the most discreet manner, which she took care not to observe again. Thus a strange but knowing relationship existed between Clara and her mama, which the latter was determined to use now that a further opportunity arose to better her own position while maintaining her daughter's. Casting herself in Clara's confidence, though the minx knew well enough what was afoot, Belinda declared her intentions more boldly in respect of Ralph Cane than might otherwise have obtained.

'You will be very nice to him, Clara-VERY nice- you understand?'.

'Oh, yes, Mama. If he should wish to kiss me, do you mean?'.

'Yes, my dear'.

'And, Mama, if he should wish to... .'

'Tut, tut, Clara, there are certain things we need not discuss. Should Mr. Cane find it necessary to-er- discipline you on occasions as your dear papa was wont to do, then naturally I shall raise no objections thereto'.

'But, Mama, he may wish to strap me, and, oh, dear, if he does so I shall have to take my drawers down'.

'I do not doubt it, my dear, but that is a problem which has caused you little offence in the past and need not do so now. The better that you present your bottom, the more engaging will be his interest. Naturally, you will report all such occasions to me'.

'Yes, Mama, as I always did'.

'Always, Clara?'.

'Well... almost always, dear Mama!'

With that neither could suppress a laugh, for both had certain fond memories of all that had passed and were as lewd in their minds as ever they had been, though all was cloaked in the most discreet of conversations as is proper in society. Only when bibulous did they let their tongues run on a little, for both had a great taste for fine wines. That, though they little knew it, was to prove their undoing.

CHAPTER 16

Having prepared her ground plan with some care, Astrid took herself promptly the morning after Patricia's initiation to see Julia, to whom she naturally divulged all her news. Listening intently to her pupil's every word, and even to the different nuances in her voice, Lady Tingle expressed her appreciation of all and even gave her student a few further hints which she knew would be thoroughly absorbed.

As to the matter of Lady Smithers, a frown grew upon Julia's beautiful features. But that was rapidly dispelled when Astrid relayed to her the scheme she had decided upon. Indeed, Julia was much pleased to hear her use that very phrase, for it showed that Astrid's steely intent was no less than she had supposed. Even so, there was one service that Julia could patently offer and this she did without demur-in fact, with mischievous pleasure.

'This, my dear, will solve your outstanding problem', she averred, handing Astrid a small phial containing a colourless liquid. Upon sight of it, and learning of its powers, the voluptuous young lady all but purred.

'You will forgive me if on this occasion I do not stay, for I wish not to delay matters lest Papa entangle himself further', she remarked, receiving thereupon a kiss for her words.

'You have but to relate to me all that passes and that will be reward enough, Astrid. The temporary obstacle of this tiring woman being removed, I have no doubt that you will then enter fully into your domain', Julia observed in seeing her visitor-who so short a while before had been carried kicking upstairs in that selfsame manor-to the door. Julia's pride was thus great in Astrid's rapid advancement, both knowing well enough that each would share the other's future pleasures.

Alas for Astrid, her return was much delayed by virtue of a broken hub at the rear of her carriage, which caused her to return as lunch was being served. Being met on her entrance by Patricia, she learned then that their papa had gone out shortly after Astrid's departure and was thought even now to be in Lady Smithers' domain. Receiving this intelligence, Astrid flushed with annoyance but then gathered her thoughts.

'Even so, we shall pay our visit', she decided. And since matters were as they were, she partook of a leisurely lunch with her sisters, Jemima being much disappointed that she was not to join them on what she thought was but an afternoon's drive.

'You will have your pleasure later, Jemima, though perhaps sooner than you think', Astrid consoled her. Becoming pettish at this, Jemima tore from her arms and ran upstairs, slamming the door of her bedroom. 'Oh, dear, she will have to be spanked', Astrid observed sadly to Patricia, though with such a twinkle in her eye that her sister laughed.

'Who shall do the spanking, Astrid? She has such an adorable bottom'.

'A chore, my dear, that must be undertaken. Perhaps I shall give the task to Papa, but much depends on how he has behaved. We shall see', Astrid murmured as the two made their way to their carriage. John escorted them, casting hopeful eyes on both their swaying bottoms ere at Astrid's bidding he deposited a box on the spare seat of the carriage.

'Shall you be needing me tonight, Miss?', he asked upon seeing them settled within.

'What need could I possibly have of you, John?', responded Astrid in a distant manner which quite caused his face to fall as the carriage wheels rolled forward. Inwardly excited at the manner of her plan, she was yet outwardly cool, which caused Patricia to dissolve into a waiting silence for she had still not fully accustomed herself to her sister's manner and all that had befallen. One question, however, could not but help tumble from her pretty lips as their journey began.

'If Papa is to spank Jemima, what might befall?', she asked, recalling all the conversations of the previous night.

'Why, my dear, what would you expect to fall? His breeches?', Astrid laughed. 'No, my pet, he will not be in such freedom as that, but fret not upon such details. For the nonce we have other matters to attend to. If Papa is already there then I think it wise that we should not make a frontal entry, but make our enquiries of his presence more discreetly. As I recall, we may circumvent the house and approach it by way of field and grounds at the back'.

'Should we not look foolish, though, if we are discovered?'.

'I, Patricia, will never look foolish', Astrid replied grandly. 'We have come to play a little surprise, have we not, upon dear friends and acquaintances we have not seen for long. Were we to be discovered, it shall be seen as playful'.

'I still do not know what we are really at, Astrid'.

'Oh, you sillikins, I have told you repeatedly. We shall make our gift of wine-the very finest from our cellars-and await events. Wait upon them and profit from them. It may be as well, perhaps, that Papa is there', Astrid said, narrowing her eyes.

'Oh!', declared Patricia in utter surprise, though she did not dare venture any more questions and indeed was still rather wrapped up in the fervent memories of John's prick shunting back and forth most pleasurably in her cunny the night before. It fretted her a little that Astrid seemingly did not intend to repeat the performance immediately at least.

'Another twenty minutes or so and we shall be there', Astrid said comfortably, for there was rising confidence in her at the success of her mission not to say a sense of mischievous excitement at what she intended to bring about. Not only would she succeed in severing any bonds that might obtain between her father and Lady Smithers, but she might henceforth have the lady herself subject to all her whims, not to say Clara as well as young Ronald Smithers. The whole idea made her hug herself with pleasure. The countryside all about them looked more verdant and inviting than ever.

It was not at that very moment the countryside which to Ralph Cane's eyes presented itself as inviting, but the attentions of Belinda and her daughter, Both had imbibed not a little wine in order to prepare themselves for the event the while that Ronald had been given strict instructions by his mama to remain in his room. Dutifully he obeyed, though ever wondering what the presence of Mr. Cane might mean. His mama frequently overawed him, for he was two years junior to his sister, who accorded him less of her time than did his mother. So he busied himself with his books rather than with thoughts of pleasure, which he was certain he could never obtain while he was under their eyes.

'You have not been a naughty girl today, have you, Clara?', Belinda was asking coyly, having arranged herself on one side of her intended inamorato while Clara herself perched on the other, her cheeks not a little flushed.

'A trifle, Mama, but surely I shall not be strapped for it? I am sure that Mr. Cane is a kindly man and would not wish to sting my poor bottom'.

Quite amazed, Ralph listened to these brief discourses while being unable to prevent his eyes from roaming occasionally over the twin pumpkins of resilient flesh that the low-cut front of Clara's gown revealed. They were as enticing a pair as ever he had seen, though once more he was torn between the desire to master such a fetching young lady and the opposite one of being mastered himself.

'Her papa had to strap her regularly, you know', simpered Belinda, laying her hand on his thigh quite close to a certain prominence that had arisen in his trousers.

'Yes, he did', expostulated Clara with a pretended pout, 'and he took my drawers down and made me hold my dress up to my waist. I had to turn all about in front of him while he lectured me most severely and-oh, Mama!'.

'Yes, dear?', enquired Belinda, who had rehearsed this moment with her thoroughly the while that they had been tippling.

Thereat, making much ado of being shy, Clara turned and buried her face in Ralph's shoulder, so permitting him an even deeper view of the delicious chasm between her tits. Indeed, one of her perky brown nipples rose to his view from out of the confines of her décolletage even as she spoke. Conical in shape and seemingly ever erect, it looked most enticing and caused his prick to quiver the more.

'M... M... Mama, Papa would make me stand in front of him with my dress held up and he would pat my bottom with one hand and t... t... tickle me in front with the other'.

'That, my pet, was merely to make you pay attention. Do you not concur, Ralph?'.

So saying, Belinda passed her hand lightly but boldly over his penis which by now was threatening to burst his trousers, this causing Clara to giggle and to press her lips as though by accident to the side of his neck.

'Ah, yes, perhaps, indeed!', stammered he.

'Mama, I always wriggled when Papa tickled me', Clara murmured, passing the tip of her tongue between her lips so that it tickled Ralph in turn and made him feel quite dizzy.

'Of course, Clara, it is fitting that a young lady should do that in the private presence of her Papa. It were better perhaps that he had taken your drawers off completely that you might present a better posture for your strapping'.

'Oh, he did, Mama, frequently, though I would blush exceedingly for his hands would then pass of necessity all about my bottom and thighs and I would clutch at him in my shyness while he then divested me of my gown and chemise for he ever insisted that I need wear nothing but my stockings and boots for chastisement'.

'AH!', exclaimed Ralph at this juncture, for by devious squirmings of her fingers Belinda succeeded in loosing three of the front buttons of his trousers. She then passed her fingers over his stemming cock beneath, though her movements were so gentle and subtle that all seemed to be happening most naturally.

'Well, my dear, to be taught to present yourself properly is fundamental to a young lady's deportment. Do you not think so, Ralph? Get up, Clara, and show us how well you were taught, for it may well be that a future papa will need to have knowledge of your aptitudes in disciplinary matters', declared Belinda boldly.

There upon a positive gurgle escaped her intended swain as Clara rose from the seat on which the three had huddled and, turning about, upped her skirts to offer closely to his view as perfect a pair of bottom-cheeks as ever he had seen. Belinda then released his upstanding pego fully and massaged it gently in her grasp.

The effect upon Ralph was naturally electric, for so well did Clara bend and dip her back that not only her proud nether cheeks but also the fig of her cunt were presented to his heated gaze. Passing her fingers down under his throbbing tool and feeling for his balls, Belinda drew them out in turn and cradled them lovingly on her palm.

'What think you, Ralph-should she not be taken to her room and strapped for this? The naughty girl drove her papa to distraction, I do believe. Move back a little closer, Clara, since you have been well taught to do so', uttered Belinda while Clara artfully brought the backs of her knees to touch Ralph and thereby all but presented her nether cheeks to his mouth.

'Why... I... I... I... ah, my dear, ooooh!', stammered he, feeling Belinda's hand grow ever more persuasive.

'Splendidly formed, is she not? But then her frequent strappings and indeed her papa's other fond attentions did much to ensure the perfect conformation of her bottom, dear', murmured Belinda. 'She had good cause to sit upon her papa's lap often enough for certain comfortings after her chastisements, did you not, Clara? Come, be truthful, girl, for I am sure that for all our future benefits we would both wish you to be so'.

'Yes, Mama, I was a little naughty', uttered Clara in a would-be trembling tone, 'for I frequently sat upon papa's p...p...p... LAP... like this- OOOOH!'.

Having accompanied her words by actions, Clara- to the throbbing joy of Ralph-now ensconced herself fully down upon him so that his stout penis, which Belinda quickly released, stuck lewdly up between the tops of her stockinged thighs and poked its purplish head enquiringly about, causing him to jerk with pleasure.

Thus, in fact, was the tableau that obtained when a knocking was heard upon the door down the hall. Bereft of servants who might answer it-for Belinda had knowingly dismissed them for the day-all three sat for a moment as if frozen in their attitudes, though there was little cold about the conjunction of Clara's warm thighs with her would-be stepfather's pulsing cock, causing her to have many excited memories of the past.

Without, stood Astrid and Patricia, the latter blushing and the former calm. They had seen all via the latticed window which they had reached silently from the rear of the house, being as much assisted by the absence of servants as Belinda had thought herself to be. Astrid weighed the visions of what she had seen warmly in her mind. Her papa's tool was as thick and doughty as she hoped it might be, but it was not for these two wantons within to enjoy it and hence she raised the knocker again and let it fall resoundingly, while nudging her sister.

'Straighten yourself, Patricia, and endeavour to look calm. What you have seen is the future and not the present', Astrid declared somewhat mysteriously, though the more that Patricia thought about the remark afterwards, the more she blushed. A certain scuffling was heard within and then at last the door was opened, presenting a much-flushed Clara to their view.

'Is Papa within? We heard that he had visited', said Astrid, who unknown to Clara was as well aware as she that she was wearing no drawers.

'Why, yes, he is conversing with Mama-upon business, I do believe', replied Clara, who appeared to be guarding the doorway rather more jealously than politeness allowed.

'Indeed, yes, I imagine so. We will not dally long, Clara. We thought only to bring you a present of some wine. Shall you accept it?', Astrid asked. Turning about as she spoke and not waiting upon a reply, she motioned to the coachman, who shuffled forward from the rear and deposited a box upon the steps. 'It is rather heavy-a dozen bottles-Papa will carry it. Fetch him', said Astrid then in a slightly sharper tone which made Clara stare at her and then step aside.

'Oh, yes, indeed-a dozen bottles-heavy', repeated Clara somewhat stupidly, for she knew not how to act in such a contretemps.

Brushing past her, Astrid strode towards the doors of the drawing room, which Clara had left revealingly open, though not so much so that Ralph did not have time to cover as best he could the evidence of his erection.

'Papa, dear, I have brought some wine for our dear friends', exclaimed Astrid while donating a smile to the bemused Belinda, who endeavoured to regain her wits and would as soon have seen Astrid at the other end of the world at this moment.

'Wine, yes, ah', repeated Ralph stupidly, his cock prodding so fiercely up under his trousers that he was at great pains to try to conceal it from the gaze of both Astrid and Patricia, who had now joined her.

'Wine? How sweet of you', cooed Belinda, though the words stuck in her throat.

'The very best, for I know you have a taste for it-as we do also', added Astrid hastily. Moving within, she seated herself demurely and gazed as if appreciatively all about while her father, scuffling and somewhat red-faced, laboured with the box and knew not where to put it.

'In here, Papa. I am sure that Lady Smithers will not mind', called Astrid gaily.

'Why, good heavens, no, what a pleasure it is', responded Belinda, who even in such a moment could not resist examining the label upon the first bottle she drew out as Ralph deposited it upon a table. 'Chateau neuf du

Pape, 1862-a splendid year, such a fine bouquet!', Belinda said.

'A rich body, too, I believe', responded Astrid coolly, casting her eyes slowly up and down Clara as she spoke.

'You must of course partake of a glass', Belinda said, seeing here-despite the inappropriateness of the interruption-a fine chance to inveigle herself with Astrid and Patricia. Indeed, the more she quickly thought about it, the better it became and all at once she began to fetch glasses from the sideboard.

'If I may, I will take sherry-it becomes me better at his hour. You, too, Papa', declared Astrid, casting as fierce a glance upon him as ever she had bestowed. The very piercing of her eyes betrayed better than any words the fact that she had not failed to espy his uprisen condition.

'Ah, yes, sherry, if we may, Belinda', he gurgled.

'Of course. Will you open the wine, dear? What a pleasant family party this can be', cooed Belinda while turning about to attend to the sherry and to smaller glasses for the three.

'Dear Ronald, is he not here?', Astrid asked casually, which question caused Clara to flutter as if she had just remembered his existence. He was at his studies, as ever, she declared, but would be fetched forthwith. Soon enough indeed-even as the glasses were being filled-he appeared, rather taken aback that he was permitted to join in anything and being much taken with the appearance of both Astrid and Patricia, each of whom were careful to give him the most winning glances.

'Well, what a pleasant surprise this all is', averred Belinda, who already saw herself now all but at the head of the two families with an obedient Ralph being occasionally diverted by the allure of Clara's bottom.

'Is it not?', responded Astrid warmly, adding to Belinda's surprise, 'I have long thought that we should all be closer together. How pretty Clara has become. Her dress suits her admirably for it shows off some of her best attributes. Have you not noticed, Ronald?'.

This remark taking all a little aback, so boldly was it uttered, that a little silence fell. His cheeks flushed, Ronald nodded and gulped down more wine. The twin halves of Clara's tits, rising from the low cut neck of her gown, did indeed present him with a more revealing view of her beauties than he had ever been vouchsafed before. Stimulated as he was by the wine, his cock stirred a little.

'Ah, yes, it is perhaps a trifle daring', Belinda ventured uncertainly, though thankful that both she and her daughter had not got to the point of taking their dresses off when Astrid and Patricia had arrived. Her voice sounded oddly blurry.

'Not at all, Lady Smithers. A girl should learn to display herself. We are all perhaps too modest in our ways, do you not think?', Astrid asked.

That something strange was occurring was evident now even to Ralph, who for long moments past had been trying to gather his wits and to quell the urgent thrusting of his cock. Perhaps it was his imagination, but Belinda seemed suddenly to have slumped in her chair, her hands becoming vaguer in their movements. Her eyelashes fluttered, a sigh escaped her, and then to his immense surprise her arms drooped and her glass- fortuitously empty-fell to the floor.

'Ma-ma-ma-ma', came then a plaintive wail from Clara, who felt the walls revolving around her and her vision becoming distinctly dim. Ronald, too, appeared to have sunk into a torpor.

'By jove-what?', exclaimed Ralph foolishly, possessed momentarily of the thought that it was he who was drunk and seeing visions.

They are tired perhaps, Papa. Their exertions have been too much for them. Pray, wait outside in the carriage. I will see to them. Your own coachman may proceed. We will all travel back together', Astrid said crisply and stood up.

'Exertions, yes, what?', responded her sire stupidly, for now all three of their hosts were utterly inert and appeared to have passed into a deep sleep. Hustled outside, he was only too glad to escape and made little of the fact that the front door closed behind him.

'Now, Patricia, make haste. Undress Clara while I see to her mama'.

'Oh, Astrid, yes', Patricia stuttered. She could not believe it was happening, though her sister had described all to her thoroughly enough. To her pleased surprise, Clara was easy to undress, wearing as she did only her gown over her stockings and boots. Having slid to the floor, she lay there, breathing softly, as in turn did Belinda, whose heavier curves caused Astrid a trifle more bother at first until she had denuded her in turn, though leaving on her drawers, which she carefully drew halfway down her legs.

Blushing and suppressing giggles as she surveyed their two voluptuous forms, Patricia was then urged to assist Astrid in making Ronald ready. Lighter of form than his mother, his laced-up boots proved more troublesome than anything, but finally all was done and three naked figures lay inert.

'Now, my pet, to the main purpose of the exercise. He is to be put half upon his mama, with his left leg well entangled in her drawers. Come, help me push his foot down between her drawers and her legs-so!', declared Astrid triumphantly, lifting and rolling and pushing Ronald until he was positioned as she wished him. His face lay upon his mother's large, pale breasts, his mouth so placed to one of her thick, brown nipples that the merest movement would suffice to bring it between his lips. His cock, a limp worm, nestled its knob close to the mouth of her cunny while his balls rested on her right thigh, a sight which caused Astrid's eyes to gleam and Patricia to titter.

'Oh, it is small!', Patricia uttered.

'It will grow bigger', Astrid replied confidently. 'Bring now Clara closer to them both, indeed right beside them. Lift her right leg and lay it over theirs. Good. What a fine tangle! Come, Patricia, we must not linger. The effects of the potion do not last long. Ten minutes more and they will be stirring. Go and see to it that Papa is not restless and I will follow'.

'Yes, Astrid. Oh, what unimaginable things are happening!'.

'Nothing is beyond imagination and few things beyond attainment, Patricia. Go, dear'. Pausing then for a few moments, Astrid bent far over and,, inserting her hand between Belinda's lush thighs, gently stroked Ronald's cock. To her perfect delight, it stirred faintly and within seconds showed the first signs of both thickening and extending itself. Gently, then, the movements of her slim, tapered fingers continued, much as one might caress a kitten. As she had suspected, Ronald's penis, although small in repose, had much to commend it when stimulated. A hollow groan escaped him as the pink-purplish knob of his weapon emerged gleaming from the tautening skin that surrounded it and poked blindly against the rolled lips of his mama's slit.

Telling herself that she had done far more than her duty demanded, and that the stronger powers of Nature would now take their course, Astrid wiped her fingers delicately on a napkin and made her way out, closing both doors of the drawing room so that the three were truly immured in their temporary stillness.

Striding out to the waiting carriage, her footsteps seemed to her lighter than ever before. On one seat sat a rather bemused Ralph, while, facing him, but not daring to give him many glances, was Patricia, whom Astrid settled beside.

'There are matters, Papa, we must discuss', Astrid declared as the coach then rumbled forward. 'Lady Smithers is, I fear, given to somewhat unseemly behaviour'. So saying, Astrid laid one hand, in the lap of Patricia's dress and by devious but slight movements of her fingers caused the hem of her dress to begin to rise. Feeling Patricia stiffen in surprise, Astrid gave her a little warning pinch that first made her jerk and then sit still again, her cheeks flushed.

'Ah!', exclaimed Ralph, for whom the world was once again turning topsy-turvy.

'Particularly unseemly', averred Astrid. 'I would not deem it-proper were you to visit here again. Such behaviour cannot be countenanced. You will not, I am sure, wish to arouse my displeasure'.

'Eh? What? No!', gurgled her papa, who from his vantage point opposite was endeavouring not to fix his eyes too obviously upon the deliciously rounded knees of Patricia as they now slowly emerged while Astrid most casually continued gathering up Patricia's skirt.

Her lips wobbling as if she wished to speak but could not do so, Patricia dimly heard the voice of her sister coming to her as first her stocking tops were revealed, then the creamy pallor of her thighs, and finally the crotch of her drawers.

'A quite wanton woman-totally unsuited, Papa.

Gulping, Patricia felt her thighs being urged wider apart, and she closed her eyes tightly.

CHAPTER 17

For the entire journey, Patricia could not bring herself to disobey Astrid by moving or covering her modesty. In equal plight was Ralph Cane, for his elder daughter, having spoken briefly, maintained a silence that remained unbroken. Thus his gaze flitted constantly from the view beyond the carriage window to that between Patricia's open legs. In consequence, his condition did not abate, as was plain to both the girls. Upon descending at last on their arrival, his gait was seen to be somewhat awkward.

'I would speak with you, Astrid', he declared hoarsely as they entered the house.

'You may have audience with me, Papa, yes. I need time to change. Attend my room in our hour', she responded grandly, and without a further word swept upstairs to Jemima's room, whence plaintive squeals and the steady slapping of a palm were to be heard for quite five minutes.

Some miles away, meanwhile, Ronald had been the first to stir. Something tingled and throbbed on his person and this he found, to his unutterable amazement, was his cock, whose knob was lodged at a slight angle between the lips of his mama's slit. Gaping all about him in a bleary fashion, he then naturally espied all-his mama's bewitching nudity and that also of Clara, who lay doubled up beside them, her shapely leg having slipped lazily down from over his own. Naturally, deeming himself to be experiencing a most vivid dream, Ronald groped tentatively about Belinda's superb thighs and found the feeling much to his liking. Awkwardly thrust as it was between her drawers, his leg ached a little and he most slowly and wonderingly freed it by pushing her most intimate garment down farther until it had been worked off over her shoes.

At that, Belinda stirred and moaned, much to the frozen horror of Ronald, who remained breathlessly poised over her, the crest of his penis moist from the warm exudations that had oozed from her cunny during their unconscious state. To his vast relief, however, she opened not her eyes but in fact opened her legs the more, as though to seek a cooling draught of air between them. This, the exposure of her entire dark bush to perfection, merely made her son's stiff cock twitch the more. Moving by stealth and quite fearful of the consequences, he laid himself full upon the sumptuous resplendence of her nudity and with increasing wonder and excitement began to lick around her nipples. Passing his left hand out tentatively at the same time, he sought also to caress his sister's warm, round bottom, which was well poised for such an exploration.

As for Belinda, her mind was bubbling with dreams, most of which were of an extremely erotic nature. Emerging a little into consciousness and feeling the weight of a naked male body upon her, she deemed it vaguely to be that of her late husband and sought to caress it. Foraging with her hand blindly between their bodies, she found Ronald's stalk and moved her be-ringed fingers about invitingly. This alluring touch naturally being quite explosive to Ronald, he moved his cock lewdly in the loose clasp of her fingers, which by instinct then nudged it down against the rolled lips of her slit.

Not unnaturally, Ronald now deemed the invitation to be complete and without thought or caring as to how the three of them had got into such an exciting situation, he urged his cock within the delicious furrow while by teasing movements of her fingers his Mama blatantly encouraged him to do so. In a trice, his pego well inserted in the hot, moist haven, Ronald passed both hands under the glorious globe of her bottom and began fervently caressing it while meshing his lips into his mother's own ripe ones.

At this, Belinda became more fully awake. Her eyelashes fluttered and her own two hands in turn sought his muscular buttocks and drew him into her more fully. Her nipples, erect and tingling, brushed beneath his chest. Inserting his tongue in her mouth, Ronald began to pant loudly while moving his penis back and forth in the heavenly clutch of her well-furred nest.

'Oh, darling, fuck me nicely', murmured Belinda hazily, at which point Clara came to and espied the gentle heaving of their bodies. Belinda had her thighs spread wide and her knees drawn half up so that her shoes could take purchase on the carpet in a manner that allowed her to churn her big bottom about in a manner as lewd as it was exciting.

'You naughty things! Oh!', exclaimed Clara, who then with a little shriek found her own moist cunny explored by her brother's fingers-a caress which caused her to fall back again so that her bare shoulders touched those of her mama.

'Clara, you silly, let Papa do it', husked Belinda, remaining in the land of the past until she then opened her eyes and saw who was upon her. Alas, the dear lady was by then in such a pitch of fervour that naught save the entire assemblage of local society viewing the proceedings could have stopped her. Her arms fluttered wildly, her mouth wet and open under her son's.

'Oh! Oh! Oh! R... R... Ronald! You naughty boy-oh!', she blathered to the accompaniment of the slight squelching sound of his prick easing back and forth in her juicy cavern.

'Ma... ma... MA!', groaned Ronald, whose searching fingers were also deliciously moist from foraging all about in Clara's slit.

'OOOH! AAAAAH!', they groaned together, neither ceasing to wriggle their bottoms in the hazy lust of the moment as the tempestuous peak of their pleasure waves approached. Couching himself more fully upon her bumpy curves, Ronald flashed his buttocks faster, causing his balls to slap resoundingly under her bottom. Unable to resist, Belinda wound her arms tightly about his slim but manly form and responded with equal jerks of her hips the while that their tongues ran greedily together. In a trice nothing could prevent the throbbing outpourings of Ronald's gushing tribute, nor that of Belinda's, who soaked his cock and balls as well in the frenzy of the moment.

After much heaving and kissing, all then was still, and a pleasurable silence reigned. Clara herself joined in, having attained to orgasmic bliss herself in the excited melee. Their eyes then confronting each other's more fully than had been possible in the mists of passion, all were a little more subdued and Belinda was forced to urge Ronald from off her so that she could sit up.

'What is afoot? Oh, I do not understand!', she cried while Ronald boldly passed one arm about her waist and with his other hand caressed her swollen titties.

'Hush, Mama, for no one has seen', he murmured, which appeared to mollify both mother and daughter, who rose up and gazed all about at their abandoned clothes.

'What of Mr. Cane then-and his daughters-OH! did they SEE?', Clara wailed, only to receive a slap from her mama, who found her ample bottom pressed warmly against her son's cock as he stood behind her. The touch of it to her groove being not unpleasant, she pretended not to notice its presence.

'Of course they did not, you fool. They are long gone. We must all have partaken of far too much wine, though how we came to be in this condition I know not', Belinda uttered. Giving then a simpering laugh, she endeavoured all too feebly to escape the clasping of her son's arms about her waist for she could feel already the renewed stirring of his prick which, by most blatantly her bulging bottom invited. Putting one finger in her mouth-a posture she had always found to be delicately inviting-Clara giggled.

'Mama, you are both very naughty. Why, Ronald's cock is sticking up again at your bottom'.

'Indeed, darling Clara, and it will stick up against yours soon enough', her brother laughed, thrusting out one arm to draw her to them. His mama's evident acquiescence increased his boldness while his cock, now fully risen, urged its tempestuous desires against her out-thrust cheeks. With those words also, Belinda deemed with many inward quivers that he sounded not unlike his Papa, which revelation she found as astonishing as Clara.

'Oh, Mama, Ronald must not do it to us, must he?', simpered Clara, her bare tummy now being pressed to her mother's hip as her brother held them both. That her question was really an invitation was easy enough for all to divine, and hence Ronald hesitated not to forage with one hand under his mania's plump cunt while fondling Clara's pert bottom.

'No, really, Ronald, we should not let you. Oh, pray, let us dress', Belinda murmured weakly while her belly urged the titillation of her fingers, which found her mount sticky still with his sperm.

'In a moment, Mama, but, come, let us sport a little first, I beg you', demanded Ronald hoarsely, for being young and vigorous his balls were ready yet for a second and third bout, and his excitement at the glorious turn of events was such that he began urging them step by step towards a sofa.

'No, no, no, Ronald! Oh, Clara, do stop him!'.

'I cannot, Mama, he has hold of me, too. OH!', exclaimed Clara, who then found herself tumbling down onto the silk-covered seat with her mother's weight de-sending upon her.

'Ah, Ronald, NO! Oh, you dare not!', cried Belinda, whose bottom, being lifted as it was to straddle her daughter, became prey to her randy son's intentions.

He, scarcely knowing what he was at, saw only the bulging invitation of her hemispheres and worked the flaming crest of his weapon eagerly between them, bringing a moaning cry from his mama.

'Wh... wh... what is he at? Oh!', cried Clara, who was now half-smothered by the agitated pair, her mother's knee being pressed up between her legs.

'He is in my b... b... bottom-OOOH! Stop it, Ronald, what a naughty thing to do! T... t... take it out! WHOOOO!'.

'Oh, Mama, let me get it right in', groaned Ronald, who found his stiff penis most invitingly half-buried in a tighter orifice than her cunny had presented. Gripping her weaving hips, he rammed manfully forward and with a quivering sigh found himself so fully sheathed that Belinda could only moan her pleasure while. Her pins having all fallen out, her hair clouded all over Clara's face, tickling her mouth and nose so that she sneezed. Taking the opportunity of the moment, and having no need to hold his mama, who was fully corked on his prick, Ronald held himself full in her hot, clenching bottomhole and raised his sister's legs about his mother's waist so that Clara hung beneath, her cunny teased by his fingers. At that, he began to pump his charger back and forth to the perfect delight of Belinda, who found it an even more comfortable fit than her husband's, had been.

So, panting and gasping, they ran their second course, uttering at the last the most abandoned cries while the sofa creaked and shuddered and Ronald's flaming rod injected Belinda deeply with his bubbling sperm. Her features hot and perspiring, Belinda then allowed him to withdraw his cock slowly to the sound of a faint PLOP! as the gleaming knob emerged and all sank down, Clara squeaking her protests until she was allowed to wriggle out from under them.-

Naught sounded then but the ticking of the drawing room clock while all three finally disposed themselves and stretched their tired limbs not without a certain satisfaction.

'Indeed, Mama, you are the naughtiest of all', exclaimed Clara pertly, for she was rather a little put out that Ronald had not fancied her charms the more, though her eyes noted well enough that his cock would evidently soon be ready for a third entry. Seeing her sly glance resting upon Ronald's cock and balls, Belinda laughed indulgently. The cares of the world seemed to have melted from her for the moment and memories of all her past pleasures had been wickedly revived by what had occurred.

'Perhaps I am and perhaps I am not, Clara. It was ever my pleasure to watch you being well fucked, dear, and I am quite sure that dear Ronald will sport between your thighs ere another half-hour has passed. Come, you silly, put your lips to his cock as you were wont to do with dear Papa and bring him well up again!'.

Ralph Cane, meanwhile, had fretted for one long hour. Whatever

Astrid was about, it could not possibly take her all this time to wash and change her attire, he told himself pettishly, yet he dared not stray from his study until the sixty minutes had passed. Unknown to him, of course, the period of waiting imposed by Astrid was a deliberate one. She had enough to think about in terms of plotting and planning, for all was now clear to her and she had few doubts as to how Belinda would have succumbed by now to the lascivious call of Nature.

Undressing slowly and having laved and dried her lovely curves, she drew on first a pair of black-silk stockings, which she drew up tightly by means of suspender straps that dangled from a fetching little corset. This latter garment left her breasts fully bared, as she intended it to. Drawing on then a pair of black-silk drawers in the directoire mode, which left an enticing gap of thigh flesh between the material and her stocking tops, she arrayed herself finally in boots and surveyed herself in the mirror. All that she saw pleased her. Drawing in her slender waist even more tightly, the corset gave full flow to her hips and an even more impudent thrust to her bottom. Above, where it encircled her snow-white skin, a rim of black lace flared, tickling the under curve of her bared tits slightly, in a way that made her nose wrinkle with pleasure.

At the junction of her swelling thighs, the drawers fitted tightly and sufficiently so to indicate the rich plumpness of her mount and the bunching of the wad of curls that surmounted it. Though naught of her cunny itself, nor the cleft of her bottom, was revealed, all was clearly delineated in the most teasing manner. Applying perfume to her armpits, where further curls showed, Astrid then loosened her hair. Letting it fall about her shoulders, she brushed it luxuriously, delighting in the sheen that the bristles produced until all was to her satisfaction. Teasing her veiled cunny with her fingers in the lightest manner, she stood open-legged before her mirror and regarded herself frankly.

'With whom shall you pleasure yourself, Astrid? Whose prick shall your cunny and bottomhole receive?', she whispered with mischievous languor to her reflection. Jemima's bottom had come up a perfect rosy pink under her spanking and by the gradually softening of her howls and the twitching of her pretty legs and tummy, Astrid knew well that she had come. Dear Jemima must have the juicing of a male soon, one whose balls were full and would inject her richly. Patricia must equally be served, for the darling girl had displayed herself well in the carriage, even though with her drawers on.

Leaning forward, Astrid implanted her lips upon those of her reflection and swirled the moist pink tip of her tongue in a slow circle around the glass, leaving a clouded imprint upon it. In doing so, her eyes hazed and her finger moved faster between her thighs, rubbing the silk all about her aroused clitty. Having imbibed a full half-bottle of wine in her room since her return, Astrid found herself caught between two itching sensations. She wanted both to come and to piss and, with a sense of curiosity that aroused the sharper points of her seeking mind, both seemed equally inviting.

Thrusting her hand down into the front of her drawers, she felt her wet cunny luxuriously and churned her hips. A dizziness came over her, making her wobble on the high heels_ of her boots. Then of a sudden she gathered herself and, withdrawing her hand which was sticky and moist, adjusted her drawers tightly once more and drew in a deep breath. The image of Julia seemed to appear in the mirror before her.

'Control-always control', Julia appeared to whisper, and then her vision faded.

Astrid shook herself and still her trembling. Yes, it was true. The greater prizes were to be won thus. There would be orgies in which they could indulge themselves, as Julia had said. Would she wish to? I am not necessarily as Julia is, Astrid told herself pertly, and was then surprised by the thought, which gave her much to reflect upon. Striding to the bell pull, she drew upon it, which in moments brought Crissie hurrying in.

'Have my father come to me', Astrid announced, her breasts jiggling firmly as she drew on a filmy black robe, the hem of which flirted about the tops of her stockings.

'Yes, Miss', responded Crissie in awe, for, despite all that had passed, she had never heard the young lady of a household give such an order before. Stern fathers were not called to the presence of daughters, but vice versa. The world was all a-tumble.

At the maid's flurried exit, Astrid tightened the robe about her so that it left each and all of her curves revealed. Her breasts gleamed milkily through the gauze of the robe and her bottom uttered itself with bumptious arrogance, the light material moulding its bulge closely. Moving to her bed, she shifted a pillow and drew from beneath it her black-handled whip of many thongs. Then, standing motionless and with her legs straight and apart and her demeanour proud, she waited for the door to open again.

CHAPTER 18

Entering nervously and tentatively as he did, Ralph Cane absorbed the voluptuous vision of his daughter with the awed gaze of a man whose eyes are opened for the first time upon the world.

'Close the door and lock it! There is something you wish to ask me, Father?'.

'What... what... what has come about I do not understand, Astrid. Such a change has come over you as I fail... .'.

'Be silent! Come-come here, closer. This whip that I carry is no mere plaything but one that will scourge your buttocks if I wish it to. There are no questions to be answered nor none that may be put. Doff your jacket and place it down. Quickly, now!'.

'My dear, if you would but explain yourself, quavered her sire, who, despite all, felt a rich stirring of excitement in him at the imperious rising and falling of her breasts and the strong straddling of her thighs, the like of which he had not seen since the glorious days of his aunt's dominant postures. His coat falling, he made to retrieve it from the floor and then quickly stilled himself under Astrid's gaze.

'I to explain!', she said, moving her lips in a sneer, though inwardly her loins and belly rippled with pleasure. 'You, who would have deserted your daughters and left them bereft of their inheritance, deserve no explanations. It is but for you to henceforth obey', Astrid stormed, her eyes flashing in such a manner that he bowed his head. Thighs trembling, he felt the over-proud erection of his penis blatantly evidencing its rise through the cloth of his trousers in a manner that his jacket could no longer conceal. Through the fine gauze of Astrid's gown he could perceive the sharp perking of her nipples and the full brown aureoles of crinkled flesh that surrounded them. His knees felt weak and his mouth grew dry.

'I know not wh... what to say, my dear', he stammered.

'It is as well that you do not, Father. Your behaviour has been reprehensible in all respects. A sense of weakness and lack of purpose clouds the household. I propose to disperse it. To this end shall I henceforth rule. My dictates will become your wishes, unspoken as the latter must be. You will seek for nothing that I do not offer you, yet neither cruelty nor scorn are my intent. You have but to signal your total obedience to my commands and all shall be well. Kneel, Sir!'.

At that, her father sank to his knees with a groan, his nostrils twitching as he inhaled the subtle mixture of perfumes that emanated from her body. Smiling to herself, Astrid loosed the tie of her robe slowly and allowed the frail garment to flutter to the floor behind her, where it lay in a limp, black pool. Raising his head hesitantly then, he gazed with awe upon the proud, naked jutting of her breasts and such hints of delight as her sheathing drawers revealed.

'You may kiss my thighs', Astrid murmured distantly, moving full over him as she spoke and then once more placing her long, shapely legs firmly apart.

'Oh, my dear-my dearest!', croaked her father. Reaching his trembling hands up, he sought to clutch the backs of her thighs but received for the gesture a sharp swishing of the thongs across his back.

'No! You do not touch, Father! Lay your lips but once in homage to the skin of my thighs and then remain upright. Your cock is well up, I see, but it is not for the purpose of assuaging it that I have called you. There! It is done. I see well enough where your eyes are cast. It is for that purpose that I have retained my drawers. Up with you! Stand still!'

Scrambling to his feet and dizzy from the impress of her lips upon her smooth, velvety skin, Ralph Cane gazed upon his daughter with such a lust as he could scarce contain. Yet Astrid had judged him well by now. His downfall had come from the moment he had intruded upon her whipping of Patricia. Had he wished- and had she indeed been weaker-he might then have taken command. There were men who would have done, but Astrid knew in her heart they too could be finally quelled by a knowing woman who feared not to stride her true path. Watching him teeter slightly on his feet, she compressed her lips and moved in tigerish fashion around him, flicking contemptuously at his buttocks in a way that made him groan and flinch.

'I b... beg you, Astrid, dear!'.

'I have no doubt that you do, Father. There are treasures in your own house, are there not? Alas, you have come late in the discovery of them. Be wilful and you will receive nothing, for Patricia and Jemima are as tightly under my control as you. Do you not wish it so? Speak the truth!'

'Yes! Yes, Astrid'.

'A confession fully made at last, but I do not intend to doff my drawers in token of it, as you may be wishing. I mean not to spoil you, Papa. There will be certain pleasures for you, attendant on your obedience. Remove your clothing now and be not long about it. I wish to see this lustful equipment you are evidently intent on displaying to us'.

'Astrid, you shame me!'

'Far from shaming you, my dear, I excite you. Let us not bandy words. Show me your cock and balls upon this instant or I will truly whip you. Down with your trousers!'.

Mouth wobbling in amazement and cheeks flushed, her father hastened to obey, not failing to see that Astrid moved her hips alluringly as he displayed himself. Moist with perspiration, his hands trembled as he finally divested himself of his shut and stood naked, his penis pronging up his belly. Allowing her eyes to reply hotly to his, Astrid held the handle of the whip warningly against his buttocks and weighed his heavy balls in her palm though she deigned not to touch his cock, which quivered in an intensity of longing for her caress. Its girth and its length pleased her, full-veined and throbbing as it was. Again her hips moved sensuously, causing her father's hands to clench in abject longing. Yet, recalling vividly that his aunt had frequently so handled him, he remained still.

Astrid's voluptuous little movements were caused not, however, by desire but by the fact that she longed more and more to relieve herself. The tension in her thus grew, for the retaining of her bladder caused her a particular sensual pleasure such as she had experienced before his entry. Turning about and making every footstep measured so that her silk-sheathed bottom-cheeks surged and rolled deliberately, she reached the window and gazed for a long moment out of it in a seemingly pensive mood. With each second, the tension of desire grew in her, yet she sustained it. With each second, too, her waiting sire swayed upon his feet, feeling all at once foolish, lewd, and humbled as his soul had so often cried out for him to feel.

Glorious as a goddess, Astrid then turned and allowed him to drink in the jellied wobbling of her tits and the sensuous appeal of her thighs and hips. That he had somehow maintained his silence was to her liking. It boded well.

'Lie upon the bed, legs together and your arms at your sides', she commanded in the crispest of tones that brooked no refusal.

In that moment, perhaps, Ralph Cane thought that heaven was truly to be. As indeed it was, though not immediately in the manner around which his lustful thoughts raged. No sooner had he settled himself in the very centre of the bed than Astrid sprang. Coming full upon him, she parted her legs about his head and, facing his feet, splurged the cheeks of her knickered bottom full upon his face, bringing a grunt and a groan from her father as he sought vainly to suck in air. The melange of scents that now assailed his nostrils was truly divine. Astrid's perfume mingled with the musky aroma that exuded from her cunny while yet from between her squashing bottom-cheeks a different effluvia faintly tickled his nostrils.

Not moving at first as his groans sounded, Astrid then settled herself more firmly so that his nose thrust into the silk between her half-moons. Her hips stirred slightly, but not sufficiently to displace her. The tickling heat in her cunny was now growing apace and she knew she could not much longer withhold the call of Nature. Hearing his snorting increase, she lifted herself but half an inch to allow his lungs to suck in air and then descended her bottom majestically once more. The moment was nigh upon her and she comforted herself mischievously-but also with a heated blurring of desire-that her father well deserved that which he was about to receive.

Moving her hands up slowly, she first cupped the snowy globes of her breasts, savouring as might a lover the silky, heavy orbs before brushing her thumbs back and forth over her well-risen nipples. The muffled gasps that came from beneath her she ignored and but tightened the grip of her knees against his shoulders.

'Julia!'.

The name came silently and as in both greeting and homage to the one who had converted her to full womanhood. The surface of her belly rippled and her nostrils flared, her bottom-cheeks so tightening that they nipped the tip of her sire's nose.

Red-faced beneath, under the enclosing darkness of her bottom and with his prick pulsing madly under her dimmed gaze, Ralph Cane felt at first a slight trickle pass through the silk of her drawers and lave his mouth. At his spluttering then, Astrid smiled angelically. The sight of his wavering cock, with its swollen crest, no longer interested her but remained a distant image in her mind. She had begun to piss and the itching delight of trying to control it stirred her senses madly. Her bulbous bottom moved, squirming and rubbing over his nose, mouth, and cheeks. In the dressing table mirror that faced the end of the bed, Astrid could see only the upper half of her nubile figure, but it sufficed. Above all, she could see her own beautiful, glowing features and the poking of her stiff nipples, rosy brown through her slim fingers.

The moment was now-the moment of the male's complete submission to the victorious female.

'GURRRR!', Ralph croaked beneath her. Splashing, sparkling, and hissing, her golden rain inundated his face, flooding his nostrils and his mouth with an acrid sweetness that stung his skin. Had it not been for his own choking sounds, he might have heard from above him the contented humming of Astrid as she released herself fully and with total abandon until her drawers were as soaked as was her father's face.

'HAAAR!', she shuddered happily to herself and gave her splurging bottom a final, wet wriggle before daintily raising her hips and moving off the bed with the lightest of feline movements. Groping about blindly and sucking in both air and the golden tribute she had rained upon him, Ralph twisted all about and then made to rise, his palms sweeping madly across his thoroughly wetted face.

'Lie! I have not told you to rise!', Astrid snapped. She wanted now to come, but she did not intend to afford herself the pleasure in sight of him. Wriggling her soaked drawers down, and completely disregarding his presence, she dried herself thoroughly with a towel which, held between her thighs, covered herself as she then faced him.

'Go, Father', she intoned coldly, observing as she did so how fiercely his cock was standing.

'Oh, my God, Astrid, I will do anything!', he cried, rolling off the bed and casting himself at her feet, where his mouth slobbered over her shoes.

'You may be brought to, Father', she responded distantly, though the impress of his lips through the thin leather of her boots made her toes curl agreeably. It would be nice to have him suck her toes, she decided, but such a little treat could come later.

'Astrid! If you would but... .'.

'What?', she asked in a tone that might have cut paper. That he dare not reply directly she well knew. He sought, no doubt, to ask and therefore to speak the words of his desiring directly, but Astrid knew better than to offer even that distant satisfaction. 'Go! You have disgraced yourself sufficiently. Dress quickly for I wish to wash', she said curtly. Withdrawing her foot from beneath his slavering mouth, she turned and displayed her naked bottom to him boldly, the cheeks rich and full where they rolled in to form their deep and mysterious cleft.

'Astrid! Astrid! I would give anything!', he implored on his knees behind her.

Remaining perfectly still and within but a foot of him, Astrid permitted herself a smile that he could not see.

'Anything, Father? You will give everything!'. Her bottom-cheeks quivered and tightened as she spoke. 'It will not henceforth be in my nature to tell you anything twice. That I forgive you on this one occasion you may count as your good fortune for the day. What have I told you to do?'.

'To go... but I wish.... Ah, how may I express myself? I know you not and yet I know your better now than any other. Permit me to be humble in your presence, my darling'.

'Permit? I command it, you fool. You have a good cock, Father. It will be put to use. Remove yourself now or I shall summon Crissie'.

'Ah, you would dare to! I believe it! Give me but the grace to let me dress myself.

'The sooner the better, Father', Astrid replied languidly. Stepping forward, she seated herself at her dressing table and began brushing her hair, the movements of her arms bringing her tits to wobble and jiggle delightfully. He could not but see their alluring movements as he strove to dress, a task made the more difficult by the rampant stemming-up of his prick. Turning then about on her stool, though ever careful to keep the particular treasure between her thighs muffled from his view, Astrid surveyed him scornfully.

'Go to your room and then bathe, Father. You look utterly disgusting'.

'Yes, my dear. Pray, if you deign to call me again... .'.

'I may not do so for days. Be mindful of your ways, Papa. Such pleasures as I may finally see to it that you are accorded will be not of a wanton nature. You are here to serve. The more you accustom yourself to the idea the better it will be for you. Were I to call Patricia in now and disrobe her, what would you do? Speak quickly!'.

'N... n... nothing, my pet, save at your bidding'.

'Excellent! You appear to have imbibed something at least of what I have said. She has a sumptuous bottom has she not?-and quite delicious thighs. You will dwell not upon such thoughts, however, but the severity of my attitudes should I find your behaviour at any time remiss. All affairs of household, moreover, are now fully in my hands. That is understood?'.

'Yes, my love, exactly, precisely'.

'Good. You may count yourself fortunate that matters have changed. The days of our dull lives are over. What think you of Crissie? Is she not a pretty wench?'.

'Eh? What? Crissie? Ah, yes!'.

Swinging about once more in a manner that permitted her sire a dazzling but lightning view of her pouting cunny, Astrid addressed herself once more to her own reflection.

'I shall put her to you tonight, Father. You have pleased me more than you think, though judge that not as praise but as a mere commendation which in any event I may withdraw upon my whim. You will be brought to her-not she to you. Go now', Astrid repeated yet again, her tone becoming so sharp that in but a moment the door had opened and closed and she was left once more alone. Rising and casting on her robe again, she summoned Crissie.

'Have John come to me!'.

'Yes, Miss, on the instant!'

No sooner had the maid vanished than Patricia hesitantly appeared, knocking first with great timidity. Her cheeks were pink, her lips parted.

'Dear Papa is utterly wet! What has come about? He gazed at me most furtively and then vanished into his room', Patricia exclaimed.

Astrid sighed. 'It is not given to you, Patricia, to ask questions. It is I who will inform you, if the mood takes me. Let us say that Papa has partaken of the waters and will not be seen again until dinner. Run a bath for me, dear. I intend to go out later'.

'Where, Astrid? May I come?', Patricia asked, again forgetting all that she was told about putting questions.

'You may not. You may, however, amuse yourself in my absence by instilling a little further education into our darling Jemima. The sweet child is quite bubbling for experience, but she must be taught a little more before she has it-as must you, Patricia'.

'B... b... but, I know not what to do. I wish not to chastise her'.

'Of course not. Why should you wish such a thing?', asked Astrid coldly. A tap sounded outside the door which made her toss her head in annoyance that any interruption should intrude upon her discourses. 'In a MOMENT, John!', she called and then turned her attention once more upon Patricia. 'There will be a little sport tonight, Patricia, after I return, late though the hour may be. Crissie is to have a good, thick prick sheathed in her cunny. It will do her a world of good. I may ask you to attend upon it'.

'Oh! But who? I mean, that is to say-oh!'

'Really, dear, you sound exactly like Papa. Would that I put you to it instead'.

'D... d... d... I don't know!'

'You will know soon enough, pet, and may take good fortune there from. The veils of modesty within and without you are not completely broken. When they are, I believe you will be as lustful a wench as any. Do you like being called that? A wench?', Astrid laughed merrily and kissed her solemn-looking sister on the mouth. At that, Patricia tried to gather herself, for she wished now above all to be as Astrid was.

'I would like to do it again, yes', she said boldly.

At that, Astrid laughed again and ruffled her sister's hair. 'That is to the good then, though I believe I may have to tie you up still. Papa is quite fervent to put his cock into your nest'.

'Oh!', exclaimed Patricia and rushed from the room, quite forgetting her attempts at self-possessiveness and all but knocking the waiting valet over in her passing.

Summoned then within, John's eyes literally gloated over the erotic spectacle that his lightly clothed mistress presented. Even so he knew better by now than to do anything but stand in a position of humble waiting.

'Do you know how to open windows, John?'.

'Eh, Miss. To effect an entry, as they say? Warrant I do. It takes but a thin knife blade and a bit of caution and then... .'.

'That will do, John. Secure such a knife, or rather two, in case one becomes broken. Dinner will be taken an hour early tonight. Tell cook'.

'Yes, Miss, but what am I to do with the knife?'.

'Bring it with you, you fool. You are coming out with me after dinner!'

CHAPTER 19

Through the dark lanes at nine-thirty that night Astrid's carriage rumbled, while John, sitting motionless opposite her, wondered mightily at what was afoot. Astrid had told him nothing save that they were to pay a visit and that he must obey instantly her every word. Modestly clothed in a dove-grey gown, his mistress looked utterly bewitching and with the full bloom of health upon her-which in fact was exactly as Astrid felt. Clutching a tubular leather holder, which, until that day had housed her father's telescope but now enclosed her favourite whip, Astrid wondered with distant amusement whether or not she would have to use it. Whether or not she did, three more would be gathered into her fold, for she suspected well that the undoubtedly arduous exercises of the day would have rendered Lady Smithers and her kin tired if not completely drowsy and more completely subject to her will.

Left his instructions curtly, her papa would now be conning over the more practical details of intentions she had put forth to him and which he yet little understood. Much leatherwork was to be ordered, including several very small saddles and bridles of which he certainly could not see the purpose. That a saddle would cloth his own back and those of a few other males would be beyond his ken. Such riding exercises for the 'studs' were imperative, Astrid deemed. The females would take to the saddles and ride them around. Jemima would giggle much at the idea but would soon get used to it. There were various ladies, too, who could be firmly saddled and then urged from the rear by a firm cock if they showed signs of refusing their riders.

The stables were to be enlarged and rearranged, Astrid had also decided, for the more she thought upon things the more inventive she became and quite hugged herself with glee at that. Her father's bemusement had been utter.

'It is not for horses, Papa, but for disciplinary purposes', Astrid had deigned to explain. 'There will be stalls for males and others for females.

That is all I intend to tell you. I will brook no delays. The drawings of such scarce require the attendance of an architect. Summon builders tomorrow and I will instruct them. Such plans as you can draw need only be rudimentary, nevertheless I shall expect to find them done on my return'.

'What are we at, Miss?', John enquired when they arrived at the residence of Lady Smithers, which Astrid was pleased to find in darkness.

'A matter in which I am sure you will find some pleasure, John. The coach is to wait here. I do not want it to be heard approaching the drive or we may be undone. Did you bring Lucifer 鈥樤? We shall need to light a lamp within'.

'I 'as everything, Miss, including the ropes and straps you give me. A fair lark this seems to me. I don't fancy it if we are caught'.

'Be silent, you fool, we are not burglars. My intent will be made plain soon enough. Come, we will enter through this window. It belongs to the drawing room and therefore I shall know exactly where we are. Can you slip the catch?'.

'I'm trying, Miss-it's a bit stiff.

'As you are, too, John, I see. There-it is done-you are a useful fellow. Climb within, find a lamp and light it, and then open the door to me. It will save me spoiling my dress'.

Within but two minutes, Astrid stood again within the house, though this time it brooded a silence of even greater promise than it had done earlier in the day. Entering the drawing room by the light of the lamp that the valet held, Astrid looked carefully all about and was amused to see a pair of drawers, which she well knew to be the property of Lady Smithers, lying at the back of the sofa. John, having not missed them either, picked them up and allowed himself a quiet chuckle.

'There's been a rare do here, Miss, by the looks of it'.

'There will be another shortly. Listen to what I have to tell you. I well suspect that we shall find the three occupants abed together, or, if not, then two at least and one in his own bed. We will proceed quietly upstairs and come upon the lady of the house. Her son and daughter will give us no trouble, I believe. The girl is quite tasty, John, and I will see that you have your reward of her in due course. That apart, I expect you yourself to treat them with the respect that is due your betters'.

'Of course, Miss, I won't do nothing until you say. A nice shape, is she, if I may make so bold to ask?'.

'You will see soon enough, but the question is nevertheless impertinent. I have mentioned the possibility merely to give you a mite of encouragement. Be quiet upon the stairs. I know the lie of the place for I have visited before. There, along the corridor, that is the main boudoir where I am sure we shall find an enervating scene. Open the door silently for me and then place your back against it when I am within. Now!'.

Such cries of alarm then sounded as turned into wailings from Belinda and Clara of the utmost astonishment. Naked, they lay abed with Ronald between them. Having indulged themselves earlier in the day, Belinda had seen no reason why they should not continue the sport. Of the three, Ronald held the most petrified silence as, with a single gesture, Astrid tore down the bedclothes and disclosed all that the trio had already made themselves thoroughly acquainted with in their amorous romps.

'My God, what is afoot?', shrieked Belinda, sitting up and gazing fearfully at Astrid and the brooding figure of John, who barred the door.

'Oh, Mama, we are lost!', wailed Clara, who crossed her legs but could otherwise riot cover herself for all their clothes lay pell-mell on the floor.

'I find you, Lady Smithers, as I had expected-in the very pit of sin', Astrid declared, brandishing her whip in a manner that caused Belinda to fall back again and all three to cower.

'How d... dare you enter my house!', Belinda nevertheless managed to bluster.

'Dare, indeed! Would I not be complimented by society for uncovering what takes place here? By morning all would know of your wanton deeds were I to loosen my tongue. The very state of the sheet is evidence of your libertine raptures. This gallant youth has ridden you both no doubt to distraction and lies exhausted. Come, Ronald, rise-you need have no fear. Come to me-stand by my side'.

'Mama! What is she going to do?', Clara sobbed.

'I know not! Oh, that we had some protection! Ronald, stay with me!'

'He will not', declared Astrid crisply, flicking her whip about Belinda's bare feet as she spoke. This caused that lady to shriek with dismay and Ronald to scuffle immediately off the bed, whence he brought himself hesitantly to the proud figure of Astrid. 'Beside me, Ronald-face the end of the bed as I am doing', Astrid murmured. So saying, and while Belinda's face grew positively purplish, she slid her free hand beneath his cock and dandled the limp worm.

'A fair-night's work have you done, Ronald? Whom did you mount first in bed?'.

'Ronald, speak not!', cried Belinda, who, making to rise, received a hissing of the thongs about her nips that brought her to double up and squeal. Clara, affecting total hysteria, rolled upon her face and beat at the pillows. Immobile with amazement meanwhile, Ronald felt his cock stir and thicken in the engaging warmth of Astrid's hand, which stroked him gently and persuasively, a phenomenon that his mama stared at with hooded eyes and red cheeks as she rubbed herself.

'You beasts! You will suffer for this!', she wailed.

'Not I, Madam, nor you, provided that you bend to my will. That, or total disclosure of your sins is but the small price you have to pay. Bind them together, John, face to face!'.

'NO!', shrieked the pair simultaneously while Ronald, trembling and starting, was held in check by Astrid's warning hand, which squeezed his now risen penis tightly, causing his eyes to screw up. Such a flurrying took place upon the rumpled bed then as seemed to make the very house shake, but, being quick and eager on the matter, John had leapt upon both, gripping their hips between his brawny legs while their hands beat in futile resistance.

'You dare not! What are you at! Oh, mercy-save us!', screamed Belinda, who found first one wrist and then the other attached to Clara's so that they were linked beyond hope of escape. Turning about and humping his strong buttocks down upon them, John then attended to their ankles and lastly, by again adjusting his position, wound a rope tightly about their waists so that their bellies, breasts, and faces were pressed close, and their howls filled the room.

'Enough, John, they are well secure. What think you of them?'.

'A nice pair, Miss. Good bottoms on both, and nice firm tits. Can I have my pleasure now, Miss?'.

'A little but not too much. They are scarcely virgins nor are either modest. Get behind Lady Smithers and put your cock to her first. Be sure you do not come for I want you to give Clara a ramming also. Their cunnies will have been well oiled enough already'.

'My God, if you let a servant do THIS!', Belinda screeched, though, doing so right into the ear of her daughter, she caused Clara even more dismay.

'Where your son had slid his poker, so may others follow, Lady Smithers. Play not the hypocrite with me. You will take pleasure from it, though I propose not to observe the spectacle. Have at her, John, while I attend to this young man. Come, Ronald, we will retire into privacy'.

'No! AH!', came then a monumental shriek from Belinda, as with the closing of the door upon the exit of Astrid and Ronald, the valet unbuttoned and drew down his breeches, presenting to her view as long and thick a cock as ever she had seen.

'Oh-woh-woh! Mama!', yelled Clara, nearly splitting her mother's eardrums in turn. Closing her eyes, she buried her hot face in Belinda's neck while the fat cheeks of that proud lady's rump were taken firmly in hand by John, who was in high glee at being allowed to attend to them in private and wondered how long his luck might last. Unable even to wriggle her hips, and thoroughly outraged at being approached so intimately by one who was not of her own class, Belinda suffered with an initial sense of horror the nosing of the bulb of his prick up under her bottom.

There John found a pair of lovelips as ready as any to receive. Rubbing the head of his charger all about and gaining much lubrication thereby, he cupped her large and arrogant bottom more firmly and drove up with all the 茅 lan of a man who has nothing to lose but his sperm. Even so, he was mindful of Astrid's admonitions and therefore kept it a-throbbing in the sleek enclosure in such a manner that a bewildered Belinda found the experience a more positive pleasure than her cries and sobs of apparent anguish indicated.

Not at all put out by her waitings-and, indeed, rather excited by them-John began to rod her with long, slow strokes that made her

well-fleshed bottom smack repeatedly against his belly. The two being so firmly joined, he was then able to pass his hands beneath and over their waists and explore the smaller and tighter glove of Clara at the same time, causing her to whimper and jerk, though in the process the minx found her nipples ever tingling and stiffening against her mama's.

'Ooooh, oooh, oooh, Mama! How h... h... hateful!', Clara whined.

'HOOOOO!', came the breathless response from Belinda, who was in the course of receiving as sturdy a cock as any she had experienced and one that was a mite larger even than her late, dear husband's. Ever having had previously the freedom of her limbs, Belinda found this a truly strange sensation and one that she was aware of surrendering to by such little jerks of her bottom as gave assent to the wicked act. Foraging with his forefinger in-between the cheeks of Clara's inviting derriere, John had found now the rosy aperture, which had been sufficiently well explored in the past for it to succumb to his invasion. Within a second, his digit was buried to the first knuckle, causing Clara's jaw to drop and a low moan to issue from her lips.

Feeling then the most warning of tickling sensations in his embedded cock, John withdrew it regretfully and somewhat to the dismay of Belinda, who had been about to come. Clambering over the writhing pair with his big prick bobbing wet and lewd, he took position behind a shrieking Clara and nosed his knob up within her furry grotto while clasping both to him again.

'Mama! Save me!'.

'I cannot, my darling, oh!', moaned Belinda, for the rubbing of her daughter's quim against her own then proved the last straw and with a divine shudder she quivered out her liquid pleasure in little rivulets down her thighs as Clara whined and jolted to the thrusts of John's stout pego.

Such sounds as emanated from the boudoir came to Astrid's ears as the very music of voluptuous pleasure. Having entered Ronald's bedroom with his cock still in her grasp, she held him thus before her while lecturing him quietly.

'You are not afraid of me, Ronald?'.

'No, no, no!', he stuttered quickly, while with her other hand Astrid suavely caressed his balls, 'but, oh, poor Mama and poor Clara!'.

'Poor, indeed. Ha! They are having sufficient pleasure of it as they have with you, my boy. You are a handsome enough youth and well furnished, as I see. Fear not that you are to be robbed of your pleasures, my dear. I mean only to see that they are in future conducted properly. How your cock quivers in my grasp, and yet I suspect it has loosed its sperm a good half a dozen times this day! Such virility promises well, Ronald. Listen to me closely and attend. You will be brought now into my service as a serving male-not a servant, my dear, but one who will nevertheless abide upon my wishes. There will be females enough to take your cock. You will be at stud to them, Ronald, well fed and well housed.

On occasion I shall allow you a free rein in order to assure myself that your training has not been wasted. Put on some clothes now, for you are to follow me'.

'Wh... wh... where shall we go? Oh, but I do not understand!'

'Understanding is not requisite. Obedience is. Will you be whipped, you naughty boy?', asked Astrid, coursing her thongs smartly around his rear as she twisted him about.

'No-OUCH! Oh, it stings! What of Mama? What of Clara?'.

'They will accompany. Separation is not intended. Far from it. You will be put to them again from time to time. The prospect for you is not a displeasing one, provided I have your total obedience'.

SWEEE-ISH! sounded then the thongs while Ronald leapt in the air, cock waggling, and holding his bottom, a cry of dismay coming from him yet again.

'YEEE-OW! Yes! Oh, don't do it again!'.

'What a ninny you are, despite your fine prick! I shall have to toughen you up, my lad. Get yourself attired now and wait here'.

With that, Astrid strode back unhesitatingly to the larger boudoir, where John's cock was slewing juicily in and out of Clara's cunny, she having already once inundated his prick in her excitement.

'All right, John, loose your come in her and then withdraw'.

'Oh, Miss, I been dying to. AAAH!'.

Somewhat with distaste, and yet with a hint of amusement playing about her lovely lips, Astrid watched his face screw up and his buttocks tighten. Slapping his muscular belly hard against Clara's hot rump, he injected her thickly with stream upon stream of his manly outpourings while she, quivering and gasping, received an abundance such as her papa had occasionally donated to her. Mingling her juices with his own, she became dizzily aware that the experience was not so hateful nor horrid as she had thought, and her cunny tightened greedily upon his still-pulsing member.

'Enough, John. You have had a pleasure greater than I intended for you. Cover yourself, untie the pair, and take the girl to see that she gets dressed'.

So much however did Clara kick and struggle in her fretful dismay that John was forced to carry her from the room, naked as she was, while enquiring where her room might be with all the ,born solemnity of one who knows his station.

'Stop it, stop it, stop it!', Clara was heard to moan, though without much conviction in her voice.

Astrid turned then her attention to Belinda.

'You... you have shamed me forever!', the latter moaned, though the risen state of her thick nipples and the moist condition of her cunny spoke of pleasures that denied her words.

'Be quiet, woman, or I will have John whip you. Deny not that you were found in sin! Even so, I am prepared to treat you with discretion- more, I might say, then you deserve. I know well your plottings to secure father's fortune, and that you will not. Quite un-meritoriously, however, you will find yourself somewhat compensated thereby. I intend to move you this very night into my own house'.

'What? You intend to kidnap us? Dear God, what is to happen?'

'Tush, woman, and make not so much fuss of the matter. My house-as indeed it now truly is-is larger by far than your own. You will be well accommodated there, as will Clara and Ronald. As to this mansion, I might find uses for it or we will have it sold'.

'Robbers! Oh, dear heavens, you intend to rob me as well!'.

'Balderdash, Lady Smithers. You will receive every penny from the sale, if such occurs, and I am by no means certain that it will be necessary. As to your comforts, they will be greater than you already obtain. Jewellery you will not purchased. I suspect you have an abundance of it already. Fine clothes shall be yours, some such as you will never have worn before'.

'Wh... wh... what are you speaking of? How can this be?'.

'The matter is simple, as I have already advised Ronald. Pretend no longer, for it will get you nowhere, that you have not enjoyed the

pumping of his virile young cock in you, as I suspect you also did the servant's. I am no moralist such as society would purport to believe in. I abide by my own rules, which in themselves are simplicity. They call for calmness and obedience, a total submission of body and soul'.

'Oh!', exclaimed Belinda, covering her face.

'Yes, my dear. You will find it not a difficult path to follow under my guidance. You are an attractive woman still. I know your passions. They will not remain unsatisfied. The males will be at stud to you under my control. Your own whims will be occasionally exercised at my discretion. The progress you obtain in these matters will eventually assure you a greater freedom. I have use for one such as you. Rise and clothe yourself now, for you have no choice in the matter'.

I cannot do such things-I cannot! OH!', Belinda shrieked, as once more the whip sang its song about her thighs, making her curl up and squirm madly.

'What a bottom you have-truly magnificent! You will make a fine mare of occasion in the stables for the male slaves to mount. Up, woman, and let us have no further nonsense or your tale shall be told throughout the county on the morrow!'.

ENVOI

A strange procession indeed made its way into Astrid's house an hour later. Patricia, rushing down, stared at all in wild surmise. Clara bit her lip and knew not where to look. Belinda returned Patricia's gaze with attempted arrogance, which melted rapidly as she was urged forward along the hallway. Wide-eyed and trembling, Ronald had his freed cock held in the almost maternal grasp of Astrid's gloved hand.

'Lady Smithers will be put in the blue room, Patricia. Make sure that all is comfortable for her. Clara will abide in the room adjoining yours. Ronald will be housed for the moment in one of the upper rooms. Escort Her Ladyship up. The other two will follow. See to it that they are fed before being put down, then return here. John, you will go about your duties'.

'Yes, Miss'.

'Yes, Astrid'.

Removing her elbow-length kid gloves slowly, Astrid watched the little party ascend. Belinda had made less trouble in the carriage than Astrid had thought might be the case, but she sensed well enough how her mind was working. Once within the house, she believed, perhaps, that she might somehow take control. Astrid's lips curved with amusement at the thought. Tomorrow morning Her Ladyship would be thoroughly whipped, as would Clara and Ronald, preferably with the three of them bent over side by side. Their training proper could then begin.

Humming to herself, Astrid indulged in a glass of her favourite liqueur and then summoned Crissie, who had been kept out of sight upon the entrance of the trio.

'Crissie, I mean you to be pleasured tonight. Where is the master?'.

'In his study, Miss, still. He seems to be hard at work on something'.

'Upon my demands is he hard at work, Crissie, as you will shortly be, with your bottom well up, Miss, and no nonsense from you'.

'Oh, Miss, you intends to whip me again and I ain't done nothing!'.

'Of course you haven't, and I do not intend to. Must you have always been remiss in your duties to have your bottom warmed and tingled? I believe you know better, Crissie. Come here and let me feel you. How nice and warm you are! How round and silky it is. Have you ever had a cock up there, between your springy cheeks?'.

'Lawks, no, Miss, it would be too big. It were tried once but he couldn't get it up and anyways I squealed and struggled so much my mother came running and all was discovered'.

'Well, now, what a comedy that must have been! You must not be so rambunctious, Crissie. I promise that tonight it will not go up your bottom, though you will be put to such exercises later. You shall have a fair poking in your cunny, my girl, but you are to remain perfectly still on all fours while taking it. Otherwise I shall indeed whip you until you howl. I have your promise on it?'.

'I'll try, Miss. Will it be John?'.

'No, it will not be John. He has spilled sufficient of his potion for tonight. Go and bathe yourself now and put on a clean chemise and stockings. You will look at your prettiest thus. Brush your hair, for I mean to have you tidy. Go then into my room and wait. You are to position yourself well on the bed as I have told you- head and shoulders down, bottom up. You little devil- your cunny is moistening at the thought of it'.

'Oh, Miss, if I dares say it, I love to have your finger there, you do it so nice!'.

'And with my tongue, too, no doubt. I may raise you yet above the elevation of your present station, Crissie, if you please me. Just wriggle your rump a little when it is put in-let it be lodged full, and then remain still. If you are a very good girl and abide by my wishes, I may let you pleasure me afterwards. Would you like to lick me a little, Crissie?'.

'That I would, Miss. It would be a fair honour. I ain't never tickled a lady with my tongue before, though I've thought of it'.

'You must tell me later who that was and what brought on such thoughts, you little wanton. You may use the second bathroom to lave yourself. Do it thoroughly, for I want delicacy and cleanliness, Crissie. Go!'

With the servant's fluttering exit then, Patricia appeared.

'Lady Smithers is in some agitation, I fear, Astrid. Oh, the questions she poured upon me!'.

'I trust you answered none save with absolute discretion. The night is warm, is it not, Patricia? You do not need to wear so much. Go to your room and attire yourself only in a clean pair of drawers, fresh stockings, garters, and boots. Then attend me in my room'. ,

'Astrid! Oh! What do you intend?'.

'The furtherance of your education, my dear. Hasten now or I may have displeasure with you. How you hesitate,, you silly girl. Come, I will see to you. Is Jemima abed?'.

'Yes. I did attend to her, Astrid, I did'. 'In the most amateurish way, I am sure. You may tell me of it later', said Astrid firmly, guiding her without and up the stairs, where under her unwilling gaze Patricia undressed and then attired herself so fetchingly that Astrid could not help but murmur in admiration.

'Such delicious curves, Patricia. Pull your drawers up a little tighter-and your stockings. Perfect! You would stir the prick of a statue, my pet'.

'Wh... what are we going to do, Astrid?', quavered Patricia, who felt very naughty indeed in her attire and wiggled her bottom as she walked.

'Shush, dear, you are ever at questions. Stand now in the corner by the wardrobe here while I bind your wrists behind you. Stand still! What a fidget you are! Now your ankles, pet, for I wish you not to move-nor indeed to speak', added Astrid, who then rose from her chore and swiftly placed a black-velvet gag across her sister's mouth, tying the ends behind beneath her hair.

Patricia's eyes bulged. A muffled squeak escaped through the cloth the while that Astrid, ever smiling, tidied her stockings tops beneath the tightly ridging garters that gave a slight, extra swelling to Patricia's bared thighs. Then did the door re-open and Crissie appear, wide-eyed and gaping at what she saw.

'On the bed with you, Miss!', commanded Astrid, slapping the girl's bare bottom and making her literally jump upon it, while Patricia, bound and staring, perceived the saucy rising of Crissie's bottom and the fig of her quim peeping beneath as she took up her posture.

'Farther back, Crissie, I want you farther back, your bottom just over the edge of the bed. There-so. There's a good girl', Astrid soothed, not being able to resist passing her fingers lightly under the maid's moist slit. Soft and warm from her bathing, it felt as inviting and delicious as Astrid wished it to. With a pleased sigh, and while Crissie dutifully hung her head and kept herself displayed, Astrid gazed at Patricia and mischievously put a warning finger to her lips. Positioned some eight feet from the bed and standing helpless in her bonds, Patricia bubbled wildly through her gag.

'I will not be a moment. Be still, both of you', murmured Astrid mockingly..

From a drawer she took one of Julia's gifts to her-a short, brown-leather strap with a thin, lengthy chain attached to it. Jemima had seen it on the occasion when Astrid had first opened her valise. Astrid had not told her what it was, for she deemed it rather too advanced for her younger sister's age. Patricia's education as to its use would soon be complete, for it was a penis strap, a device whereby a male could be led by the chain to a waiting female.

Moving it through her fingers, Astrid left the boudoir and proceeded to her father's study, whence came a waiting and wondering quiet. Around her, the neighbouring bedrooms echoed a similar silence, where all lay with nervous expectancy upon the breaking of a new day. All now was well and secure, and all was in her domain, Astrid told herself, as with a gentle smile she clinked the chain lightly and opened the study door.

THE END

Printed in Dunstable, United Kingdom